This is a work of fiction. Names, characters, places, and incidents are products of the author's imagination or are used fictitiously and are not to be assumed as real. Any resemblance to actual events, locales, organizations, or persons, living or dead, is entirely coincidental.

# ACKNOWLEDGEMENTS:

First and foremost, I'd like to thank God for allowing me to express myself the way that I do. I know I wouldn't be able to do what I love if it wasn't for his Grace.

I want to thank Jessica Watkins for seeing the potential in me and giving me this opportunity to express myself and share my crazy imagination through my writing. To my JWP family, I will be forever grateful.

To my family the Russells, Taylors, Bowras, Cottons, Tiptons: I love you all.

To my fans: Wow, I have fans... I think you guys are awesome. You are the reason why I stay encouraged. It's the little things you say to me that keep me going. I hope I can continue to entertain you in my own special way.

Special love sent to my sorors and Frat... Love you guys.

# DEDICATION:

I will continue to dedicate my writing to my family. You all allow me to do what I love, and I'm blessed to have you in my life. I'm blessed to have a strong foundation and people around me that support me and love me enough to tell me when my writing sucks or when it's good.

Dad, you will always be an inspiration.

JESSICA N. WATKINS PRESENTS

# Desired

*Loving an Alpha Male*

## S.K. LESSLY

# Prologue

I can't breathe.

I felt his hands grow tighter around my neck, and I tried desperately to move his fingers. He had a vice grip on me and by the look in his eyes, he wasn't letting up until he saw the life leave mine.

I'm going to die and the last person I will see is this maniac. The last smell would be his breath on my face as he watches me struggle to breathe. The last thought I'm going to have is fear and regret.

I can't believe this is happening. I don't understand what I did that was so awful that my life would end like this.

*Damn it, I'm stronger than this.*

I tried to fight him, gouge out his eyes, but his arms were too long, and I couldn't reach his face, let alone his eyes. I tried to kick him in the balls like I'd done earlier, but it was futile. It's like he has brass for balls or something.

God, what was I thinking getting wrapped up in him? I knew the moment I laid eyes on him that it wouldn't end well for me. I knew he would end me. I knew the moment his lips touched mine that he would destroy me, but I didn't listen and now... Oh God!

It's happening.

I blinked back the tears but as I felt them fall I knew I no longer had control of my body. I could feel the fight leaving my body. I could feel death circling my dangled feet. My brain was finally getting the message and starting to shut my body down.

I started to pray first asking for God to forgive me. Since I messed up in this life, maybe He'll have mercy on me in the next. I then thanked Him. I thanked Him for the good and bad that happened in my life; for the mistakes and triumphs, successes and losses.

It's crazy really; that this would be my end.

I'm dying because I fell in love with a man who said he would love me forever, but has taken my life instead.

# CHAPTER 1

## DRAKE

*Damn, if this bitch grazes me with her teeth one more time, I'm pulling my gun.*

I was really trying to concentrate on her lips moving up and down my shaft, but it's hard as fuck. I couldn't believe I let my stupid fucking cousin talk me into taking these two broads to our hotel suite. I, of course, said no. Just looking at these chicks, I knew it wouldn't end well for me. And just as I suspected I was probably going to have brush burns on my dick because she can't keep her teeth away from my skin, and blue balls that would haunt me all night.

The only fucking thing that kept me hard was the porno I'd listened to as wet smacking noises vibrated throughout the room. That's my cousin, of course. He was in the bathroom clearly getting his off while I was stuck with a fucking vacuum with teeth.

"Shit!" I said as I sat up. "We're done, darlin'."

She started moaning and trying desperately to get me off, adding her hands to stroke me. I felt her graze me again, and I shifted, trying to move from her mouth, but she gripped me tighter.

*Fuck this.*

I pulled my gun from underneath my pillow and put it straight to her head. "Get the fuck off!" I growled cocking my Glock and she, seeing and hearing that I had a gun to her head, screamed backed up and fell off the bed.

The wet smacking noise stopped, and the bathroom door opened.

"Fuck, Cuz! What are you doing?" my cousin said as I stood and pulled up my boxer briefs and black slacks.

"I told you this was a bad idea!" I yelled.

"Yeah, but did you have to pull your gun on her?"

I grabbed my shirt and starting buttoning it. "Hell yeah... Man, she tried to skin my dick with her teeth. She's lucky I don't shoot her on principle alone."

I walked by the girl, and she screamed again. "Shut the fuck up!"

At this point, she was loud enough to be heard throughout the suite. Three guys burst through the bedroom door with guns drawn. I looked at them and shook my head, asking, "What the fuck is wrong with you?"

Goon number one, Darrell, who I call "Thing 1," looked at the naked girl on the floor. "We heard screaming. Thought you guys needed help or something."

I frowned. "Really?" I shook my head and looked back at my cousin, who at this point was pulling up his pants with a smirk on his face.

*I'm surrounded by idiots.*

I moved past the three idiots by the doorway and said, "I'm going downstairs."

I started to leave the suite when I noticed her makeup was all over my light blue shirt.

*Fuck.*

I walked into my bedroom to change my shirt. Hell, while I was at it, I needed to erase her scent from my dick. I wiped off quickly in the bathroom, put on a fresh pair of boxer briefs, cologne, a charcoal gray button down shirt, and my black Fedora and walked out.

I made it to the club that happened to be inside the hotel and went straight to an open table in the corner. A pretty ass waitress with her tits on display came over smiling at me, which made me frown even more.

"What can I get you?" she asked, with hidden meaning evident in her tone.

I placed my order with the look of "I'm not fucking interested" in my eyes and sent her on her way. I reached into my front pocket, pulled out a Cuban and lit it. I've been here for two days now with my cousin, Angel, and a few of his goons from Philly. My uncle, Bruno, Angel's dad, sent us here to Cabo San Lucas as a mini vacation that, to be honest, I didn't feel I needed. I've been working nonstop at home, because of his dumb ass eldest son, Eddie, that I haven't come up for air in weeks. That didn't mean I was tired. If he wanted to do me a favor, he could let me put a bullet in Eddie's fucking head and put us both out of our misery.

I looked around the bar. What I needed right then was to get wasted so I could forget how fucked up those two days had been. Since our plane touched down, my cousin Angel had been trying to get laid nonstop. It's like he's a fucking virgin who just got a taste of pussy and now can't seem to get enough.

Angel and my Uncle Bruno are from my mother's side of the family. My father disowned that side of the family, for obvious reasons. In the last five years, I have reconnected with them. Angel and I have been thick as thieves since then. For the most part, we're always together, whether it's when I'm out on a job, or we're just out shooting the shit. Wherever there's one, there's the other.

So even though I was not too thrilled about being there, Angel was trying to make the best of our situation. The problem was finding the right kind of woman for me. I'm not complaining about the pool of women. There were plenty for me to choose from. The locals were beautiful, as well as some of the vacationers. The problem for me, so far, was that we had dabbled a little with some of the local women, and I was not really impressed.

Angel decided that we needed to grab some vacationers more so than the locals. His backward ass thinks they were there for the same reason we were so they would be more eager to fuck a stranger. At first I was with it. I mean, I won't turn down a piece of ass. But I do have fucking standards, and so far I had not found any on my level.

I was getting more and more irritated being there, and I was this close to fucking off this trip and going home. But, doing that would be a slap in the face of my uncle, and I wouldn't do that either. So I just had to make the most of it and hope the days would go by fast. I just needed to get laid properly. The women we hooked up with last night were alright, right up until I took the panties off the girl I was with. Man, I wanted to throw up at the smell, first and foremost. Even if I was a nasty fucking dog, which I'm not, but even if I was, I would've been turned off by the bush that exploded the moment the panties came down.

Ladies, I don't care if you expect a man to go down on you or not, fucking tame your shit. You don't have to get waxed, and you don't have to shave. But get a fucking pair of scissors and handle that shit. We shouldn't have to weed through a fucking forest to get to the pussy, hoping that nothing bites us on the way in.

I told you I have fucking standards, so I told her this wasn't going to work, and I left. My cousin, pissed off, followed me out. He too had standards and we weren't that hard up to get laid, or at least I wasn't. Again, my cousin was on a mission, so he found someone else to get into that night. Me; I went to my room, and fucking went to sleep.

The bar I was currently in wasn't too bad as far as the pool of women. It was packed with a live band playing some local music, and everyone was either on the dance floor or sitting at tables drinking. I surveyed the area looking for someone that would be more my speed and so far it looked like blue balls were in my future again.

I hate fucking Cabo...

The waitress placed three shots of top-shelf tequila in front of me. I took two quickly and sipped on the other while telling her to bring three more. The moment she walked away, I fit my hat closer to the front of my face, slouched and brought my cigar to my lips. I took a pull, rethinking the waitress, when my eyes fell on a vision of perfection. I watched this heavenly beauty walk apprehensively into the bar, looking around as if she was looking for someone. I really hoped she wasn't. I didn't want to have to get my hands dirty over ass, but in her case I would definitely make an exception.

She was my exception.

She slowly moved through the club, still looking around. Then her eyes suddenly fell on me. She paused and stared. I stared back through the cigar haze, drinking her in, and wondering how she would handle my dick between that perfect mouth of hers. Shit, her lips were beautiful and full and seemingly calling my name. Her eyes were slanted slightly, but I could tell they were expressive and alive. Her hair was wavy and contoured a face that I would kill someone over if only she'd smile at me. Her body was exactly what

I needed. The swell of her breasts and the sway of her hips told me I could get lost in her and fuck her until I pass out ... and she would take it all. I knew she would. Her curves, the thickness of her body is making my dick hard. Just as she turned to walk up to the bar, I saw the most delicious ass I've seen in a long time.

Yes, she was definitely made for me. I'm not a small man in every sense of that phrase. I require more of a woman and, my God, this woman was all that I needed.

Her eyes hesitantly looked back my way. It was that moment I realized if she gave me a chance, I would probably ruin her. The air of innocence rolled off her in droves. I should turn my head and find someone else to conquer. I would hate it, but I could probably find someone to halfway get into. Hell, I've done it already, so I could do it again. As I took the rest of my drink down, and the waitress brought my order to me, the brown skinned beauty finally made her way to me.

"Um, excuse me. Is this seat taken?"

I should say yes. I should tell her to find another seat. But I didn't. The smile that creased her beautiful face fucking did me in. "It's yours now, darlin'," I heard myself say.

She nodded and sat down next to me. I remained quiet, trying not to let her perfume make my dick explode. I need to keep cool. As I said, she's too sweet for me. I had no business talking to her and quite honestly she had no business being around me.

*It's time for me to leave.*

I took the rest of my drinks down and pushed out my cigar. I stood, and her eyes came to mine.

She stood too and looked up at me. "Do you mind if I ask you a question?"

I was in the midst of dropping pesos when her question caught me off guard. I moved my eyes from hers and traveled down to her lips, then to her neck, collarbone and to this set of tits that I would love to be in between right this very minute.

I cleared my throat, "Yeah, I do." I moved to leave when she stood in front of me, blocking my exit.

She ignored my brooding and said, "Are you here with someone? I mean, like are you married or have a girlfriend?"

I frowned, trying my best to give her the meanest look I could. "Why?"

She looked down at her feet, then looked around the bar before leaning into me and saying, "Well, I was ... um... hoping that maybe instead of going back to your hotel you would ... um... like to come to mine..." I moved back from her, stunned, and she quickly added, "With me, of course..."

I couldn't move if my life depended on it... I was fucking floored.

This woman, who clearly was way out of her comfort zone, is standing in front of me asking to take me to her hotel room. I gave her a once over again, and I have to say I was fucking intrigued.

My first thought was this being a setup. No way she could be this sweet and at the same time try and seduce me. But seeing the fear in her eyes and trepidation all over her body quickly changed my mind. I had a feeling tonight would be thoroughly entertaining. I might have blue balls again tonight, but to see if this wallflower could successfully seduce me will be worth it.

I smiled and moved closer to her, playing her game. "Lead the way, darlin'..."

# CHAPTER 2

## GEORGIA

*Shit, he said yes! Now what do I do?'*

His smile deepened, and I swear if I was light skinned I would be blushing right now.

*You can do this, girl.*

I kept my eyes on his and finally he said to me, "Where are you staying?"

*Where am I staying?* I frowned starting to say Cabo when common sense finally hit me. "I'm staying here on the second floor on the other side of the resort." I turned quickly and exited the bar, hoping that he was truly following me. The nerves and goose bumps that were flooding my body should've been an indication, but I still looked back periodically to make sure he was still with me.

My palms started to sweat, and I knew my hands were going the same speed as my heart was. I don't usually do this, pick up men, but this is part of the deal I made with myself when I got on the plane to come here. I'm no longer Boring-Stuck in the Mud -

Georgia. No, I'm Carefree -Throw Caution to the Wind -Georgia. I'm Get My Freak On- Georgia. I can do this. I'm in control.

We got to the elevator, and I pushed the up button. He stood next to me, and, as I tried to take a peek at him, I found his eyes searching me, undressing me. A few other people joined us at the elevator, and when it came, he held it open for me and the others there. He never smiled while we made our way to my room. He didn't have a pleasant soft, approachable face. He was hard with features that I knew meant he was no good for me. But for what I wanted, I didn't need good. I needed bad. I needed him.

The elevator ride was short. He again followed me as I led him to my ocean view room. It took me a few times to put my key in the lock, but once I did, I opened it and held it open as he walked past me. Damn, this man was walking sex and probably as bad as they come. I could tell that the moment I laid eyes on him at the bar downstairs. But what else drew me to him was pure physical. I mean, he was the sexiest man I had ever seen in my life. He was so fine, hard, and rough. I couldn't stop thinking about him taking me up against the wall of my hotel room. Hell, he made smoking a cigar sexy, and I hate cigars. And just the sight of him, slouching in his chair with the cigar in his mouth and his hat covering his eyes, made me want to jump him right at the table.

I remained at the door of my room watching him and taking deep breaths of my own. Then I finally closed and locked it. I put my back against the door and watched him look around my room.

If my friends could see me now, they would probably commit me to the psych ward. This is so out of my character, but that is the point, right? I don't want to do what I normally would do, which, of course, is to steer clear from him. No, I'm running full speed into danger.... This better be worth it.

I closed my eyes and took a deep breath again. My nerves were starting to get the better of me. I'd never been with a white man before, so I didn't know what to expect. But there was one thing I did know for sure; as I opened my eyes to look at him, the look in his dark ones as he stood in front of me exuded promise of a night I knew I wouldn't forget.

Good God!

*Okay, Georgia, here we go...*

"So... um ... I have some rules," I said trying to sound confident and in control. I'm sure, if the sound of the surf crashing wasn't wafting through the open balcony door, he could definitely hear my heart beating out of my chest.

"Okay," he said simply as he removed his hat and put it on the desk.

*Oh, those eyes of his.*

I walked further into the room. "Rule number one: Under no circumstances do our lips touch. No kissing."

He smirked. "No kissing. That sounds reasonable, considering I don't have a clue where your lips have been."

"What?!" My hands went instantly to my hips. *'This son of a bitch.'*

He put his hands up defensively. "Hey, baby, you're the one that picked me up so..."

I rolled my eyes. Okay, so maybe he had a point. I *could* be a skank.

"Rule number two?" he asked, and then started unbuttoning his shirt.

*Wait, he's unbuttoning his shirt!* My eyes watched as he slowly worked his way down his shirt, revealing a wife beater and a very defined looking chest.

"Um..." I looked up at his smirking face. *Control, Georgia. Stay in control*, I thought as I told him. "Rule number two: No foreplay."

His eyebrow curled. "No foreplay?"

"That's right. I mean, you said it; we don't know where each other's lips have been, so no foreplay."

He removed his shirt and started walking toward me. I moved quickly to my right and created more space between us.

"Rule number three: The lights must go off and stay off."

He frowned. "Why?"

I didn't want to elaborate. "Rule number four: Under no circumstances will there be any cuddling. No spooning and you will not spend the night. We are only here to share in a physical experience, and that's it. After tonight, we don't know each other...

and please stop with the nicknames like baby or darlin'. I hate pet names."

He smiled at me, and I swear to you it lit his entire face. Then that smile turned sinister as his hands went right to his belt buckle. I watched as he opened the belt and his pants, then moved toward me.

*Holy shit.*

The muscles in his chest, the flatness of his stomach, the cut of his arms; he looked like he came straight out of some muscle magazine for bad boys.

"Is that it?" he asked me.

"Yes," was all I could get out of my suddenly dry mouth.

"Good... So, since this is your show, what do you want to do next?"

I frowned, confused. "What do you mean?"

He walked closer to me. As I backed up, I felt the bed hit the back of my knees.

"What do you want to do tonight?"

"Well, you know..."

"No, actually I don't, so why don't you tell me?"

I folded my arms in front of my chest and tried to not look like I was thinking of what to say next. The smile that appeared told me that I was doing a horrible job of being aloof.

"Do you want me to fuck you?" he asked me just as blunt and to the point like he was asking if I wanted a drink of water or something.

My eyes grew wide, but I couldn't formulate words or make my lips move, so I nodded.

He moved even closer to me. "No, baby, I need you to say it. Tell me you want me to fuck the shit out of you until you can't remember your own name."

'Um... what?'

He stood still and waited... and I mean he was actually waiting for me to say it. Well, I couldn't say that... I mean, hell, I say the normal curse words, but I barely use the word "fuck"... not in this content anyway.

But I've come this far. What harm would it do to say it? I took a deep breath. "I want you to fuck me." There. Close enough...

A look of pure unadulterated lust and desire suddenly caressed his features. I knew at that moment that I was in serious trouble. He then smiled at me and said in the most seductive voice I had ever heard, "It would my pleasure."

The next thing I knew, he reached in my hair and gripped the back of my head tight. He grabbed my ass with his other hand, which caused me to gasp in surprise and lust. He crashed his mouth into mine. God... his tongue moved in my mouth with determination and greed.

There was nothing I could do about the invasion and, to be quite honest with you; I didn't want to. The feelings he stirred in me with his aggressiveness had me wanting him more than I had ever wanted anyone. And the way he kissed me... Damn, the throbbing between my legs was pulsing out of control.

He lifted me up by my ass, and I wrapped my legs around his waist. I felt the softness of the bed meet my back, all the while he never stopped kissing me. God, this man was exactly what I've wanted since I first desired being with a man.

Then suddenly, when he let me up for air, he pulled down the summer dress I wore, taking it from my body. He threw it behind him, leaving me lying in front of him with just my panties. He then licked his lips and tugged at the sides of my panties, ripping them off me with one motion... Did you hear what I said? He ripped the side of my panties apart and yanked them off my body in one motion!

We need to pause a beat to let that soak in... Holy shit! I mean, they were a pair of thongs, but they had thick straps. What the hell did I get myself into?

I closed my eyes as he captured one of my nipples in his mouth. *Oooh. What is this man doing to me?*

I was concentrating on what he was doing to my nipples until the moment his fingers entered me. I wiggled my hips to the sensation that was grappling me to death. Again, I was not ready for what he was doing to my body, making me feel things I thought

I would only read about in books. This man was feral and aggressive, taking exactly what he wanted from my mouth, my nipples, and my sex. He moved in and out of me slowly and controlled while he lapped and sucked my nipples with a need that I've never experienced from a man... *ever*.

The assault on my body was so overwhelming that I didn't know what to do. I wanted to grab his hair, but his head was shaved. He still had his t-shirt on so instead I gripped that tight. Just when the feeling of ecstasy started to consume me, I started circling my hips.

"Oh my," suddenly escaped my mouth and I arched my back into his touch. Damn, he felt so good and strong. I opened my eyes to see him looking right at me. I didn't know what to say. His eyes were so intense and overpowering. I watched this powerful man bring me to an intense orgasm with just his fingers. I closed my eyes again and let the feeling take over me as he continued to move in me. Finally, when he pulled his fingers from me, my sated eyes drifted open slowly just in time to see him put his fingers inside his mouth. All I could do was stare at him in amazement as he closed his eyes and moaned, slowly sucking my taste from his fingers.

*Shit, that was so fucking hot.*

Suddenly, he stood, reached into his pocket and pulled out a trio of foiled wrapped condoms. The packet was something I've never seen before, so I said, "Um, I have some condoms if you want to use mine instead of yours. You know, you could save yours for another time." The smirk on his face made me feel so small.

*God, Georgia you are a complete idiot.*

But in my defense, I was nervous about the brand of condom he had. I've never seen that color wrapper, and I studied them all at the drug store before I flew out here.

He did try and make me feel better by not laughing at me out loud. "I appreciate that, baby," he started. "But yours probably wouldn't fit."

I started to protest, but when he dropped his boxer briefs, the air in my lungs suddenly escaped me.

"Holy shit." I sat up on my elbows, then hands and backed away from him. "Um..." I started to say more, but at the moment I couldn't speak. There was no way he was putting that in me.

He grinned at me, pulled off his t-shirt, revealing the most chiseled body I had ever seen, bent over to remove his socks and then moved in between my legs. "Don't worry, baby. I'll make sure you're ready for me."

"Yeah? And how will you do that?"

He didn't reply. Instead, he yanked me closer to him and used his shoulders to spread my legs wide. I knew instantly where he was going. I sat up and started to move away from him, but somehow he wrapped his arms around my thighs keeping me in place.

"Um, wait remember rule number... Ohhh shittt..." My head fell back against the pillow just as his lips touched my clit, and he circled it with his tongue over and over. He then fluttered his tongue. I was losing my mind as I felt him place his hands underneath my ass, which seemed to give him more access to me.

"Can you wait... just give me... ho-ly fuckkkk..." I yelled as the most glorious sensations ripped through my body taking me, plunging me into... Oh, hell, I don't know.

It feels fucking amazing.

And his moaning... He tasted every drop of me, drinking eagerly as if he was quenching a yearlong thirst.

"Fuck, baby. You taste fucking amazing... Give me more, baby. I want you soaked and fucking ready for my dick." He moved back in and fucked me thoroughly with his tongue, bringing me to another orgasm.

*I am seriously seeing spots right now... Is that normal?*

I grabbed onto anything I could; sheets, pillows, my braids. I even put my fist in my mouth to stop myself from screaming, but he pulled my hand out of my mouth saying. "Don't do that shit. I want to hear you, baby. Tell me how good this feels."

I couldn't form tangible sounds, much less be able to tell him anything. Hell, this is the first time any man has gone down on me, and this is the first man who has made me come this many times.

I'm officially hooked. Every man needs to do this to his woman. It should be a damn requirement. I mean, goodness! He's making me lose it, and he has only used his tongue on me. Imagine what would happen when he...

"Oh shit..." I sat up just as another wave struck my body. I tried to scoot from his mouth. The feeling was so intense I couldn't take it any longer. Finally, probably having sympathy for me, he let me go but pushed me back on my back and in one quick move he was inside of me.

"Ho-ly mother of..." My eyes were large as I felt him consume my insides. I think I heard a faint wrapper noise while his tongue was inside me, but I couldn't confirm it. And to be quite frank, I didn't care. If he even thought about pulling out of me this second I would murder him. Shit, he was huge! I tried again to move back from him, but he gripped my hips tight.

"Don't move, baby. Just relax and let your body get used to me."

"God, I don't know if I can," I replied shaking my head.

"The moment I saw you, I knew you were capable of taking all of me. Just trust me, baby, and relax. I'm about to make you feel so fucking good you'll be screaming for me to go deeper and fuck you harder."

*Yeah, I doubt it.*

However, I tried to relax, like he said. I looked into his eyes and then his lips. I noticed my juices glistening all over his five o'clock shadow, and I think he knew exactly what I was looking at and thinking. He said while smirking at me, "Yeah, I don't do well with rules."

"So I noticed," I smirked back.

He laughed, and it was at that moment I knew he had the capability to destroy me, and oh I think he knew it. He started moving in me slowly at first; long and deep and it felt incredible. He moved his hips, continuing to go deep in me and hitting spots that awakened pleasures I didn't know anyone could. I couldn't take it any longer. He was driving me crazy. I started clawing at his shoulders just as he started picking up his pace.

"Oh yes! Please just… Oh God….," I panted.

Then the beating of my womanly parts started. When I say he fucked me so hard and so well; when he asked me what my name was, I couldn't fucking tell him… Arrogant bastard.

I tried ways to get him to ease up on me but to no avail. He was taking no prisoners. I bit him in his shoulder to stop from screaming, and he didn't slow down one bit. I grabbed his ass and squeezed and all he did was grunt his approval, moved my legs up further and continued to claim my body for his. I came I don't know how many times, especially when he found a spot inside me that had me cussing up a storm. I said cuss words that I've never said before, making up phrases that I knew didn't exist. And I really used the word "fuck" …like a lot.

He growled and cursed too, and I hoped to hell those were good signs. I got my answer when he placed his forearm next to my head and the other on the headboard, making his lips hover inches from mine. Feeling his breath on my face was one of the most calming things I had ever felt. I can't describe the feeling I was having this very moment. I grabbed hold of his ears, and we watched each other come apart with such force. Seeing the vulnerability and rawness in each other truly touched me. It was like we gave a part of ourselves to each other in that instant that we could never take back.

He finally collapsed on me. I instantly closed my eyes as I tried to catch my breath. I then felt him reach down between my legs, pull out of me and get out of bed. I followed the sound of his heavy footsteps as he walked away. Moments later, I heard him walk back to the bed. I thought he would start putting his clothes on, but I was wrong again. Instead, he crawled back into the bed, pulled me back into his arms with his chest against my back and covered us with a sheet.

He kissed the back of my head. Soon I heard heavy breathing coming from him.

I sighed deeply. *Yeah, he can't follow rules worth shit.*

# CHAPTER 3

## DRAKE

I opened my eyes and looked out into the darkness coming from the balcony door. I wasn't sure what woke me, but I closed my eyes and started to fall back to sleep when I felt a soft leg draped over mine move.

*Oh fuck.*

I turned my head ready to wake this girl up, so she can get out of my bed, when my eyes fell on Beautiful. That's when I remembered where I was and who was lying next to me. I lucked up last night when she walked in the club. And last night was some of the best sex I'd had in a long time. She took all of me just as I knew she would and just thinking about last night had me wanting her again.

*I should let her sleep.* No doubt she was sore from the way I was going at her pussy, but I couldn't help myself. I wanted her right this moment like I wanted to breathe. I moved my hands underneath the sheet and caressed her body from her arm to her luscious hips and ass to her thigh. Damn, she felt so good and soft. I loved the way she felt. I loved her scent. Eating her pussy wasn't on the agenda last night but smelling her desires made me go out of my mind, and I had to taste her. I wanted to drive her as insane as she was driving me.

I moved her thigh up higher and moved my hand between them. The need to have her was too overwhelming, so I coated my fingers with her juices. Then I started slow fluttering movements on her clit. I felt her start to move against my hand.

*That's it, baby. Wake up.*

When I increased the speed and started a circular motion, her eyes opened, and she stared at me blinking. I smiled at her, and she moaned, closed her eyes and instinctively bit her bottom lip.

"What are you doing?" she asked me as I felt her hips starting to pick up its pace.

"Getting you ready for me," I replied simply and increased my speed along with her.

"Mmmm... Oh, I'm about to…. Ahhhhh…."

Just hearing her go over the edge made me want to bury myself in her quickly. I entered her with two fingers hell bent on seeing her climax again.

"Damn, baby, you are sexy when you cum. Cum again for me," I told her as I changed my position to better get to her spot.

Her eyes met mine, and they stayed on me as she gave me the sexiest smile.

*That smile makes me want to keep it on her face forever…Wait, what the fuck did I just say?*

Yeah, her gaze was getting way too intense. Trepidation filled me completely so I buried my face in her neck and nibbled a spot I knew would drive her crazy. She grabbed my ears and held on, which I fucking loved. I don't know; it was just something about her and the way she touched me.

I worked her up to the point I knew she was about to cum, and I pulled out of her. I grabbed the condom wrapper, ripped it quickly and sheathed myself. I pulled her thigh up farther on my leg, positioned myself and glided into home... Shit... I mean *her*.

We both moaned at the invasion. I slowly moved in her wetness, getting the feel of her and fucking loving it. She felt amazing. Her pussy gripped me tight as if she never wanted to let me go. Our eyes met again and again I saw too much intensity in them. So fuck having morning breath; I kissed her. I had to do something before she would be able to see right through me, before she found out I was no good... if she didn't know it already.

Our rhythm stayed smooth as I stroked her deep and slow and long.

"I can't take it. Please..."

"Please what?" I asked her, keeping the torturous rhythm going.

"Please, baby, fuck me... Make me lose my mind."

Well, hell what is a man supposed to say to that? I didn't know what to say. So I didn't say shit. Instead, I fucked her like she asked.

*****

Sweat poured from both of our bodies, but I didn't stop. I was starting to crave her sound, her scent, her voice, and her desires. I wanted to please her. I wanted to embed myself in her and to her. I wanted to claim her and conquer her for myself. Damn it, this shit is fucked up... I don't even know her name.

"I'm cumming!" she screamed.

I pushed her face back down in the bed, gripped her hips tight and brought this shit home.

The moment I exploded, she did too. We both collapsed on the bed. I pulled out of her, tossed the condom on the floor and fucking went to sleep.

*****

A faint buzzing sound invaded my dreams. I suddenly realized it was probably my phone but for the first time in my life I didn't want to move. This beautiful woman lying in my arms felt right to me. Me holding her felt right. She was soft and innocent, representing everything I am not.

My phone stopped and then started again. *Shit.*

I turned my body to the side to gently slide her off of me, and then turned to reach for my pants. I grabbed the fucking thing, noticing it was 5 a.m., and answered it.

28

Sleepy and annoyed, I replied, "What?"

I heard a chuckle, and then my cousin say, "Some shit's going down. I need you to come to the room."

My interest peaked. "Yeah? See you in a minute," was my reply, and then I ended the call.

When I turned over, her body was facing away from me. I leaned into her and started kissing her shoulder lightly. She moaned her response and, damn, if my dick got hard again.

I didn't have time to play with her body again, so I said to her, "I have to go, baby."

She moaned her response again and turned to look at me.

The purity and innocence that graced her face that moment humbled me and made me feel guilty as hell. I had to take a deep breath in order to fill my lungs with air so I could talk. "Damn, baby, you are so beautiful," I whispered to her and touched her lips with mine. She smiled shyly and looked away from me. "I had a great time with you."

"Really?"

"Yeah, baby, really. Too bad this is the only night I get to play with this sexy ass body of yours." She looked at me confused, so I added while circling her nipples, "It's a shame really. I would have loved to taste your pussy again. Maybe you could've sat on my face, since you like to squirm so much; give you some control over your own orgasm. And then feast on you all night long. Then fuck you until well after the sun goes down." I moved my hand, nodded and rolled out of bed. "Yeah, that would've been some good shit don't you think, baby?" Then I shrugged and put on my briefs and pants.

"Georgia," she breathed

"What's that, baby?" I put on my shirt and grabbed my t-shirt.

"Um... My name is Georgia."

I grinned, "Of course it is." I grabbed the condom I left on the floor and threw it in the wastebasket underneath the room desk across from me and grabbed my hat. Then I walked toward the door.

"Aren't you going to tell me yours?"

I turned around to face her. "No. Rule number four, remember? We don't know each other once I leave this room." I put my hands up, "You're rules, not mine." Then I winked and left.

*****

"You're fucking kidding me," I barked.

I was sitting on the couch in the suite with my cousin sitting in a chair across from me. The fury I felt that moment was becoming completely overwhelming. I wanted to punch someone or something, which I'm sure my cousin knew it and was sitting far away from me for that reason. I've also noticed he apparently got rid of Thing 1, 2 and 3 so I wouldn't use them to take my frustrations out on. I've been known to do that a time or two.

"Cuz, I know how you feel," Angel said but I wasn't hearing that shit.

"Fuck that, Angel. You don't have a clue. You know I didn't do shit."

"I know you didn't," he countered

"So what are you telling me? Uncle Bruno thinks I fucked up?" I studied my cousin looking, for a hint of a lie, but he didn't show anything but remorse.

"Come on, Drake. You know better than that. Pops has the utmost confidence in you. He trusts you to the fullest."

I leaned forward, placing my elbows on my knees and looked at him. "Then tell me something that justifies me hiding out like a bitch."

Angel, knowing my temper sighed. "Drake, this is by no means a bitch move. You have the fucking Feds after you. This isn't some small time shit. They have you on a few counts of murder."

I nodded. "Yeah, and you know for a fact they can't have shit on me." I leaned back in my chair. "There's no way they could pin anything on me."

Angel nodded. "I know, but the fact that they're looking at you means they're looking at the family, so we have to stay low. You have to stay low. At least until I can figure out what the fuck is going on."

My head fell back and sighed. I knew he was making sense, but this was still fucked up. I knew the Feds had nothing. There was no way they could. I wasn't trying to be cocky. It was just a fact. I was that good. Alright, I'm cocky as shit, but hell the truth is the truth. I was not stupid though and cocky stupid motherfuckers are the ones that get pinched... I was a professional... I didn't get pinched. I didn't leave evidence, and I fucking didn't get caught.

With my eyes closed, I said. "How long do I have to be here?"

"Two weeks at least-"

"Two weeks?! There is no fucking way I'm staying here that long!"

"You have to give me time to work, shit." Angel looked at me, his own patience wearing thin.

I ran my hand over my head, leaned forward and looked down at my feet. "What the hell am I supposed to do for two fucking weeks?"

It was a rhetorical question, but my cousin didn't know the meaning of the word. I heard him say, "Well, shit, if I have to tell you..."

I lifted my head and saw a smirk prominently displayed on his face.

"Fuck you!"

He laughed. "Seriously, Cuz, just lay low. Don't piss in someone else's pot and the two weeks will go by before you know it."

I grunted but didn't reply.

Angel stood and walked to his bedroom. He came back out with his suitcase in hand. "I think you should get another room in one of your aliases."

I didn't reply.

"Are you going to sulk for two weeks?"

I folded my arms thinking about it, but I knew I would lose my fucking mind if I did.

"The moment I find out what's going on, I'll call you." He handed me a phone. "Use this burner phone to contact me. I got it before we left so it's not linked to us at all. If there's anything you need, you know what to do, yeah?"

I nodded but didn't reply.

"Drake," I looked up at him. He continued, "I'm going to find out what's going on. You can count on that."

I knew I could, and I told him so.

I stood, and we did the bro handshake. You know; half handshake half hug.

"Stay out of trouble," he told me.

"Yeah, you do the same. I'm not going to be there to have your back, so you're on your own."

He smiled. "Yeah, I can take care of myself."

"I know, but if it gets too hot, back off. I'll figure out another way to clear my name. I've done it before."

Angel is one of the few people that truly knew my secrets. There aren't that many people I trust, but I know for a fact I can trust him.

"I know you have, but you don't have to do that shit anymore. You know I've got your back."

Angel left out of the room, and I waited about thirty minutes before I called the front desk and asked if they had any other rooms available. They told me they had one and gave me the rate. It was highway fucking robbery, but I couldn't complain, so I booked the room under one of the many identities I've created for myself. Then I showered and packed.

After I had breakfast, I moved to my room, unpacked and went to fucking sleep. I thought about going to Georgia's room to see if she really meant what she said about us being strangers, but I didn't. I may not be stupid cocky, but I'm fucking prideful. I'd be damned if she makes me feel like a fucking idiot for wanting to be with her. I couldn't understand why I wanted to in the first place.... Yes, I do. She was a fantastic woman. I didn't know shit about her, but I just had this feeling about her. I knew she was a good person. I knew last night was a bucket list kind of thing, and I was all too pleased to be that for her. The problem was I wanted more.

That night I went to bed determined to find a warm body to get into the next day. That night though, I went to sleep thinking about one of the best pussies I've been privileged to be inside of.

# CHAPTER 4

## GEORGIA

*What are you doing here, Georgia?*

I sighed deeply and looked around one of the many exclusive Cabo San Lucas clubs, realizing that very moment that I had no business being there. Let me paint the picture for you. There were women in their twenties in the skimpiest bikinis I've ever seen, dancing and gyrating their non-existent hips for any age male that would give them a second thought. There were women in their thirties, such as myself, watching the younger women like they were antichrist, wishing they would get swallowed by a tidal wave or something, anything that would wipe them from this beach.

Me; I really didn't give a shit about the twenty-somethings. I mean, I had the same goal as the thirty-something females but I wasn't going for perfect.

The goal isn't to have happily ever after. No, my goal for these two weeks was to get my freak on and often. I wanted to remain numb. I wanted to forget everything and everyone I left behind and get lost in someone, even if it was temporary. I didn't have the stomach for anything else.

*Okay, so all I have to do is walk up to one of these idiots and say, "Hey do you want to come back to my hotel room?"* I mean this should be easy. I did it the other night.

*They say yes like that other guy did, and that's it; we can leave.*

Funny thing though, I couldn't get up from that stool I was sitting on to approach anyone like I did the night before. This shouldn't be this hard, right? All these guys here are just waiting for a female to go up to them and invite them to their rooms. But, it seems every time I think about getting up and approaching someone, he invades my thoughts.

*No, I need to forget about him. He didn't even want to give me his name.* No matter the sweet things he said to me, no matter the connection I felt instantly when our lips touched, I needed to forget him and move on.

I turned on the stool and looked out in the club. The dance floor was packed, people were sitting around tables and some were just standing and people watching. Maybe I was just doing this wrong. I needed to stop thinking about him, and focus on finding someone for my bed that night. I took it easy last night. I figured I needed to give my body a break from the pounding it took. Now I was back at it and...urgh.

Maybe I should've acted like the twenty-somethings and went out on the dance floor and shook my ass. If I did that then maybe, just maybe, I could find some young hot stud to freak on that night.

I looked around the room and sighed. Watching these young women grab the attention of the men here, I didn't stand a chance. Don't get me wrong; I'm not ugly, at least I don't think I am, and that's what matters, right? Anyway, I'm brown skin, the color of chocolate I'd say, but I've been told I'm more of a mocha color, which to be honest with you I don't see the difference. I'm 5'7" with thickness and curves that according to society and department stores, puts me in the plus size category, even though I don't look it. It's the hips and ass I say, but hell what do I know.

I wear my hair short most times, but this trip I have wavy styled micro mini-braids that come to the top of my shoulders. My eyes are brown, slanted slightly, but I think they are my best facial features, besides my smile.

I know I'm not the first choice for the majority of these men, but maybe someone would take me up on my offer. My mind suddenly drifted back to the other night and the man that seemed to see right through me. It was as if he knew I shouldn't have been in the bar, much less trying to pick him up, but the fact that he went along with everything should have told me all I needed to know about him. He wasn't someone I needed to spend any more time with. What we had was mind blowing to say the least, but that needs to be the extent of it. Never mind he made me orgasm more times in one night than I have in my thirty years of existence. Never mind that he turned my body inside out, making me feel things that

I've never felt before. Never mind the fact that he was the sexiest man I had ever seen in my life.

He wasn't good for me.

I suddenly realized I was subconsciously rubbing at the hickey he left on my chest. I shook my head and put my hands back in my lap. I turned to face the bar and my eyes instantly went to the front door just as he walked in.

Shit!

Of all the clubs in Cabo, he decides to come to this one? Really?!

I quickly turned my head and signaled the bartender for another drink. Maybe if I pretended to not have seen him, he would go away. I took a few deep breaths as I felt him get closer. He stopped and spoke to the bartender behind the bar. I watched him then move in my direction, and I was ready to ignore him fully if he came up to me, but he didn't. Instead, I noticed him go from the corner of my right eye to the corner of my left.

*What? He didn't even stop to say anything?*

I frowned and watched him look around. After locating a seat, he grinned, admiring some twenty-somethings and sat down.

*That son of a bitch!* I knew he saw me. I'm almost certain to the fact. But he didn't have the decency to just stop and say hello, or give me a nod, some type of acknowledgment?

I mean shit didn't the night we share mean anything?

I watched him pull out a cigar and light it. As he leaned back in his chair, the bartender came up to me and placed a drink in front of me. I turned and still frowning, said, "I didn't order this."

He replied without a hint of a smile, "I know. He bought it for you."

I followed the bartender's finger, and he pointed right at the son of a bitch who was now grinning and looking at me.

Smug bastard.

I gave him the finger, and I should have given back the drink or poured it out, but yeah I don't turn down drinks. I have a thing about wasting alcohol. I may not like that he bought me this drink, but damn it I'm going to enjoy it.

Alcohol and I were the best of buddies. I can hold my liquor, and I'm quite proud of that fact. Unfortunately, the two closest people in my life think I drink entirely too much and too often. I'm not an alcoholic by any means. I'll have a glass of wine when I'm grading papers to get me in the mood and mellow me out. But on the weekend, if I'm at happy hour or something, I'm going to have a good time. I don't drink and drive. My fiancé sends a car for me every time I go out to make sure I make it home safely.

I frowned at the thought of Gavin and decided to order another shot of tequila. Every time I think of him my heart starts to break all over again. I feel sick to my stomach wanting to curl up into a fetal position and cry.

Gavin Diego was who I envisioned spending the rest of my life with. He was nice, smart and successful. And he was very attractive. I mean *very* attractive. He stood at a good six feet and worked out religiously. He had beautiful brown eyes and thick black wavy hair that my hands lived in every chance I got.

We met while he was getting his Master's Degree at the university I currently teach at. We both were in the library, he studying and I was grading papers. I would see him in the library all the time, and I admired him from afar. I didn't believe he and I were compatible just looking at him and me. We were so different, but it turned out I was wrong. He actually made the first move one day by coming up to me and asking if I was a student. When I told him I was a Psych professor, we started talking and well the rest was history.

I was on cloud nine having a man like Gavin around me. He was getting his Master's in Political Science and was heavily involved in the Latin communities in Miami. At first, I thought he was way too good for me. I have a seedy and dark past, and I didn't want to tarnish him. But he would always tell me not to worry about anything. He was in love with me, and he didn't care about my past or what anyone else thought. I was his, and he was mine.

That's sweet, right? Well, my best friend thought otherwise. Maya Wilson was my ace and closest friend. We met in undergraduate school at the University of Miami. She currently works for a huge public relations company in Miami as a publicist.

To her, appearance is everything. She would always get on me about my looks, even before I met Gavin. She would tell me that I needed to work out more, watch what I eat, buy expensive clothing so they can fit my body better. I've mentioned I'm a little on the thick side. Well, the crazy thing about my makeup is I can work out all the time and my hips, ass and thighs remain big. And when I gain weight guess where it goes... Yup, it goes to my hips, ass and thighs. My stomach happens to not be that much of an issue, which boggles my mind all the time.

I love food mind you so I wasn't going on anyone's diet, but I at least went to the gym to run on the treadmill for an hour twice a day. That was enough for me, and she tolerated it. That is until she got a look at Gavin. Things changed between her and me at that moment. She started to beef up her shots of me being too big or eating too much. She'd told me multiple times what I needed to do in order to keep Gavin interested in me. She would tell me how to dress, eat, and how to speak when I was attending public engagements with him. She frowned on me drinking, and after Gavin had proposed to me, they both started teaming up on me. Suddenly, it wasn't okay that I was myself in their eyes; I had to be more. So I would try to please them both, doing everything they suggested but it seemed it wasn't enough. I was exhausted just trying to be something that I wasn't. To be quite honest, I felt like I was losing the essence of who I was. I lived with being criticized my whole life. I didn't want to marry into that. So, even though it was horrible timing, on the night before our wedding, I went to talk to Gavin.

He told me he and his friends were going out that night to celebrate his last night of freedom, so they got hotel rooms off the South Beach strip. That way no one drove home drunk and the hotel happened to be close to the church where we were getting married.

I was staying at a hotel not too far from his hotel so it wouldn't take long to go see him and come right back. So, I snuck out of my room trying to be quiet so I wouldn't wake up Maya, which was easy to do because she slept like a rock. We were staying in a two-bedroom suite so I was in one room, and she was in the other. She decided to stay with me that night to keep me company and prep me for how I'm supposed to behave at my own reception. I knew if I told her I was going to go see Gavin, she would kill me.

I managed to escape undetected, and I walked quickly to his hotel. South Beach streets were still bustling at three in the morning, so I didn't seem or feel out of place being out so late at night. The clubs were still going strong, and people were still hanging on the streets.

Once I entered the hotel, Gavin was staying in, I went straight to the floor he was on. The hallway was deserted and quiet; so quiet you could hear a pin drop and someone getting their freak on as clear and loud as if you were right in the room with them. I smiled and shook my head. But my smile soon faded when I got closer and closer to Gavin's room. The sounds I was hearing drifting in the hallway seemed to get louder as I approached his door.

*No, this can't be possible. I know he isn't having sex with someone else. This has to be a mistake.* I quickly took out my phone and called downstairs to the office. It was possible he switched rooms. I got the front desk clerk and asked for Gavin's room. A few minutes later, I heard the phone ringing in the room where the sex noises were coming from, but no one picked up. Still I didn't believe it. *Maybe one of his groomsmen switched with him or something. Yes, that has to be it. There's no way he would...*

"Yes, Gavin! God, yessss!"

The blood from my face drained, and bile started consuming from my throat. First things first, that was Gavin in there screwing someone else; I'm one hundred percent sure of that, and secondly... He was screwing my best friend.... That was her voice I had just heard giving God and Gavin the glory.

Can I ask have you ever had your life flash before your eyes? Something that you never thought would ever happen to you does and you have no idea how to handle it? Yeah, that would be me right at that very moment.

I couldn't move or breathe. I stood there placing both hands on the door, hoping that what I was hearing was my imagination; that I was still in my bed stuck in a horrible nightmare. But as the moments passed by, and the moaning and slapping of skin on skin contact continued, I knew I was in hell.

My best friend and my fiancé were fucking each other's brains out, and all my brain was capable of doing was listening.

God so many things went through my head at that moment. Should I bang on the door and confront them? How long had this been going on? Would I get off with temporary insanity if I killed them both?

Rage and hurt consumed me, and I collapsed on the floor in front of the door. I couldn't believe the man that I was going to spend the rest of my life with, the man I loved with all my heart, was fucking my best friend. And I couldn't believe the woman that I thought was my sister, my best friend, who had been there for me through so much, and I her, would do this to me.

*I'm such an idiot.*

I felt broken, destroyed and completely alone. I had no family I could turn to. Maya was the only person I had, and then came Gavin. Now the only two people I ever loved betrayed me. I didn't have the strength to walk away, nor did I have the strength to bang on that door and fight. So I just sat there and listened to them call each other's name in thrills of passion and lust.

I went through all types of stages while I sat there like a coward. I started off feeling sick to my stomach to bewilderment thinking, *Wow, he's never lasted that long with me,"* then to anger thinking, *I'm going to cut them both.*

But as you can imagine, I didn't cut anyone. I waited while they satisfied each other. I waited as they probably cuddled and kissed. I waited until 6 a.m. when I finally heard movement toward the door. I stood shakily and waited patiently for the door to open. I heard the click of the lock, and I got ready. The door started to move, and I balled up my fists...

"Please tell me you're not waiting for your boyfriend or husband?" The accented English voice that caressed my ears brought me out of my nightmare and back to the bar in Cabo. I turned my head to find a very attractive Latin man smiling at me.

I was stunned into silence for one. And for two, I was mesmerized by his looks. I mean, holy hell this guy was hot, pretty boy hot at that. He definitely was the kind of guy that should be looking at the twenty-somethings and not at me.

I was hesitant at first, but I answered, "No I'm not, but I'm waiting for a friend."

"...Ah, a girlfriend perhaps? Is she as beautiful as you?"

Now I know this is a line he's pulling. Again, I think he's too hot for me, but I want to believe badly that he's somewhat sincere. Besides, maybe this is the one for me tonight for meaningless and mindless sex. I looked at him up and down, and I was impressed. He seemed to be lean, but muscled with a great head of black hair and dark brown eyes. His complexion was flawless and amazing, to say the least. And he reminded me of my ex.

"My name is Julio." He offered me his hand.

I smiled and accepted, "Hello, I'm Maya." Not sure why I did that, but I just didn't want to give him my real name…

Julio lifted my hand to his lips and kissed it. He gave me some intense eyes and said, "It's nice to meet you, Maya."

Julio and I ended up talking for a long time. We talked about each other's lives, me not telling anything truthful and him, probably doing the same. One thing I will say, it helped me forget about the cigar-smoking son of a bitch.

I was having a good time though and Julio was a lot of fun to talk to. What I didn't feel was safe asking him to come with me to my hotel room. God, I know how that sounds. I shouldn't be doing this in the first place and talking to this guy I realized I was making a huge mistake being there. I didn't belong.

So now I just had to let Julio down easy and make my exit. Julio had at least four drinks as he sat with me. I was on my third, but they were light. The bartender wasn't heavy on the alcohol all night, so I should've been good to go when I said my goodbye.

It's crazy how being shafted by one guy didn't deter me from this plight of self-destruction, but talking to a seemingly willing participant did.

I had noticed there is something off with Julio though, and I couldn't really put my finger on it. Again he seemed very nice, easy to talk to and very pleasant on the eyes. It's just that when he smiled at me, it never reached his eyes. When "the son of a bitch" smiled at me the other night, it seemed genuine, which is why I'm pissed at him for walking by me like he did.

When "the son of a bitch" touched me, it ignited my entire body, but when Julio touched my arm a minute ago while talking to me, I felt unnerved for some reason. He seemed so honest and truthful though, which is really confusing me. Or maybe it's my gut telling me that he's definitely not good for me.

I grunted. *Where was my gut the other night?*

"Do you want to dance?" Julio asked me.

Well, hell, why not? I figure maybe if I said yes that would be my hint at calling it a night and leaving by myself. So I took the rest of the drink I had and stood. The instant I did, I felt dizzy and uneasy. The room was spinning out of control. I felt weak and disoriented. I grabbed the chair in front of me and tried to get myself together. I felt Julio wrap his arm around me and say something to me, but I swear it sounded like he was miles away.

"I need to get out of here," I heard myself say, but I sounded like my voice was not my own, and it was so far away. I looked in Julio's eyes and knew instantly I was up shit's creek.

# CHAPTER 5

## DRAKE

I've never in my life wanted to end someone as bad as I wanted to this very moment. Watching her laugh and be touched by this fucking dick was making me insane.

I know I did this to myself, but that doesn't make the feeling of killing someone go away.

I shouldn't have walked right past her without speaking. I've been thinking about her ever since I left her room. The moment I laid eyes on her, I started feeling myself. No, I'm just going to keep this real and say what really happened. I fucking froze. I wasn't sure how she would respond to me, and I didn't want the feeling of rejection from her. So instead of having balls, I bitched out, and now I'm paying for it.

I thought the moment the bartender gave her the drink that I bought her, she would come over and talk to me. Instead, she gave me the finger and ignored me the entire night. I'm in fucking hell, and it's my own damn fault.

I tried to concentrate on the other women in the club and not watch her and the gel-haired fucker. You would think it would be easy for me to do. There were some gorgeous women there, half dressed and probably willing and able to walk in the men's room for a quick blowjob. But if I was going to be honest with myself, the only mouth I wanted on my dick was Georgia's. And from the stunt I pulled earlier, I doubted she would be willing to let me get near her, much less taste her again.

So I just sat at the table alone, letting my anger build until I was about to explode. The look in my eyes and the fury rolling off me was becoming hard to control. A few women made attempts to come to my table, but I knew the look I was sporting on my face made them pause and reconsider, which again is my own damn fault.

I ended up spending an obscene amount of money on drinks, chasing a buzz that never came and almost finishing my cigar when I decided to call it a night.

*Maybe tomorrow would be better, and I can get the scent of Georgia off my mind.*

I stood and dropped money on the table. Just as I looked up, I saw Georgia stumble and grab hold of her chair.

*What the fuck?*

I was watching her all night, and I knew she didn't have enough to drink that would get her fucked up. The bartender was making some weak ass drinks, which is why I was still fucking sober.

I watched closely as she attempted to shrug the guy's arm off her shoulders and trying to move around him, but he wasn't letting her go.

Decision time came for me quick, and I thought about the ramifications if I intervened. This could end badly for me in more ways than one. Georgia could go off on me and leave with this guy, making me feel like an idiot, or this guy could make a scene, which I would have to show my true colors and beat the shit out of him, and she leaves with him anyway disgusted with my behavior.

Or this could be exactly what I think it is, and I would have to save her from God only knows what.

Seeing him drag her, and then practically carry her to the door made the decision for me a no-brainer, and I started moving quickly to the exit and to Georgia. I knew it was important that I caught her at the door where there were plenty of bystanders. If he makes it to a car, shit is going to get ugly real quick because I knew a guy like that wouldn't be traveling alone.

I made it outside the club in seconds and just in time before they were out of my reach. Georgia was still being held or practically dragged as she tried to fight but didn't have the strength to. I immediately gripped her other arm and yanked hard, releasing her from his grip while saying loudly, "Georgia, baby, you can't be that pissed I made you wait for me."

I was hoping she wouldn't fight me, and she didn't. In fact, she wrapped her arms around my neck and gripped her fingers tight together.

Feeling her being pulled away from him, the guy swiveled and charged up to me. Now normally I don't let anyone come this close to me, but I had to be smart and play this right. Clearly it seems I wasn't the only one playing it smart. Instead of invading my personal space, he looked around at the people walking around and trying to enter the club, and then smiled at me.

"Uh, I think you have the wrong person. Her name is Maya, and she's clearly with me."

I smiled back moving Georgia behind me so I could defend us if I needed to. Georgia kept her arm around my chest and rested her head on my back. I backed up slightly, putting the wall behind us instead of the door to the club, and said to my opponent, "No, actually I think you're the one that has the wrong person in more ways than one." I then squeezed her arm and pulled to get her attention. I asked, "What's your name, baby?"

"I hate when you call me baby," she slurred.

I chuckled and said my tone a little softer. "My mistake. Tell me again what it is."

"It's Georgia... Are you going to take me back to my hotel?" she asked.

I didn't reply; I just looked over at him and waited for his next move.

He didn't disappoint. He moved closer to me and said, "It would be in your best interest to butt out of my affairs."

The man was two inches shorter than me and had a leaner body mass than I did, so his intimidating stare did nothing to me. I don't get intimidated, and I have a pretty mean stare myself.

I looked at him up and down before saying, "She happens to be my affair. As a matter of fact, she happens to be mine..."

"No, I'm not!" she piped up. "And what's that poking me?"

Without missing a beat, I added, hoping no one else heard that last part, "And since she belongs to me, I suggest you move on."

"You wouldn't even say hello to me..." she mumbled.

The man in front of me was joined by two others that happened to be bigger than me in body mass and height. Since his backup arrived, he figured he'd grow a set and said to me, "You clearly don't know who you're fucking with."

"Oh no, I know exactly who I'm fucking with; unfortunately I don't really give a shit. You aren't taking her anywhere. As a matter of fact, you will stay away from her from now on."

"Are you threatening me?"

I started to smile as I saw true anger possess his eyes. He was losing his patience with me and my boldness. He puffed out his chest, and I really thought he was about to swing on me. The two next to him seemed to be ready for just that, which amused me even more. I guess this fucker was hot shit on this island.

I shook my head. "I'm not threatening you at all, at least not yet. No, this is just a friendly warning..."

"Oh, a friendly warning..."

I nodded. "Yes, a friendly warning. Georgia is mine and is not to be touched. She's marked. So, out of courtesy, I'm asking that you leave her be. There are plenty of clueless girls on this island that you can take, but she isn't one of them."

He smirked at me and looked at the two at either side of him. "Oh, well, since this is a friendly warning, okay... Go fuck yourself! You think you can boss me around, talk to me any kind of fucking way... I don't know who the fuck you think you are..."

I moved closer to him seething, "Yeah, you're right, you don't know who the fuck I am. What you need to know is she's the property of the Leonetti family, and she's protected. That means if you fucking touch a hair on her head, I will fucking destroy you and anyone else that gets in my way. I will erase your piece of dog shit ass off the face of this fucking planet without a trace left for your family to fucking mourn. If you so much as think you're going to come at me, please understand who the fuck *you're* dealing with. The name's Drake, now get the hell out of my face and go learn who the fuck I am before I have to teach you."

We stared at each other for a long moment, both giving off some serious heat. I knew how this was going to end the moment one of them made a move. I sized up all three knowing that the one on my left I would have to deal with first. He seemed itching to start some shit. The other two wouldn't be a problem. I just needed to keep them in front of me. I can't let them near Georgia.

I noticed lights flashing off to my right coming to a stop right on the side of us. The tourist business is big in this country, so any of the locals that start trouble with the tourists the police crack down hard.

Suddenly, my adversary's demeanor changed again as he backed up from me. "Until we meet again then. And best believe you, and I will meet again."

I nodded my head slowly. "I fucking hope so!"

I watched them get into a Cadillac Escalade and drive away. Once they were out of sight, I changed my attention from the fleeting SUV to the woman behind me.

"Is everything alright?" one of the officers finally made their way to us.

"Yes, sir. Everything's fine. I'm just taking my girlfriend back to the hotel." I put my arm around her waist and kept her close to me, keeping my eyes out just in case the Cadillac circled back on us. The heat underneath my shirt was easy to get to, but I didn't want to be caught actually using it. That could really put me in more shit than I wanted to be in. But if they did come back or I felt threatened, no way would I hesitate to pull it and fucking use it.

The officer was satisfied with my response and walked away.

The walk back to the hotel was painfully long since I kept stopping and checking my surroundings. I didn't want to get caught unprepared just in case he came back around to finish what he started. Georgia and I made it to our destination in one piece and entered on the beach side of the hotel. The moment we entered her room, she started stripping without any assistance from me. I watched amused as she crawled into the bed naked and threw the covers over her head. I removed my jacket, shirt and pants and crawled in next to her, putting my gun underneath my pillow. She then turned and moved to rest her head on my chest.

It was at that moment, the moment when I wrapped my arms around her that it sunk in what I'd just prevented. For sure if she was placed in that car before I got to her, she would be gone right now. I kissed her forehead and nestled her closer, closed my eyes and drifted off to sleep.

*****

I first felt the light of day fall on my face. I turned my body, not wanting to wake up when I felt something else fall on me. I opened my eyes to find a beautiful set of brown ones looking back at me with questions, puzzlement, and anger.

I moved back from her gaze, yawned and stretched. "Um... Good morning, baby."

I rose out of the bed and headed to the bathroom to take a piss, when I noticed I didn't get a reply back.

Before I walked back out, I grabbed a robe that was hanging up behind the bathroom door. I leaned against the bathroom doorway and looked at her.

I have to admit, even though she was giving me a murderous look, I couldn't help but admire how sexy she looked in the morning. Her hair was all over the place, but it didn't matter- she was still quite beautiful.

"Don't look at me like that. How did you get here? No, better yet, why are you here?" She then tightened the covers around her body to protect herself from me. "And please don't tell me we did something last night."

I feigned shock and hurt as I said, "You don't remember what happened last night?"

She shook her head, "No, I don't. That should tell you something about your abilities. Now, since you have used my body, *again mind you*, you can see yourself out."

"Wow, really? I used your body again? I clearly remember it was the other way around, sweetheart. And I have to say both nights you weren't complaining."

Despite the color of her skin, I knew she was blushing. That made me smile even more, glad as fuck I was at the right place at the right time.

"Don't worry, baby. We didn't do anything last night, but sleep," I told her. "You were too wasted for anything else. You just came in here, stripped and crawled into the bed." I put my hands up defensively, "Without any help from me."

She folded her arms and frowned. "Oh and you just had to get in the bed with me?"

I moved and sat on the bed facing her. "Well, yeah, I didn't want to leave you in the shape you were in, and I wasn't about to sleep on the floor or in some uncomfortable chair. Don't worry, baby, the moment I take your pussy again, you will be coherent and an acting participant."

Her frown deepened, showing more of a confused state than anger. "Messed up? I don't get messed up. I know how to handle alcohol. Besides, the bartender was skimming on the alcohol. There was no way I could've gotten drunk."

I didn't reply. She looked at me and asked, "Did you have to carry me home or something? I don't really remember anything."

"Tell me what you do remember."

"I was just sitting at the bar. Then you came in and didn't speak to me. You just kept walking like we didn't know each other. That was messed up, you know. I mean, I understand that I created those ridiculous rules, but after you broke like all of them, I didn't expect you to ignore me."

"Yeah, I know. I'm sorry about that; believe me I really am... but can you focus a little? What else happened? I did see you talking to some guy."

She nodded, clueless of my poor attempt of aloofness. "Yeah, I can't think of his name right now. Though I think it was probably fake."

"Why do you say that?"

She shrugged. "No reason really. I mean I think I gave him my friend's or ex-friend's name, but I really don't remember. It's so frustrating; everything is just a blur. All I remember is you. You being at the bar, then me waking up to you lying next to me."

I really liked waking up to her lying next to me. Seeing her face in the morning, I don't know how to describe it, it just felt right. I looked at her and realized I had this stupid grin on my face. I wiped it quickly and cleared my throat.

"Listen, why don't you go and take a shower or a bath. We can either get breakfast delivered here, or we can go and find something to eat." Seeing her frown and shake her head, I hoped I diverted the questions in her eyes.

She gathered the cover around her body and looked at me, "Um, I really don't want to go out. I don't feel good."

"Okay, I'll order and we can eat on the terrace." I stood and allowed her to slip into the bathroom without my eyes on her.

When I heard the water running, I reached for my pants and pulled out the phone Angel gave me. It was nine in Cabo, so it was early enough to call him. I dialed his number and heard his voice in my ear on the third ring,

"Shit, Cuz, you fucked up already?" he asked jokingly. I didn't answer him. I let the silence tell him the reason for my call. I heard him moving around on the phone, and then he said an exasperated, "Shit."

"Before you go fucking crazy, it wasn't my fault," I added.

"Fuck it wasn't your fault. I know you. It's always your fault. What happened and please tell me you didn't leave any bodies."

I chuckled. "Uh no. I didn't leave any this time, but I can't say that will be the case next time."

So I told him about Georgia, how she was the woman I hooked up with the other day. I told him about last night and what I saw, playing back the conversation I just had with her and even described the guy that was trying to put her in the car.

I didn't have to tell him what I thought about the operation. We both knew what the outcome would have been if this guy was successful. There are a lot of men and factions that prey on women who travel alone. They kidnap them and either sell them into the twenty-first-century slave trade or pimp them out, put them on drugs and make money off of them. Or hell maybe he was just going to fuck her that night and probably dump her body in the ocean when he was done.

None of those things sat well with me, and I knew it didn't with my cousin either. Human trafficking was something our family didn't take too kindly to. We never fucked with anyone that did, and if we caught whiff of it happening, Angel and I usually fucked up shit majorly.

Angel brought me out of my own thoughts when he said, "You were watching her all night?"

"Yeah, and I didn't see when the guy she was with slipped her anything."

"So what you're saying is you were watching her all night then?"

I frowned, starting to get pissed off when I heard the humor in his voice. "Fuck you, Angel."

He laughed, "Yeah, I want to meet this Georgia. She must be something to keep your attention on her all night long."

"Can you concentrate? Look, I have a plate number that might help with identifying the family that this piece of shit is a part of. Also, I think the bartender was in on it. He was the only one that could have slipped her something, which tells me they've probably been doing this a long time. I'm thinking the bartender stakes out the place, finds a prospective girl and this guy comes in and sweeps her off her feet, literally." I got quiet as I listened to the sounds coming from the bathroom. "Angel, I gave her our protection. That means..."

"Yeah, Cuz, I know what it means." He sighed, and then continued, "I'll take care of it on this end. In the meantime, can you stay out of sight for a while? And stay out of trouble? At least until I have some answers for you."

I grunted. "I can't make any promises." I listened again and still heard the water running, so I asked, "What's going on with the other thing?"

"They don't have anything... You're right about that. I have our lawyers working on it. I have someone on the inside too, so as soon as he gives me what they have, I'll let you know."

I was about to say something else when Georgia burst out of the bathroom wrapped in her towel, still wet with a horrified look on her face. I sat up and looked at her, saying quickly, "I gotta go keep me posted." I hung up and stood. "What's the matter, baby?"

The tears fell from her eyes, and she shook her head. "He drugged me didn't he?" I didn't reply. Fear flooded her body as she started to shake. "Oh God." She placed a shaky hand over her mouth and closed her eyes. More tears fell, and I started to move to her.

"You're safe, Georgia," I told her, trying to comfort her, but she just looked at me.

"How can you say that? How do I know that for sure? Oh, yeah, I'm safe in my hotel room, but I'm here with a man, and I don't even know his name. Some guy was going to do God only knows what to me, and I can't remember a thing. I can't even tell you what he looked like, or what we talked about. I don't know what I told him.... Oh God, what if I told him where I was staying? Or where I lived back in the states?"

She started pacing. I wanted to soothe her fears, but she started babbling and waving her arms around. I couldn't get a word edgewise. "God, I am so stupid... I can't believe I was almost attacked or killed or worse..." She stopped and looked at me. "Could he have sold me or something?" She shook her head and picked up her brisk pacing. "No, don't answer that. Damn it, Georgia, they were right about you. You can't handle shit on your own. You're just as weak and soft as they said you were. To think you could do this, come here and be something that you clearly are not. I mean, you get a man to come to your hotel room and he blows

61

your mind with just his touch. And you stupidly thought that maybe, just maybe, there was something there, only to have your feelings hurt the moment you see him again. That should be a hint that you don't belong here. That you deserved everything you got up to this point and probably more..."

I watched on stupefied as she kept going on and on about shit I couldn't begin to tell you I understood. What I did make out is that I hurt her feelings last night by walking past her. That bothered me more than it should. I mean, it really shouldn't, but shit it did.

I moved closer to her and said her name. She didn't hear me at first until I said it louder, causing her to jump out of her skin and back away from me. Her back landed against the wall next to the bathroom door. The water was still running, and steam was billowing from the cracked door, but we both ignored it.

I took a few deep breaths and said, "Sweetheart, I don't know what he was planning on doing to you and with you, but the point is he didn't get that chance. As long as I'm here, he won't get that chance, do you understand me? I won't let that happen. Secondly, I don't know what the fuck you're talking about, but I don't think you're stupid. You stayed alert while he was with you. You never took your eyes off him for him to have been able to slip you anything. I think you were set up a long time ago without you knowing, and that guy just came to collect."

She laid her head against the wall and closed her eyes. She started shaking again, and all I wanted to do was hold her. I brought my voice down a few and said to her, "And I'm sorry about last night. In no way did I mean to make you feel the way you did." I moved closer just as she opened her eyes. "I've been thinking about you ever since I left your hotel room that night. I just wanted to respect at least one of your rules and give you some space. But you have no idea how much I didn't want to." I caressed her face lightly with my knuckles and wiped the wetness that formed on her cheeks with my finger.

I don't do this sort of shit. I'm not a person that shows this kind of emotion. According to those that know me, I'm incapable of feeling anything but anger and hate. It's like the ability for compassion was not wasted on me. But looking in this woman's eyes; seeing how lost and scared and hurt she was tugged at me. I tried to put some feeling in what I was going to say next so she would understand me. "I know you know I'm not good for you and, shit, you're right we don't know anything about one another. But I want you to know that the night we spent together did mean something to me. I can't explain why, but it just did."

Georgia broke our eye contact and looked down at the floor. In no way did I want to break this moment. I tilted her head back up until her eyes were on mine. The intensity she gave me unnerved me, but I didn't waiver. I leaned in closer and brushed my lips against hers. I kissed her again a couple of times, raining light kisses on her lips, capturing her top lip, then bottom, then just swept my lips across hers lightly.

I inhaled her deeply, wondering what it would feel like if I were able to do this all the time. I backed away from her and gave her space. I also put space between my dick and her naked body. I didn't want her thinking that's all I wanted her for....

My eyes grew as I realized what the fuck I just thought. What the hell is this woman doing to me? I cleared my throat needing to get the fuck out before I...

"Did you order breakfast?"

"Huh?" I snapped out of my befuddled trance and looked at her. I kept my eyes on hers and apparently she was doing the same.

"Breakfast... you said you were going to order it."

"Oh yeah. Um ... No, I didn't yet. Did you change your mind about eating in? Do you want to go out to eat?"

She shook her head, "Um, no, I just..." Her eyes traveled to my crotch and the tent that was clearly evident. She looked back at my face and God, for me, said the sexiest thing from her lips... "I'm not hungry for food anymore."

She walked to me, dropped her towel, grabbed both my ears and pulled me down to her lips.

Our kiss went desperate the moment our lips touched. I picked her up, deposited her on the bed and devoured her body with my mouth and tongue. I felt her untying the robe I had on and freeing me. She took me in her hands and stroked me from the middle to the tip, rubbing the pre-come around my head, adding extra sensation. That shit was driving me insane.

It's blowing my mind the way my body is reacting to this woman's touch. I'm on fire with the anticipation of her skin coming in contact with mine. I don't care where she touches me; fuck, I just want to be around her so she can. I'm losing my mind with just the slightest gasp of breath that she takes when I touch her and how her eyes feel like they can see through my soul. I don't know anything about this woman, but shit I want to.

"Can I have you?" she asked softly, and yup I'm fucking hooked.

My body shuddered as I tried to gain control; I was failing miserably. "Baby, you're not nearly ready for me. I don't want to hurt you. And the way I'm feeling, I might rip you in half."

She smiled, then wrapped her legs around my waist. She wiggled, and the tip of my dick was touching her pussy. The wetness from her warmth coated me as she brushed me along her sensitive bud. She had no idea the sensation she was causing. She closed her eyes and arched her back, giving herself to me, encouraging me to get lost in her. When she moaned the most erotic sound I've ever heard, she fucking undid me. I couldn't stop if I wanted to; I slipped into her wetness as slow as I could and moaned as her tightness smothered me.

"Wait a second... Please," she whispered, and I obeyed.

She looked in my eyes and I hers. I said to her because I didn't know what else to say at this moment, "Drake Lincoln... Thirty-three, born and raised in Philly. I love all things Philly, except cheesesteaks and those fucking Rocky movies. I have a brother and sister who I fucking hate and parents that I don't speak to. "

She smiled at me and grabbed my ears again... God, why do I love when she does that? "Georgia Sayers... Thirty, born in Baltimore, but currently I live in Miami. I love to eat, hate to work out, and I have no parents."

I couldn't help but mimic her expression. "It's very nice to meet you, Georgia."

"You too, Draaake," she replied, barely able to speak my name as I started stroking her long, slow... Just as I knew she liked.

# CHAPTER 6

## GEORGIA

Okay, so I needed to pause, *again*, just to let what I'd just done a few hours ago resonate.

*Whew...*

I was sitting there stunned in silence for numerous reasons. First being, I just had unprotected sex with a man that I barely knew. I wasn't even thinking when I attacked him. That is so unlike me but oh my goodness the way he kissed me and spoke to me had me on fire. My lips quivered and throbbed with a deep need that it seemed my body felt only he could quench. The need for him came over me, and I needed - no, I desired - to feel his hard body on top of me. I wanted to feel him inside me, claiming me. And, hell, I longed to feel his touch, his lips all over me, and he didn't disappoint.

He came inside me multiple times, and I didn't stop him. He tried to pull out, but I gripped him tight and wouldn't let him go. He was making my body convulse and cry out in ways no one has ever managed to do, and that astounded me.

I reached for the picked over fruit from my plate as I sat across from Drake on my patio off my room. Drake, which, by the way, his name fits him so well, had just told me everything that happened last night. Which is the second reason why I'm stunned. Just when he described the man that tried to kidnap me, I remembered the name he gave me... Julio.

Excitement radiated from him as he reached for his phone. He instantly started talking freely and adamantly as if I wasn't in the room. He was so comfortable and open with me it scared and shocked me all at once. So I tried to take my mind off his conversation and looked out onto the ocean. These past few days had been crazy, to say the least. Hell, this week had been insane. But I really needed to make a decision on where my life was going to go from there.

The moment I got home what the hell was I going to do? My life was completely wrapped up in Gavin and now suddenly it wasn't. School was out for the summer, and I didn't make plans to work that summer because I was going to come home a married woman. We had a home to find, and I would've been completely busy being Mrs. Gavin Diego. Instead, I'm going home to unanswered questions, embarrassment, and humiliation. The thought of being with Gavin was a stretch for me in the beginning of our relationship. I second-guessed us from the moment we met. But Gavin showed me how much he cared about me, how much he wanted me. So I figured, finally this was it; I've finally found someone to love me for me.

Oh, how I was I wrong.

I glanced over at Drake again and thought about the short time I've known him. This man had managed to spark more emotion from me than Gavin had, and we were together for years. Could that be the reason why he cheated on me, because in reality I wasn't sexy enough for him because I wasn't desirable? If that's the case though, what am I doing different now than what I normally do? Why is this man still here next to me with so much promise of passion in his eyes? What does he see in me that Gavin doesn't?

"Baby!"

I blinked and realized I'd been staring at Drake for Lord knows how long. I felt the heat rise from my neck to my face; thank goodness I'm dark. I diverted my eyes quickly and looked down at my shaking hands. "Did you forget my name already?" I asked him.

"No, I didn't, but you seem to not respond to your name when I use it. Besides, I think you like when I call you baby." I looked at him and saw that smile that seems to always light his face up.

I rolled my eyes but deep down, down in the pits of my soul, I feared he might be right. But that can't be. I've always hated when men call women those pet names like baby and sweetie. It drives me bananas. It's a false sense of security and acceptance a man gives a woman. I mean, whoever told men that women take baby, honey and sweetie as words of endearment must have been really hard up for a man's attention and acknowledgment. For years, I'd decided that's not going to be me. I wouldn't let a man call me baby and sweetie and smile and grin in their faces, especially when they use the word freely for any other woman that walked by.

So while I'm frowning, thinking of all the things I just mentioned, there is one truth that I don't want to admit.... I do actually like when he calls me baby and sweetheart... It's something about the look in his eyes when he says it and the sound of his voice. His voice gets all gritty, deep and full and oh-so-luscious... Yes, I think the sound of a man's voice can be luscious. The right bass, deepness and inflections in a man's voice can break you down and make you weak, vulnerable and under his complete control.

It can make your panties wet with desire the moment your name leaves his lips.

I sighed, looked back up at him and found him smirking at me. "Oh, what's so funny, Lincoln?" The smirk suddenly disappeared and was replaced with furrowed brows and a darkening of his already dark eyes. Watching this transformation caused me to adapt his expression a minute ago. "Oh, it seems I've struck a nerve. You don't like being called Lincoln, I take it."

His jaw tightened as he kept his eyes facing the ocean. "No, I don't mind being called that. Not at all."

I started to tease him more when he used his own deflection tactics and said, "What's on your agenda today?"

I shrugged. "I don't really have one. I mean, I had planned on hanging by the beach, or going sightseeing, but considering what almost happened to me last night, I might just stay here in my room for the rest of my vacation."

"Well, listen, I planned on doing some snorkeling or scuba diving, maybe even some parasailing today; you're more than welcome to join me…"

I shook my head vehemently. "Oh, no, that's sweet of you really, but I don't think so."

"Why not?"

"Huh, for one, I'm afraid of heights…"

Drake just shook his head. "Okay, I get the heights thing, but what do you have against scuba diving and snorkeling?"

I sat up straight and leaned in closer to him. "Um… first of all, there are sharks out there… And I know there is some statistic that says there is a one out of twenty chance that a black person can be bit by a shark… So how many white people have been attacked so far? I'm not becoming a statistic."

He chuckled. "First of all, there is no such statistic out there. Secondly, the part of the ocean you would snorkel is safe. You will not see any sharks."

"Yeah and how do you know?" I folded my arms.

"Because I do it all the time. Besides, if you do see some, I'll protect you. Come on. You have to at least give it a try. I promise you won't regret it."

I was so tempted. Really I was, but … I don't know… Looking at his handsome face, sincerity dripping from his eyes, I just couldn't shake that feeling of doubt. I didn't want to make the same mistakes with him that I did with Gavin. I know you're probably thinking I could just hang out with him, no strings attached. Problem with that is... and this is embarrassing to admit but... I'm starting to really like him.

This is absurd. I can't like someone this much and barely know him. No; what I'm feeling is completely physical, and I just can't handle that right now. So I said to him, shaking my head, "No, really. That's okay. You don't have to waste your vacation with the likes of me. Really I'll be fine. But I would like to thank you for, you know, helping me out last night. If it wasn't for you, there's no telling what could have happened. So I really appreciate it."

Okay, so I didn't mean to sound so dismissive, but I didn't know what else to do. This Adonis of a badass spells nothing but trouble for me; I could taste it. As a matter of fact, the overwhelming feeling to taste him is constantly threatening to consume me.

I moved my eyes from his face as he said to me, "So are you telling me you don't want to hang out with me?"

Annoyance fueled me, and I darted my eyes back to his and rolled them. "Oh, come on, Lincoln. You really expect me to believe a man like you really wants to hang out with a woman like me?"

"What the fuck is wrong with hanging out with you?"

I stood. "Are you kidding me? Do you want me to spell it out for you?"

He stood. "Please do that shit because I'm so fucking lost right now."

I stared up at him, watching that tension in his jaw expand to his shoulders and now his fists.

As I felt my erratic breathing take over, I knew he could sense my fury as well. I mean shit, how hurtful could it be to make me explain why a man like him just doesn't belong with a woman like me.

Drake, as if hearing my thoughts, shook his head, "Don't you even fucking say that fucked up shit in your head."

I turned my back to him and walked over to the edge of the balcony. *Just take a deep breath and do what you need to Georgia...*

Without facing him again, I said, "As I said before, I definitely owe you for helping me last night. Really I do. And if there is any way I could pay you back, please let me know but... I'm fine now. You can go about your business and go snorkel to your heart's content and smoke lots of cigars until your lungs give out and find a hot young twenty-something to take back to your room. There is no need to waste time on me."

"Wow... that was uh... Yeah, that was some kind of fucked up shit to say to me."

I turned around and crossed my arms, "How do you figure that?"

"Well, for one, I've admitted to you that you've been on my mind since the first night we slept together and you actually think

I'm only here out of obligation for saving your sweet ass? Let me tell you something, sweetheart, I don't do obligation. If I didn't give a shit about you, I wouldn't be here, and I wouldn't have said shit last night when that motherfucker was dragging you to his truck. I'm not that fucking honorable." He walked toward me. "I'm not the kind of guy that wastes time doing shit just for the fucking hell of it either. I'm asking to spend time with you because I fucking want to…"

"…Yeah, well I'm not the kind of girl that guys like you just hang out with so…"

He frowned lowering his voice in that gritty, deep way that is screwing with my head. "Baby, what kind of shit is that? Who the fuck has been filling your head with this bullshit?"

"It's not bullshit."

"Oh, yes the fuck it is, sweetheart. You are by far the sexiest woman I've seen in a very long time. You're fucking gorgeous as shit and sweet as fucking apple pie. Why wouldn't I want to spend my time trying to figure out new ways to make you blush? And, baby, there is nothing else I want to do more than make you blush."

*Ho-ly shit…. Yup, another timeout…*

Sorry, but no man has ever spoken to me like that… like ever… What the hell should I say? I turned my back to him again, gripped the railing and closed my eyes. My head dropped to my chest as I took a few deep breaths. *Sexy as shit? Really? Me?*

Getting in my own head made me miss the moment when the space between our bodies disappeared. My breath quickened, and I felt my heart bullying my ribs to beat out of my chest. He placed both of his hands on the railing too, placing his arms on the outside of my body, caging me between the railing and him.

The body-scent radiating from him was making me lose my mind. The closer he got the more shallow I breathed.

He sighed deeply and said, "I don't know who's been feeding you that shit you just insulted my ears with, but I don't ever want to hear you say that around me again. You're radiant day or night without any effort. You make me want to be here, and that's why I asked to spend time with you."

God this man...

The hairs on my arms and neck reached out in anticipation of his touch, my chest constricted, waiting for me to finally let air inside. Please... someone help me... oh this man...

"Why don't we make a deal," he said close to my ear. "You clearly came down here alone with an agenda. Let me help you with it."

My throat went dry instantly. I cleared my throat and said hoarsely, "What do you mean?"

He leaned in closer and the moment his fingers brushed along my shoulder my body screamed, "YESSSSS!"

Drake moved my tank top strap slowly down and bent, brushing his lips on my shoulder.

"You want to forget whatever you're running from. You want to let go, be someone you're not and maybe have a vacation fling, right?" His lips traveled slowly along my shoulder to where my shoulder and neck meet, his voice getting deeper, smoky, downright sinful and... "You want someone to fulfill your deepest desires and most intimate sexual fantasies, something that no one has ever been able to do for you." I closed my eyes and gripped the railing as tight as I could to keep from dropping to the balcony.

He moved to my other shoulder, lightly grazing his lips there, slowly traveling up to my neck. "I can make you forget whatever shit you left at home. I can help you escape, even if it's only for a little while... Isn't that what you want? Isn't that what you've been craving for since you got here?"

I closed my eyes trying not to hear the voice inside my head screaming to say yes...

Oh...I want his hands on me, touching me, caressing me, claiming me... controlling me. I want to feel the power he yields over me by just the simplest of touches. I want... Oh God, yessssss! There it is!

His hand finally touched my stomach, moving my t-shirt up and placing his palm on my bare skin. He rubbed and caressed me as his lips and teeth gently stroked and nibbled on some of the most sensitive spots on my neck.

"I will do whatever you want me to do to you, baby; all you have to do is tell me. I want to make all your fantasies come true. I want to make you feel coveted, wanted and desired... Can you let me do that for you, baby? Can you let go and let me be that for you?" He then ran his tongue along my ear, kissed me lightly and then whispered, "You don't know how much I want to be that person for you. Make you scream out in ecstasy. Prove to you how desirable and sexy you are." He moved even closer to me, and I automatically leaned against him. I felt his hand that caressed my stomach move to caress the under part of my breasts, brushing a nipple. Then he moved his other hand way down past my navel to under my shorts and panties to confirm my inner most secrets were revealed.

My hand instantly went to his wrist to stop his assault, but the moment his fingers felt my wetness, he plunged into me and started moving slowly.

"Let me help you become the freak I know you are... Damn, baby, you are so wet ... You love when I touch you, when I kiss your body, don't you, baby?"

I inadvertently started moaning my response until I heard that small voice say, "There are people watching you." I looked around frantic seeing if anyone was watching us... I mean, it wasn't like we were hidden from view....

"Lincoln, stop, please. People will see us."

Drake moved to my other ear and licked the outer part of it, then sucked on a sensitive spot just behind my ear that I had no idea existed. I buckled quickly and grasped behind his neck for balance. "Please…"

"You want me to stop?" he asked low and guttural and God so sexy.

I nodded yes but said, "No."

"If you don't want anyone to see you, you better come then… because I'm not stopping until you do."

He continued to break me, to claim me, to… damn it, I can't explain what he was doing. I just knew I didn't want him to stop. I wanted to not like what he was doing to me. We were in broad daylight and, even though, there were no kids around, I still didn't want anyone else watching him get me off-f-f … Oh, the hell with it….

I started grinding my hips against his hand, chasing the feeling that was building through me slowly. A slow exhilarating moan escaped from my mouth softly and just as he pinched my nipple I drowned in ecstasy.

Just then, I heard some commotion below, and I saw an older couple close enough to know exactly what Drake and I were doing. To Drake's credit, he did move his hand from my shorts back to my belly and hugged me in just enough time for the couple to look up and see us.

I of course was breathing out of control. "I can't believe you just did that."

"If you give me a chance, I can show you what else I can do." He kissed my shoulder and then let me go. I turned around and saw he was just as affected by what he just did. I reached for him, but he kept backing away from me.

"I'm going to go take a shower... be dressed in an hour." He turned and left me standing, wanting. I heard him moving about in the room, then I heard the door shut. I, of course, am yet again completely stunned.

# CHAPTER 7

## DRAKE

"Oh my goodness! I've never had that much fun in my life." A brilliant smile greeted me as we got out of the cab we took from the marina. I know I don't know too much about this woman, but already I've coined her smiles specifically for me.

She laced her fingers in mine as we walked to the hotel. For the past two days, we'd been going nonstop; from sightseeing to riding ATVs to snorkeling. Yeah, I finally got her to do it, and she's fallen in love with it, as I knew she would.

We made it to the elevator and as she spoke to another couple about the sunset cruise we took. I took that moment to admire her again for the umpteenth time that night.

I'm amazed at the quiet beauty she possesses. She never flaunts it, but she is sexy as hell. Her personality, her character, makes her even more unbelievably sexy to me.

Tonight she wore a short black dress that showed off her thick ass legs, stopping at just above her mid-thigh. She wore her hair down, and it was curled around her oval shaped face. Her smile though... Wow... I think it could move mountains if she really wanted it to.

When the elevator came, I possessively grabbed her and brought her close to me. The man and woman that came on the elevator with us seemed nice, but I don't trust anyone, and the fucker that was looking at Georgia's tits I liked even less. But I remained calm. I didn't show my true colors that night or any other night, though I was tempted multiple times.

The moment we hit her bedroom, she was under attack... I attacked her lips first; getting lost in their feel, their touch giving me the promise of a night where we have yet to hold back from each other. The feel of her, the scent of her is like a drug. I can't get enough of her body, of the sounds she makes when I'm inside of her. How she has no inhibitions with me. She's not ashamed of her body when she's around me, and I love that even more.

I slowed us down, savoring her body as I removed her dress. She wore black sequin bra and panties. With the combination of her four inch heels and the look of pure and utter desire encompassing her face... *shit...* all I wanted to do was make her unravel in my arms. I licked my lips slowly thinking of tasting her slowly as I walked her backward to the bed while removing my shirt and unbuckling my pants.

"Tell me what you want," I told her, looking heavily in her eyes. Make no mistake I wanted to conquer her tonight... and every night for that matter. I wanted to please her; I didn't lie about that, but I also had my own selfish reasons. I couldn't help the desires to lose myself in her. It would take over if I let it and I can't afford to that. Her body, her moans and her taste is what's driving me though. I can't get enough of her, and I'm fucked up about it. But I'll deal with that shit later. My goal was to make her forget whatever she's running from, and I've been doing that since I mentioned it the other day. Tonight though, I felt like seeing how she could handle being in control.

She stared at me thinking about how to answer me. I knew that, so I decided to give her a little push. I slowly moved to her and began to move the straps of her bra from her shoulders down her arm. I lightly caressed her with my lips, moving slowly against her shoulders and up her neck while my hands traveled along her waist up to her breasts. I yanked her bra down hard, popped her breasts out and brought my lips to her nipples. I sucked, licked, massaged, and squeezed them both with inhibitions nonexistent. She started writhing and rubbing her thighs together while gripping my arms tight. I moved my hand down into her panties to stroke her, knowing that was what she wanted, as I moved back to kissing her neck. I felt her cream the moment I circled her clit, and I knew she wouldn't be able to take it anymore.

Georgia gripped my shoulders tight as her shoulders picked up. "Drake, please...," she moaned.

"I can't hear you, baby. Tell me what you want," I whispered close to her ear. "Do you want me to taste you or just fuck you?"

She really didn't have an option. I was doing both. I didn't just want to be inside her. I craved to taste her. Shit, I wanted to taste her so fucking bad that I was losing my fucking mind.

I was about to take over when I heard her say softly, "Yes, I want you to taste me."

I stopped kissing her neck and looked at her. It's been too long since I had her. Well, it was just this morning that I claimed her, but I still needed it. I needed to feel her tight around me. I wanted to please her until she too lost her fucking mind. An idea popped in my head, and I went to pull her panties down. She helped by lying on the bed and lifting her ass so I could take her panties completely off. I dropped my pants as well as my underwear, and as she moved backward up the bed, I followed.

I didn't waste time. I kissed her once on each of her inner thighs. Then I moved to her core, and my tongue and lips brought her to the climax she was craving. After she came down from her high, she started going over the edge again and started moving away from me. I fucked her mind up in that instance as I gripped her thighs in my arms and flipped us both to where my back was on the bed, and she was straddling my face.

She gasped loudly and looked down at me, stunned. "Drake, what are you..."

I moved us both up the bed without letting her move from my face. I smacked her ass and said before I sucked and fucked the shit out of her with my tongue, "Fuck my face, baby... Give this pussy to me the way I like it."

She didn't know what to do at first until I started moving her hips for her. The moment I heard her moan, I knew it wouldn't be long before her hips would be bucking my face.

I don't do this often. Hell, I have to truly like you to even go down on you. For me to be doing this was fucking with me yet again and still I couldn't think about it. Tonight this woman was mine. Tonight I was going to make her scream my name until she gets fucking hoarse and loses her voice. Then I'm going to still keep going at it until she passed the hell out.

"Oh God! Drake, please...." She cried as she came apart again and again. She found that rhythm as I knew she would, and she learned to give herself the pleasure she craved. But I craved more. I need to be inside her. I couldn't take it anymore. I pushed her body down to where her pussy was close to my dick, and her lips were inches from mine. Georgia grabbed my ears and kissed me just as I rammed home and sated into the best pussy I have ever had. I told myself to go slow, but she felt too good. So fuck going slow...


*****


"Drake, are you awake?"

I opened my eyes to find hers looking at me through the dark. We'd just completed, I think, round three and she was still lying on top of me. I'd grown accustom to her sleeping on top of me. It's something about us being skin on skin that soothes me.

"Yeah, baby, what's up?" I answered groggily.

She rested her chin on my chest and started making circles using her fingers.

She hadn't been hesitant to express herself around me, so the pause she was taking was causing some alarm. She needed a little push it seemed, so I caressed her back and ass, "What's going on, baby? What do you need to ask me?"

She sighed but didn't reply right away. I grabbed another pillow and put it behind my back and neck so I could see her better.

She met my eyes and said finally, "Will you tell me something about you that you've never told anyone?"

*Shit.*

I watched her. She gave me those intense eyes again and, even though it was dark as shit in the room, I knew they were heavy with doubt, worry, and fear.

*Shit.*

*Deflection tactic time.*

"I thought we weren't doing this, baby?" I asked slowly, trying not to sound heartless. I mean, I am most times, but I didn't want her to think I was a complete heartless SOB.

She nodded her head and looked away from my eyes.

*Thank God.*

"Yeah, I know. It's just…"

I sat up more, putting my back against the headboard, and she ended up straddling my hips.

She inhaled and started off speaking softly; apprehension and emotion laced her voice. "When I was fourteen, I got pregnant. It wasn't by choice; the act of getting pregnant mind you… but there I was, and there was nothing I could do about it. I couldn't tell my family… God, my life would have been far worse than what it already was. I couldn't do that, and I couldn't keep it either so… I decided to end my pregnancy…" She looked down and outlined my abs as she stared absently at them. "That was one of the hardest things I'd ever had to do, and it haunts me every day, but I just…"

I didn't reply… I mean, shit, what could I say to that?

"The problem I faced though was that I was a fourteen-year-old with no money. I mean, how am I supposed to pay for an abortion, right? So I did what I had to do… There was this uh… this guy in the Baltimore neighborhood I grew up in named Jay Rock. He was well known in the street, so I went to see him for a job. He was the only person I could go to. He ran the streets in Edmondson Heights, my neighborhood, and it would be suicide if I went anywhere else." She chuckled uncomfortably and added, "He took one look at me when I asked for a job and laughed… He said, 'Nobody gonna pay for you, mama. Go on somewhere.' I should have done what he told me, but I begged him. He then looked at me, licked his lips and then he did offer me a job... Well, I wasn't doing that either, so I told him that I could sell for him. I explained since I was a big girl who stayed quiet and to herself, no one would suspect me. I could blend in when I wanted to or be a ghost if I had to. I figured I could do this for him..."

She chuckled softly and shook her head, "Well, as you can imagine, he wasn't going for it, but I was so adamant that he gave me a chance. I tell you, when I came back to him with his money and a smile on my face, he hired me right then and there. I was only fourteen years old, and I sold drugs for two months... Man, I was sitting pretty, you know? I thought this was going to be my chance. I was going to make a run for it, leave that awful house that I lived in and take care of myself. I proved I could do it, right?" She shook her head then looked at me and shrugged, "I was making a killing. I hid my money in the backyard over where my family kept their pit bulls. No one bothered those dogs but me. They were mean and vicious, but the only one that could be near them was me, not even my parents could get close. I fed them and walked them, so when I was out in the streets, they were my bodyguards."

"The success I was having gave me a plan for myself and Jay Rock helped me. He kept me under his wing, letting everyone know in the neighborhood, 'Don't no one fuck with Baby G'. Rumors got around on the street, and I was watched closely by Jay Rock's rivals, but no one ever stepped up to me. The police didn't believe I was capable of doing what the rumors said, so they never bothered me either. I still stayed to myself, and I remained quiet. I never flaunted; I had money and never ran my mouth. But I was observant and very careful, and I think that's what Jay Rock liked about me."

She squirmed again in my lap, but I didn't notice. Instead, I was taking in everything she was saying and even the things she wasn't saying. I did feel her move off my lap and sit between my legs on the bed, still keeping her legs draped over mine. She started tracing my abs again; eyes on my torso, "There was this one day Jay asked me to come by his headquarters. He usually picks some abandoned apartment building in the neighborhood to house his stash. So I typically was careful when I make my way to him. I took different routes and watched my back to make sure no one was following me. And I did that. I swear no one saw me coming, and I wasn't followed. So I got there, and he asked if I would run some errands for him. So I did that. I was gone a long time, and when I made it back, he was on a heated call with someone. Jay Rock was always on the phone cussing and yelling, so I didn't think nothing of it. When he got off the phone, he looked at his crewmember and said, 'Yo, put Dawg, Spank, and Lateef on alert. Those muthafuckas don't know who deh fuckin' with. I don't think they'd be stupid enough to start some shit, but jus, in case, I wanna be ready.' He then looked at me and nodded his head, 'Stay low for a while, Baby G, aight? I'll call you when the block is cold; you got me?'"

Her eyes traveled to mine. "I nodded to him and was about to say something when the shit just hit the fan. I mean, one minute, all his boys were just milling around, watching porn on TV, playing video games, counting money and then ... Bam! Gunfire just erupted..."

I could imagine exactly the scene she was describing. I'd hit places like that multiple times, and I also know what the end result of that raid was. I rubbed her thighs to try and soothe her. I knew whatever she saw fucked her up pretty bad. I could see the emotion overcome her and tears gathered in her eyes. They only fell the moment she closed her eyes.

Her voice lowered when she spoke next. It didn't matter how close we were; I could barely make out what she said. "God, Drake, all that blood... I've never seen anything like it. I mean bodies just dropped left and right. Bullets... men screaming in agony, cursing, pleading, begging... I mean, some of them were executed without prejudice. I wasn't naïve. I knew what Jay Rock and his men were, but it still bothered me, you know? It was awful...When it got quiet, I thought the coast was clear, so I rose up from my hiding place and was met with a gun placed right against my forehead. I've never seen so much evil in a man's eyes. That day, I swear Satan was standing before me. I couldn't move from the look in his eyes and only blinked when I heard a click from the gun. But still I couldn't find my legs, so I stayed there as he pulled the trigger over and over again. I saw him bend down and grab another gun lying around. He quickly pulled that trigger too, and nothing happened. He got frustrated and yelled, looking on the floor for another gun to shoot me with, and I finally found the will to move and cut out running. As I ran, I saw a gun just lying there next to one of Jay's men. So I picked it up and blindly shot it behind me. I didn't look back. I just kept firing as I got clear…"

I instinctively touched her face with both my hands and tried to remove the sadness as each tear fell. She opened her eyes and just looked in mine. Seeing the pain in her eyes pissed me off to no end. I was literally figuring out how I would find this motherfucker and rip him to fucking pieces.

"There were at least sixteen bodies lying in that house from the aftermath… but there was only one that died at the hands of me."

"I'm so sorry, baby," I said softly.

She started shaking and trembling. I didn't know what I could do to ease her. I kept caressing her face, rubbing her arms, just trying to soothe her as best as I could.

"I ran for two blocks before the cops stopped right in front of me. I was covered in blood, and I still had the gun in my hand." She shook her head and frowned. "I can't begin to tell you why they didn't shoot me on sight. I mean, I saw them stop in front of me. I saw them draw their weapons and point them at me, but I just stood there. I didn't move. I couldn't. I don't know if I passed out or what, but the next thing I remember is waking up in the hospital."

She fell silent that moment still trembling. I was enraged at this point, and I wanted to ask her about her family, but she said, "The cops didn't get much out of me because, hell, I didn't see much. I told them how the men came in and just started shooting. I didn't know who they were or why they were there. They asked what I was doing there, but I never answered them. They had my prints on the gun, but they also had prints from the owner too. From all the evidence, they gathered, the DA decided not to charge me. When the cops brought me home and told my family what happened, we had an understanding. They stayed away from me, and I stayed away from them."

"I was so scared, Drake... I was so afraid that Jay Rock's people would think I set him up, and they would come after me. I was afraid that the other crew that got killed would come and retaliate on me too. I barely ate; I barely slept... I didn't have to go through with the..." She paused, and I knew what she meant. She sighed, "Sometimes I just wish I died with everyone else in that place... God... I took a life, Drake, and I can't seem to shake that fact... I sometimes see his eyes in my sleep, and I think he's not dead... When you told me about that guy trying to kidnap me... I just know I'm a goner if they get me..."

"I won't let that happen, Georgia, I promise you." I pulled her into me and turned our bodies to where she was lying under me. As I turned her though, she broke. She just cried out in agony and pain, as if this shit just happened to her instead of it being seventeen years ago.

"Listen to me, what happened that night in that house wasn't your fault. I know those kinds of people. Jay Rock probably had a long-standing beef with them, and they were probably watching him for a long time. So don't beat yourself up about that, and don't you dare fucking feel sorry for the son of a bitch that you shot. Baby, he had no soul, no heart... He was going to kill a fourteen-year-old because you were just there. Believe me, he wouldn't have lost any sleep, so you need to stop letting it bother you now."

"I can't help it..."

"I know, baby, but try. Try and think about the good shit you've been able to do in your life that justifies you still being here... being alive."

She scoffed, "Yeah, like what?"

"Like, hell, I don't know... You've graduated from college, you're shaping young minds as a professor, you've gotten the rare opportunity to be fucked by me; I mean, take your pick..."

She started laughing. If I wasn't secure in myself, I would have taken it personal. I smiled at her, hoping I was getting her back.

She covered her face from me with her hands, groaning, "Ugh... I don't know why I told you all of that. I'm sorry."

I moved her hands and kissed her cheeks, her forehead, her eyes, and her lips. I caressed her face and said, "Baby, it's okay. I understand why you've shared that story with me, so don't worry about it. I'm honored. I really am..."

And I did understand why she told me. The way she's given herself to me these last few days, I knew she hadn't done this with anyone else. I could feel that every time I was inside her. She needed to justify doing this, giving herself to me in the way that she has. I can't be a stranger to her, she can't be a stranger to me, so she figured if we share something about each other that no one knows about, we'd kind of solidify a relationship that was above any we'd experienced with anyone else. It made our arrangement easier to cope with in her eyes.

It was my turn to share. I didn't want to, but as she continued to recuperate in my arms, I had no choice. "Ever since I was born, I've been a rebel. It's hard for me to follow rules that inhibit me to get what I want. I've done a lot for the sake of my wants as a kid. I've stolen things I wanted, I've cheated to get what I want, and I've beaten the fuck out of anyone that stood in my way."

Her red eyes searched in mine. For what, I didn't know, but I kept my eyes on hers so she could get what she needed from me. I caressed her face, wiping the wetness and just wanting to touch her, to mend her somehow.

"My parents, as you could imagine, weren't thrilled to have me as a son. I'm the youngest, and my siblings reminded me all the time that I was an afterthought as I grew up, so I made sure they regretted having that one more child and sibling." I chuckled and added, "I wasn't ever sent to juvie or anything like that. I was smarter than to get caught. I only surrounded myself with smart people, and if they did some dumb shit that could get me caught, well... Let's just say I cut them out of my life."

"I did manage to graduate high school, and I thought about college, just to fuck with my siblings and my parents. But instead I thought of another way to do it. My brother, Daniel Jr., is about six years older than me. My sister, Julia, is four years older than me. They, of course, are very close, and they actually followed in my parents' footsteps. My father is an Assistant Director of one of the divisions of the FBI. My mother works for NSA and is rubbing elbows with high-ranking officials in the government. So being the ideal children, my siblings decided to follow in my father's footsteps and joined the Bureau fresh out of college."

"So what I did to fuck with my family is join an agency that would piss them off every time they thought about it... I joined the CIA."

"You're a CIA agent?"

I chuckled at the size of her eyes. "Oh no, not anymore, but for twelve years, yes, I was. The CIA doesn't recruit kids fresh out of high school, but I ascertained a certain amount of skills growing up that they couldn't possibly pass up, so at the age of eighteen, I was trusted with the life of spies."

"So you're estranged from your family because you joined the CIA?"

I sighed and just looked at her. This was something that I didn't want to tell her about. Only Angel and my Uncle knows about my past, and it took me months before I confided in them. I really could make up anything at this point, but I didn't. Instead, I gave her the exact same honesty she gave me. "Well, they don't like me for a number of reasons, but for me, it is a lot deeper than that. So..." Georgia sat up a little, placed her back against the backboard and hugged the pillow to her. I laid on my back and put my hands behind my head. I looked up at the ceiling and continued, "I need to explain that I was really good at what I did for the agency. They would call me for most of the sensitive assignments, and I would do whatever I needed to accomplish the goal they wanted. If I didn't like the job or I felt something was up with the assignment, I wouldn't do it. I worked alone, so I didn't have a problem bailing on a job. I mean, the powers to be might not approve, but fuck them... Well, not to go into details, but I was told to capture and bring a very important witness to an undisclosed Embassy. I was specifically told to do a snatch and grab clean. So I went to where the subject was and planned on doing just that. But when I got there, someone beat me to him, and they killed him."

I heard her gasp so I looked back at her, "Are you okay with me telling you this?"

She nodded, and I added, "Baby, I need for you to say the words to me. Are you okay?"

"Yes, Drake, I'm okay... I'm not shocked that he was killed... I mean, I was, but I was more shocked that someone beat you to it."

"Yeah, me too. So I got out of there as quick as I could. Well, the problem was this person was some big hotshot, something that I didn't know, and someone planted evidence that pointed right at me. I mean, the moment I made it out of the apartment where the body was, the police were already there. I barely got out of the country with my life, then to find out that my own country was selling me out to take the fall for this fucker. My superiors complained about me, had written documentation that I was mentally unstable- shit that they have never told me, and accused me, in writing, for shit I didn't do. I've never seen any formal or informal complaint on me until that moment."

"They set you up," I heard her whisper. I nodded my head and didn't reply.

The shit they did was still fresh in my mind. It had happened about six years ago and just like Georgia that shit was still warm.

"What did you do?" she asked.

I took a deep breath, "Well, I did what I was good at. I got to the bottom of the shit and cleared my name by finding the person that set me up."

"Did that person get arrested?"

I didn't want to answer her question. This was too much for me to share, but I heard myself say, "No, baby, he wasn't arrested, but I can tell you that I took care of him none the less."

It was her turn to be quiet, and I let her. This was a lot for her to take in.  She just told me about killing someone and seeing all that blood and bodies, and I just indirectly told her that I had committed that same sin.

"So your family, they didn't help you clear your name?"

I chuckled, "Oh, no, baby... they were the main ones trying to bury me.  They believed everything that was being said about me and probably still believe that shit.  They were condemning me more than the CIA was... So much for loyalty, right?"

"Wow. I'm sorry, Drake."

I rolled, propped myself up on my elbows and forearm, and faced her. "Baby, don't waste your sorry on me, okay?  I've done some fucked up shit throughout my days in the agency. But what's fucked up is how they treated me after all I had done for them. The fact that they were saying I was unstable and shit, fucked with me. So I got out of the agency and never looked back."

"Has your family found the error of their ways and tried to mend what they've done?"

"Not in the way that you think. My father said, 'Well, what did you expect from us? You joined up with that agency and that's all they do is set up their own people.' He didn't take accountability for his part or my siblings and mother.  So I say fuck them every chance I get, and I continue to shit on them when necessary."

"What if they change? Would you forgive them? What if they need you one day? Would you help them?"

"Baby, I don't know if I would. It would depend. I'm not an honorable man. If you fuck with me, I will fuck with you far worse than you could ever imagine. I'm not ashamed of that fact at all. So it would take a lot for me to do it. I'm all for the loyalty thing. If I give you my trust, I expect it in return. Fuck that up, and I will forever be your enemy, and honestly, baby, you don't want me for an enemy."

I let that sink in for a bit before I added, "You don't have anything to worry about that though."

"Yeah... I guess I don't..." She turned from me, got up and walked into the bathroom.

I closed my eyes and laid back on the bed.

*I'm such a fucking idiot.*

# CHAPTER 8

## GEORGIA

I got up early the next morning and unraveled from Drake.

Last night was emotional, to say the least. I mean, I really don't understand why I gave up all that information to him. He claimed he understood, but I really wished he'd elaborated more. I've never in my life repeated any of that to anyone. My past was just as I said-mine. No one would understand the dynamics of my family life and those that do pretend to would fail at it.

The story of my life is typical of any female growing up in one of the worst neighborhoods in Baltimore. My neighborhood, Edmondson Heights, was filled with abandoned buildings that drug dealers used frequently as well as addicts. There was crime of all kinds but mainly it was the drugs that brought the area down.

Both my parents were addicts and barely around to take care of me. My mom wasn't always an addict. I have memories of her taking me to the park, baking cakes for my birthdays. I remember her taking me to school. My mom was the glam girl. She always dressed very well and smelled pretty; that's what I remember of her. We had food on the table, and I had almost anything I would ever want. We weren't living in Edmondson during that time. We lived in a pretty nice area of Baltimore, at least that's what I remember. I also remember visiting my grandparents a lot back then.

I can't begin to tell you what happened. I mean, one minute my mom was happy, smiling and laughing all the time. Then the next she was sad and crying all the time. She started to wither away with each passing day. She stopped caring about looking nice, smelling nice. She stopped caring about taking me to the park and making dinner.

Then the random men started coming. She stopped taking me to my grandparents. One day, she came and got me from school and instead of us going to our nice apartments, she took us to this rundown high rise in Edmondson Heights. Still to this day, I can't tell you what happened that changed her. My mom never told me, and I never asked.

I watched my loving-life mom turn into a bitter fiend in less than a month. Her boyfriend, who she told me was my father, became her supplier, pimp, and executioner. She long forgot about me. I used to have to find something to feed myself, if there was anything in the cabinets to find, and I used to walk back and forth to and from school alone. My school was far, and it took me a long time to get there on my little legs. I passed by street hustlers and gang bangers every day. I wasn't afraid though. Seeing them was like window dressing for the neighborhood I was in. But I refused to miss school. School was my way out. It was my escape from the hell that was my home.

Coming home from school one day, I found my mom dead on the steps of my apartment complex. I ran into the apartment to get my father and found him lying on the couch dead too. I was nine at the time, so I just called the cops and waited. It took them a few hours to come. When they did, I became the ward of the state. They threw me into some house in the neighborhood, and I went from hell to completely hopelessness. The two people I had to call mother and father were horrible to me and the six kids they housed. Mother called me fat and told me I would be nothing but a whore or a fiend just like my mama. Father tried his best to see me naked every chance he got. I wanted to leave, especially when I was attacked, but after that thing with Jay Rock, I couldn't do it. I stayed there until I was seventeen. The day I turned seventeen, I left for college and never looked back.

I don't tell anyone my story because I don't need sympathy from people. I never let my past hold me back, but it became the reason for my future. What always seems to happen though is I surround myself with people that truly care nothing about me. I mean look at Gavin. I loved him and thought he felt the same way. But when I think about it, the constant "Georgia, do this" or "Georgia, don't do that" or, which, by the way, is my favorite, "Georgia, why can't you be more like Maya," it was obvious that he didn't love me for who I was. I don't know what he thought I could be, but clearly I wasn't the woman for him. If I were, he wouldn't have banged my best friend.

Couldn't he have had sex with another woman? On our wedding night with the maid of honor is so freaking cliché. And Maya, I thought she was family. That's what she would always say to me, that I was the sister she never had. But at the end of the day, as with most people in my life, she stabbed me in the back.

I think I need to re-evaluate my lifestyle and the people I keep close to me. My problem is I open myself up too soon to people that haven't even proven themselves worthy of my love, worthy of my heart. That needs to change. And maybe it should start now.

I moved into the bathroom and took a long shower, trying to figure out a way I could tell Drake that I didn't want to hang out with him anymore. However, whatever plan I tried to think of, I just didn't like the outcome. I didn't want to admit it out loud, but I loved being with this man. I loved the way he looked at me, how he touched me. He was possessive at times, but there were those times where he just let me be myself.

But I had to keep this in perspective. This was just an arrangement that wasn't going to last. When we go our separate ways, I will never see him again.

I closed my eyes and let the hot water fall over my face to hide the tears that were starting to fall. I didn't want this to end. I wanted forever with this man, but I knew for a fact he was probably not good for me. He'd said it multiple times, and from the first night I met him, I knew he was bad for me.

I should be thankful that this would end soon. But part of me, the wanna-be rebel side of me, wanted him desperately. He was like that decadent chocolate cake that you know you shouldn't eat, but it keeps calling for you, baiting you, and you can't resist just a bite, and as always, one bite is all it takes, and you're hooked.

I got out of the shower and wrapped myself tight in my towel. When I exited the bathroom, Drake was asleep. I stood there and studied him. He seemed so peaceful in his sleep, so less threatening. Watching people move out of his way when we were walking through town was always comical to me. It was obvious that he was used to it though, so I could only imagine how he was in the states.

But to me, right now at this very moment, he seemed harmless.

"Are you just going to stand there and stare at me?"

I jumped slightly and smiled. He opened his eyes and looked over at me.

I don't know how he does it but all he has to do is look at me, and I swear I melt.

I cleared my throat and moved to the chair furthest away from him. "Are you going to sleep the day away?"

Drake watched me closely until I sat down and crossed my legs. He smirked and said, "Really? You're going to sit all the way over there?"

"Yes I am..."

"Why? Afraid of what I might do?"

I ran my hands through my braids and answered honestly, "Yes."

"Baby, you know I wouldn't do anything you didn't want me to..."

I nodded. "That's what I'm afraid of."

Drake laughed and removed the sheet from his glorious body. I stared at him, eyes wide. It didn't matter how many times I'd seen him naked, I still had to pay homage to his greatness.

Drake walked over to me, and when he got close, he knelt in front of me. He moved my legs apart and positioned himself between them, bringing his hands to the folded part of my towel.

He said to me, "Never be afraid of what you want, baby... especially not with me." He opened my towel and the hunger suddenly took over his features.

"Drake..." I said softly.

"Yeah, baby?" he replied just as low as he moved and started featherlike kisses between my breasts.

I took a few deep breaths. I was already feeling the effects of him being so close to me. The anticipation was evident through my body. I wanted him to touch me; the problem is I wanted it all the time.

He slowly continued his assault down my stomach, and I instantly grabbed him by his ears with both hands and stopped his movement. "Wait... Can we get out of this room? I know where this is going, and I also know once you kiss me, we'll be at it again for another hour..."

He grunted, "At least..."

"Yeah, so please can you save your assault on my senses until later? I want to go snorkeling." My heart was pounding in my chest, and I knew I was drenched, waiting for some Drake loving, but I was serious. I knew what it meant to be ravished by Drake, and I needed to stop myself from getting attached. I needed to keep this whole thing in perspective, right? Or at least try anyway.

Drake leaned into me and kissed me. He didn't deepen it, and when he parted from me, he smiled. "No problem, baby. We can do whatever you want... But please be on notice; I will continue this assault on your senses, as you call it, tonight." His finger went along my lips, then down my chin. He moved in to kiss me again, and I almost said forget snorkeling... Drake is just that good.

# CHAPTER 9

## DRAKE

As the cool ocean breeze touched my face, I leaned farther back into the cushion of the lounge chair, sitting on the patio off of my room. The nicotine flowing through my system combined with my smoke filled lungs had brought me to a state of calm after the storm that was Georgia Sayers.

Fuck, that woman was a piece of work. She was full of energy and life, and wouldn't you know it; she could practically drink me under the table. We had spent the last four days getting very familiar with what Cabo had to offer.

Since I'd managed to get her to snorkel, she was hooked, and we'd been going every morning bright and early ever since. We'd continued to take tour after tour; from learning about Los Cabos culture and history, to submarine tours to tequila tasting. We'd swam with the dolphins, took Kayaks out on the Sea of Cortez, and she even got me to whale watch with her.

Besides the shopping and the sightseeing, being with her had been an adventure. I had talked more in four days than I had in years. The nights that we shared had been eventful all on their own. We had partied hard, going to multiple clubs and getting shit-faced. Then we'd go to her room or mine and have mindless drunk sex. It'd been a long time since I'd had drunk sex, but those last three nights had been uh... something else.

I said this woman could drink, and I'm not lying. It took a lot to get her drunk, but once I did it, she let go completely. She was fun, exciting, sensual and fucking amazing. We danced all night and fucked each other's brains out until the sun came up. We'd gotten intimately familiar with each other's bodies so much that I could tell the moment when she was aroused just by looking at her.

The reaction she had on me blew my mind, and I couldn't get a hold of it. I couldn't understand how I responded to her so well. The only thing I could think was, *She's changing me.* Now I wouldn't say she'd changed me completely. I still had my dark, twisted urges, but I didn't sightsee, I didn't swim with fucking dolphins and fuck if I whale watched. But just seeing the excitement in her eyes, the life in them, I couldn't turn her down.

I felt the phone that my cousin gave me vibrate on the table. I quickly reached for it hoping he finally had some news for me.

"What?"

My cousin chuckled, "Damn, am I interrupting your night with the glorious Georgia?"

I sighed. I regretted telling Angel about Georgia the very moment her name left my lips that the other day.

"I hope you're telling me some good news or that you got the information on that piece of shit that tried to take Georgia."

,

"Well, yes, I do have some news, but I'm not sure you'll think it's good."

I sat up. "You found the son of a bitch shot in the fucking head with his brains splattered all over the place?"

"Well, no. Actually I haven't been able to find any action down there that you mentioned or the guy you described. The car was a rental and the name it was under came back with a bogus. Cabo is pretty clean, as far as crime goes. I don't know, Cuz. Are you sure she just wasn't fucked up? Or maybe she was taking something and didn't want you to know about it?"

I shook my head. "No, I'm sure about that. Georgia isn't the type. Besides, the woman can drink and hold her own. I told you the bartender that night was serving weak ass drinks, so I know for a fact she wasn't fucked up. No, there has to be some reason why he was trying to take her."

"Well, if there is, I haven't found one. Why don't you find the bartender and ask him?"

"Yeah, I've tried that. He hasn't been to work since that night."

My cousin paused a beat, and then said, "Do you have a name?"

"Manuel Agosto."

"All right. I'll check it out to see if I can find out something about him based on your description."

"Yeah okay. Keep me posted then... I'll talk to you later."

He cleared his throat. "Uh, don't you want to hear the news I have?"

I frowned. "I thought you already told me the news?"

"No, I said the news I have to tell you is good news, but you might not think so. That shit wasn't it."

"Well, stop pussying around and just tell me."

He chuckled again before he said, "You're clear to come home."

"You shittin' me?"

"Nope. The lawyers got back to me, and the Feds have nothing. They claimed they were slipped the information, but none of the evidence they gathered matched to you. Also the people that you allegedly took out, I know for a fact you didn't. The family had no beef with them, so you are good to come back."

I took a drag on my cigar and smiled. Finally, I get to go home and leave this... Oh shit...

"Yeah, bittersweet, isn't it?" Angel added as if reading my thoughts.

I didn't reply.

"Pops says he needs you home ASAP though."

I nodded my head self-consciously. "Yeah alright. Get someone to book me a flight some time tomorrow and text me the info."

"Will do. See you then," I heard Angel tell me before he hung up the phone.

If my Uncle said he needed me home ASAP that only means my cousin Eddie is into some shit, and he needs me home like yesterday. I knew I was going to have to take the next thing smoking out of there if I could.

Shit... I didn't want to leave Georgia there by herself. Even though I'd been looking out for any backlash from the other night, it didn't mean she was safe. I didn't like having loose ends, especially since Angel didn't get any information on the three goons from the truck.

Georgia told me she wasn't leaving for another two days, and I knew I couldn't wait that long.

*Fuck.*

I heard my door open, but I didn't turn around to see who came inside- I knew it was her.

"Hey, I've been calling the room for the last ten minutes. Are you okay?"

When she stepped out on the balcony, my eyes went to her, and I froze. She looked fucking amazing. Her braids were up and away from her face, giving the world full view of her beauty. She wore eye makeup that made her brown eyes come alive and gloss on a pair of beautiful full lips that made me want to devour them every chance I saw her. But the dress she wore...

"Damn, baby, you look beautiful."

I stood on shaky legs... Wait, what? *Get a fucking grip, Lincoln.*

I shook my head to clear it and walked toward her. She absently ran her hands down the front of her dress and looked down.

The dress was a white strapless dress that started just at the bottom of her neck and traveled down past her hips and thighs, caressing her body like silk. It contoured every curve of her hips and stomach, falling to the ground with ease. Her heels brought her almost eye level, which was a fucking turn on all by itself.

She smiled, her eyes averting a direct look into mine, "Drake, it's just a dress."

She's finally gravitated to calling me Drake instead of Lincoln, unless she's pissed at me or wants to get a rise out of me. I have to say, I prefer it and, to be honest, I love hearing my name leave her lips. Hearing her say my name while trying to get my attention, or in the middle of us claiming each other's body, seems to always make me want her more. She doesn't know what I am or what I do, and she doesn't have a clue about who I am. So I let her say the name that most men in the world would never use and live to tell about it, and no woman has parted their lips to say. It's the power I gave her, and she doesn't have a clue what it means.

When I finally got to her, I cupped her cheek in my palm, and she put her head down.

*No, no, that won't do.* I tilted her chin up, so she had no choice but to look at me, and damn if the intensity in her own eyes was causing me to want to look away.

But I don't. This may be the last night I have with her and I want to make this count. I wanted to embed myself into her soul so she never in her life forgets about me.

"Georgia, you are beautiful, strong and sexy as shit. This dress is just enhancing what you already possess, baby." I looked at her lips, daring myself to touch them. I knew if I did, she would be out of this dress faster than I'm sure it took her to put it on. "You. Are. Stunning."

She gave me that smile that I would kill for and turned away from me.

"Come on, baby. Let's get out of here," I said to her, saving each of us from what undoubtedly was starting to happen between us.

We took a cab to the Marina of Cabo and found a romantic Italian restaurant, with outdoor upscale dining and a fantastic view of the marina and the sun setting. The moment we arrived, valet greeted us and led us inside. We didn't have to wait that long, which I was thankful for, and a hostess escorted us outside to a small table in a corner with a panoramic view of the bay.

Every table was sitting outdoors, using the marina and the horizon as its wall, paintings, and décor. There were tall lamps that illuminated the area as the sun set, giving this place even more of a romantic feel. Yeah, if Angel had seen me there... This woman was definitely changing me.

Our conversation was light. We managed to maintain that throughout the time we spent together. We shared childhood experiences, favorite cartoons as kids and movies we liked to watch- that type of shit. She asked me how many girls I banged in high school, and I just made up some number and told her. Chicks threw themselves at the bad seed when I went to school but rarely did I bite. I don't like to be used by anyone unless it's on my terms, of course.

Dinner came. She'd ordered a simple spaghetti dish, and I had the beef tenderloin with Pacchero style breaded pasta, Mozzarella tomatoes, and organic pesto. The food wasn't half bad, and the wine we drank wasn't half bad either.

I felt my phone vibrate signaling a text message. I knew it was my cousin giving me my flight information for tomorrow. I hadn't figured out a way to tell her that I was leaving yet. For some reason, the words just wouldn't form in my mouth. I knew I needed to tell her. I was regretting the moment that I had to just as I heard her say, "I plan on going home tomorrow."

The way she blurted that out took me by surprise. I was actually stunned, especially since I was sitting there trying to figure out how to tell her the same thing.

I took a sip of my wine as she added, "I know I said I was going to be here for another two days, but I think it's time. I can't keep running from my problems, can I?"

"No, you can't," I finally said to her. I signaled for our waiter with my wine glass as I said to her. "What are you running from exactly?"

It was her turn to take her wine down fast. When she sat her empty glass down, she looked at me. Sadness colored her face that put me on edge. I knew this wasn't going to be a story that I would like. It seems the life this woman has led was one she didn't deserve.

She took a deep breath and said, "Well, I'm running from my fiancé."

Yeah, I wasn't expecting that shit...

"I'm sorry; you're what?" I know my tone was a little harsh but fuck... What the fuck?

I leaned back in my chair and looked at her. She shook her head quickly and moved to touch my hand, but I moved it. She said, "No, Drake, please don't think..."

"Yeah well, help me fucking think, Georgia, and really quickly." This was fucked up...

She took another deep breath as my fucking blood pressure started to rise.

"You're not fucking talking fast enough," I told her.

"The night before my wedding, I found out my fiancé was cheating on me." She blurted that out so fast that I barely made out what she said.

"What?"

She sighed again and moved her chair closer to me. She inhaled, closed her eyes and repeated what she said slower.

I didn't reply, but my temper calmed.

"My relationship with Gavin was good, or so I thought. I mean, we had problems but, all in all, it was good."

"Was he the one filling your head with bullshit?" I asked her.

She shrugged and shook her head, "Yes and no."

"Then your relationship wasn't good, Georgia."

She blinked at me a couple of times, and then said softly, "I know."

Yeah, I knew I was being an asshole but shit, I needed a minute to grab some sensitivity for this shit.

"Anyway, so yeah, I did finally realize that maybe he and I weren't really good for each other. I mean, I felt he loved me, but he loved me only if I ate or drank what he wanted and spoke how he wanted. I was losing myself, and I wanted to talk to him about it. So the night before our wedding, I went to see him."

She went through the whole story of how they met to how she was losing weight to look better for him; she stopped drinking and just became someone she didn't recognize. I wanted to tell her she was fucking stupid for doing that shit, that he clearly didn't love her, but I found some restraint, not sensitivity, and kept my mouth shut.

When she got to the night before her wedding, I was on edge. I already wanted to fucking kill this man for causing her pain, but I didn't expect what she told me.

"So let me get this straight, you went to his hotel and heard someone having sex in his room?"

She nodded. "Yes, and I know what you're going to say. I thought it myself. I thought maybe someone else was in there..."

"...Well, yeah, baby, it's plausible."

115

"Uh huh. But when I heard the girl call his name, or rather scream his name, all doubts went out the window. And when I heard my best friend's voice call his name..."

"Shit, your best friend was the bitch he was with?"

"Yup."

"Wow, baby. I'm sorry..."

She took more of her wine, and I poured more in her glass. She seemed to need it. I asked her, "So what did you do when they finally came out of the room? You were there waiting for them, right?"

She got quiet all of a sudden and, knowing what I've learned about her, she probably didn't wait around. So I said for her, "You left, didn't you?"

She nodded, "Yeah... I mean I waited the whole time, listening to them but when the moment came for me to confront them, I bailed. I got to the exit so fast they didn't even open the door all the way before I was gone. But I saw them. I saw her hug him, and I saw them kiss through the exit door glass." She shrugged. "So I went right to the airport, turned my phone off, removed the battery and went to claim our tickets for Cabo. We were supposed to come here on our honeymoon."

I reached for my cigar and asked her, "Okay, so the man thought he was getting married that day, but you were nowhere to be found. I'm sure he tried to call you too, but you turned off your phone. Did he come here looking for you? I mean, he had to have seen that you claimed your ticket."

She nodded. "Yeah, I'm sure he saw that, but this wasn't the hotel we booked, and I didn't use my name to book my room."

I raised my eyebrow. "Oh yeah? How did you manage to do that? You have fake ID?" She nodded, and I couldn't help but laugh. "Seriously, baby, you have a fake ID?"

She reached into her small purse and pulled out her wallet. She then pulled out two items and handed them over to me. One was an ID card by the name of Chloe McDaniels. The picture was of her, but a little younger than the woman before me. And the second card was a credit card in the same name.

I was fucking impressed, to say the least. She smiled knowing that fact and added, "I had someone in the neighborhood make that for me when I went off to college. I tried to look older in the picture, but I was only seventeen at that time."

"Damn, baby... And you don't think 'what's his name' knows about this?"

"No, I never told him, and I never told Maya. Chloe is my little secret. Sometimes when they used to get on my nerves, I would escape for a few days. I would get a hotel room somewhere and just relax for a few days, turn off my phone and just get myself back together."

I sighed and shook my head. No one should be in a relationship and have to fucking disappear in order to gain some sanity. And she was going to marry this clown? Still unable to find my sensitivity gene, I said to her, "Baby, I hope you don't take this the wrong way, and I'm going to try and say this as nice as I can… Baby, the people in your life have fucked you up. For you to think being with this motherfucker was healthy proves that something isn't right. Baby, no one finds a reason to escape being with someone because they were getting on your nerves.  You stop taking your best friends calls or tell her to butt out of your fucking life, but you don't escape using a false name to do it."

"And that pussy you were going to marry; you didn't need him. If he didn't see how amazing you are just the way you are, fuck that motherfucker, understand? You tell him to go fuck himself. You don't alter who you are for no-fucking-body. That shit ain't healthy, number one. Number two, that shit ain't fair to you."

The look she had in her eyes after my tyrant told me I wasn't very subtle. Hell, the looks I was getting from people at the tables around us told me the same. But Georgia surprised me. Just when I thought she was going to start to cry, she actually smiled.

She said to me, "Wow, that was… um… your idea of trying to be nice?"

I leaned back and took the rest of the wine. I needed something stronger at this point.

I answered, "Yeah… That was my nice."

She shook her head and said, "I would hate to see you when you're not nice."

"Yeah, you would."

I let that hang in the air a bit before I said, "Look, baby; bottom line, the fucker doesn't deserve you. You can take what happened and learn from it, but don't let it eat at you."

"I know. I'm not. I'm just tired of running from it. I came down here to prove to myself that I wasn't what they claimed me to be. I can be fun and spontaneous."

I laced my fingers with hers and brought her hand to my lips. I kissed her softly and said, "Baby, you are that and so much more. You just need to find someone that can appreciate all that you have to offer."

The sorrowfulness that came over her made me feel like shit. I know what she wanted and hoped for, but I knew I couldn't give that to her. She doesn't deserve anyone like me; she deserves better.

Deflection time...

"Well, it looks like you aren't the only one heading home."

"Really?"

I nodded. "Yeah, I'm being summoned back to Philly."

She took her hand back, and half-smiled at me, "I'm sure you're happy to get back."

"It's a double-edged sword, baby, but yeah I'm glad to get home. Sleep in my own bed... shit like that."

The waiter came that moment, and she declined getting dessert. I even asked if she wanted to walk along the beach together, but she told me she wanted to start packing, saying she had an early flight. So when we got back to the hotel, I walked her to her room.

I'm not gonna lie; I was disappointed she didn't want to spend more time together. I could have tasted her pussy one last time, but I'm not that much of a heartless SOB. I understood.

I did kiss her though. I kept my hands along the sides of her face and just used my lips to show her how much I was going to miss her... because I was.

When I parted, I looked in her eyes. "You take care of yourself, Georgia. It has been a fucking pleasure..." She grinned and put her head down, her way of blushing, and again... I was gonna fucking miss her.

I stepped back and let her enter into her room before I went to mine.

I didn't have shit to pack, so I went to the bar and put down a few before calling it a night. This vacation turned out to be a pretty good one. I had a little drama, but no bodies this time, which I think was good for me. I met a beautiful woman and had the best sex of my fucking life. And if I weren't a bastard, I would have given her my number and took hers. I would've promise to call her and maybe even fly her to Philly, meet the family and all that but... I'm a bastard so... The way we said goodbye fit the perfect ending to a perfect vacation fling.

The next morning, I was sitting on my flight; drink in my hand and eyes closed. In about six hours, I planned to be deep in my bed, fast a-fucking-sleep. Goodbye beach, hello fucking hell.

# CHAPTER 10

## GEORGIA

I sat in the airport, not knowing what the hell I was doing. The Philadelphia skyline looked back at me over the horizon.

"How did I get here?"

Well, here's how...

So I was waiting to board my flight back to Miami, feeling the effects of Drake withdrawal and regret that I didn't have the guts to have one last night with him. In order to take my mind off him, I turned on my phone. I had a ton of messages, mostly from a very angry Gavin and a few from that bitch of an ex-best friend. She had the audacity to cuss me out for not showing up at my wedding... Yeah, after she fucked my fiancé. She is a piece of work.

So I was sitting there, and my phone lit up with a number I didn't know. I typically don't answer numbers, I don't know but I thought that it could possibly be Drake calling me. I didn't know how that would be possible since we didn't trade numbers. Wishful thinking, I guess.

"Hello?"

"Hello? May I speak to...," I heard rattling of papers in the background, "... A Georgia Sayers."

My heart started to pound out of my chest. This sounded like a professional call. Gavin did threaten to sue me for the cost of the wedding he lost, so I thought, *Shit.*

"Uh hello?"

"Oh, I'm sorry. Yes, this is she," I stammered.

The man sighed deeply. "My, young lady, you are a hard woman to get in touch with. I've called and left a few messages, or tried anyway, but your message box was full. Sorry, I'm rambling. My name is Mr. Dennis. I'm with Hardwick and Lieberman based in Philadelphia, Pennsylvania. I'm calling you on behalf of Mr. Gregory Sayers."

Confused as to whom Gregory Sayers was, I asked, "Okay, excuse me for being ignorant, but who is Gregory Sayers?"

Mr. Dennis paused slightly, and then said, as if I was slow or something, "Well, Ms. Sayers... He's your father..."

So I quickly changed my flight, got the address to Mr. Dennis' office and there I was. He promised to stay in the office until I arrived. As I made it to the baggage claim area, I saw that apparently I had a car waiting for me as well.

The ride downtown seemed to take forever and, maybe it was my anxiety, but the time also dragged. I haven't a clue what all this was about, but when he told me who my father was and that he left a will with me named in it, I had to come just to see if this was a hoax. Knowing my life and luck, it was.

I watched the city go pass me. With each person we passed, with each car that drove by, I looked to see if I would catch Drake driving by or crossing the street somewhere. But that wasn't the case.

I made it to the law offices of Hardwick and Leiberman, and I took a deep breath before I got out of the car.

I traveled up to the fortieth floor and made my way to the office. A secretary was there to greet me. She led me into a conference room where I heard a loud, deep voice seemingly very upset bellowing from the closed door.

"How the fuck do we know who this broad is? I mean, where the hell has she been all this time? Didn't she know dad was sick? What the fuck, Anthony?"

When the secretary looked at me with a sheepish smile, I almost wanted to turn around and leave. But I didn't. Instead, I stood up straight, took a deep breath and followed the secretary to the door of the conference room.

When it opened, I found the source of the loud, deep voice instantly. He frowned at me and looked me up and down with a bit of disdain evident in his body language. The man was tall with broad shoulders wearing a dark blue suit and crisp white shirt. From seeing Gavin in multiple suits, I could tell the suit wasn't cheap.

The expression on his face wasn't welcoming though, but he looked to be a few years older than I was, with a dark complexion and brown eyes that were slanted slightly like mine. They were hard, and skepticism occupied them, but it looked like, when he wasn't frowning, he was a very attractive man.

My eyes fell on two women that were also in the room. I couldn't tell anything about them, except they both were very pretty and the same complexion as the guy with the frown. I could see they were related.

"Ah, Ms. Sayers?" My eyes went to a slightly overweight white guy with glasses, pale face and hair combed over, trying to mask the fact he was losing the hair battle with himself.

He moved to me and stretched his hand out to me. "I'm Mr. Dennis. I hope your flight was a pleasant one." I forgot to add, I flew on his dime.

"Oh, yes it was. Thank you for the tickets and thank you for the ride here."

"Oh, it was no problem at all. I couldn't have you trying to get here on your own."

"Yes, thank you."

"Come sit down. We have a lot to cover, so let's get started with introductions. I know you have a lot of questions. I hope to have them answered tonight."

I moved hesitantly to the table and found a seat far away from the brooding man. I smiled at the two women who were equally dressed in expensive clothes. I looked down at what I was wearing and wished I actually listened to Maya and bought better clothes.

"Where have you been all these years?" the frowning hot black guy asked me.

"Greg, give the girl a chance to explain," one of the women said, and then looked at me.

I looked around the room freaking clueless to everything and answered, "I've been in Miami…" I looked at Mr. Dennis. "Sir, you told me that you would explain everything, which is why I'm here."

"Yes, Greg, can you please have a seat so we can get started?" the woman asked.

Greg reluctantly sat down but kept a heavy eye on me, quite frankly they all did.

"Ms. Sawyer… Georgia; can I call you that?" Mr. Dennis asked.

I nodded after hearing sucking of tongues, at my name I guess. "Fabulous. Okay, so as you three know, your father was not traditional, so he just wrote a letter with instructions on how he wanted his estate divided…"

*Estate? What the hell is going on?*

"He first addresses Gregory Junior, his son. " Mr. Dennis cleared his throat and read, "'I have a separate letter for each of my children, leaving them particular instructions and a portion of my estate. So I'm not going to waste time going over that. Gregory, you're head of the family now. I expect everything to run just as smooth as if I was still there. We planned for this day, son, and I expect you to carry on the family. Make necessary choices and decisions with the backing of the entire family. Just because you're the head, you still have to make moves, and it's the neck that turns the head.  Listen to your neck...'"

Yeah, I was lost, but I tried not to show it.

He continued. "But what I want to talk about is my daughter, Georgia."

"What?!" I blurted.

Mr. Dennis looked at me and smiled. He then continued to read, "'I know you, Greg, Dara, and Deidra have a lot of questions. Son, I know you're looking as if you want to kill someone, but your anger is in the wrong direction. Georgia didn't know anything about me or any of you.  Out of respect for her mother, I stayed out of Georgia's life. When I finally found her again, I didn't know how to introduce myself as her father, so I continued to stay away. It was what her mother requested of me.'"

I, as you can image, was stunned.  I didn't know what to do or say, so I stayed quiet. The lawyer continued, "'Georgia, I know you are wondering how I could be your father.  My lawyer has the necessary arrangements to get your blood tested with mine for your proof, but I assure you, I am your father, and you are my daughter.  I met your mom a long time ago, and I fell for her hard. She was a wonderful woman with a heart pure of gold.  I was in Baltimore for about six months, and I spent all of my time with her. It was at that point I fell in love... I loved your mother.'"

Mr. Dennis paused, put down the page he read and started with the second page, "I had to go back to Philadelphia on other business and I promised her I would come back, but circumstances prevented me from keeping my promise. The next time I saw her, you were five years old. She told me she tried to get in contact with me for years, but I never responded. That's when I told her that I had gotten married. I found out I was having a son and decided to make a life with his mother instead of her. She stared at me confused for a long moment. She never knew about my life here in Philly, and I never planned on telling her. That's when she told me to stay away from you and her. The pain I caused her ate at me for years to come, and I regret ever putting her through that. But what I regret most is not being around you. I never got to see you that day I came to visit. I missed graduations, birthdays and holidays, and I feel horrible about that. I wish I could have done more for you, and I hope you know that..."

"Stop..." I cried out. I was crying uncontrollably as finally, finally I figured out what drove my mom to self-destruct. It was his rejection. Everyone looked at me as I stood.

Mr. Dennis called after me, "Georgia..."

I shook my head, "Enough, I don't want to hear anything else that man has to say," I bit out.

Greg Jr. stood, his eyes filled with anger, "You will respect my father..."

"I will do no such thing. That man turned his back on me on my mom...," I started.

"Your mom should have kept her legs closed instead of trying to get a kept man...," Greg spat.

"Fuck you!" I turned and stormed out of the room unable to control the tears, the anger and most of all the hurt I was feeling. See how my life ends up? I can never get ahead. It seems the moment I do, something knocks me back down.

I heard Mr. Dennis coming after me, but I saw a set of steps and took them. So glad I decided not to listen to Maya and get expensive clothes... my jeans, sneakers and "I love Cabo" t-shirt was just what I needed.

When I got to the bottom floor, I found the ladies room and hid there until I was able to stop my heart from beating out of control.

I threw water over my face and stared at myself in the mirror. My red, pained, and puffy eyes greeted me back. "This is so fucked up."

"I'll say."

I jumped clear out of my skin as I saw... what was her name?

"Deidra," she said to me as she walked completely into the bathroom.

I guess I should have escaped first instead of hiding.

I went to the paper towel dispenser and wiped my face.

Deidra turned out to be tall like me and actually a bit older too. She looked at me through the mirror and said, "You look like my grandmother... or rather our grandmother in her younger days."

I didn't reply. She sighed deeply and turned to face me. "I'm sorry for my ignorant ass brother. He's so quick to use words to hurt people as a coping mechanism when he's hurting himself. He lashes out and I'm not saying what he did was right or making excuses for his behavior, but I just wanted to first apologize."

She shook her head and smiled. "Wow, you are a surprise, I tell you that much. I never thought you were out there because if I did, I would have tried to find you. I don't know if my father ever tried, but I would have made him. I don't know if you were alone growing up or how it was for you, but I can tell it wasn't good."

I squinted my eyes at her, and she added, "I'm a therapist. It's my job to see in people's minds. Anyway, I want to invite you back upstairs. I promise my brother will behave. I'm the oldest and quite frankly, I don't care how you got here. You're blood, and I don't need a stupid test to see that. I can see it in your eyes that you're a Sayers, but I understand if you want a test... I'll even understand if you don't want any parts of us too. But don't make that decision based on that idiot upstairs. You seem like a pretty great person, especially when you told told Greg to fuck off. He's not used to that, so I really hope you do stay around." She put her hands up. "But no pressure... If you still don't want any parts of my father or us right now, I totally understand. Just know you have family waiting for you."

Deidra turned around and left.

I looked at myself in the mirror again. I thought long and hard about what she said and well... Yeah, I went back upstairs.

*****

It was a cold, brisk Saturday night, and I was trying to understand why I was wearing this short ass dress in this freezing cold weather. For some reason, I was dressing like I was in Miami when I'd been in Philadelphia for the last few months. Dara of course said it wasn't cold, but then I showed her the temperature in Miami in September and she just said, "Ah yeah. Well, okay, it's cold."

I'd been in Philadelphia the entire summer getting to know my siblings. I ended up getting the DNA test done just for my sake and Greg's, and it came back ninety-nine point ninety-nine percent. I was Gregory Sayers' daughter. In a matter of days, I found out I wasn't alone. I actually had family.

So I stayed to get to know them and decided to teach a course online that year, allowing myself more time with my family. *My family...* that sounded so strange to say, but being around them wasn't strange at all. I met my grandparents, and when my grandmother took one look at me, she just smiled and embraced me. She said, "I knew the moment I saw your eyes. You're my grandbaby."

So let me give you a rundown: My father never looked for me. I guess he assumed that I was well taken care of and didn't imagine my mother would fall apart like she did. I was glad that my father let it be known in his letter that my mom didn't know anything about his so-called family in Philly. It felt better knowing that my mom just trusted and gave her whole heart to the wrong man. She paid for it.

Wow, that sounds so familiar.

I shared some of my story with my siblings, not all of it but some, letting them know where my anger stemmed from. Greg, hearing what my mom went through never said anything else about her sleeping with a kept man. He stayed loyal to his own mother, which by the way I met one day. It was awkward, to say the least, but she was cordial to me. By the way, Greg is only older than me by four months.

I found out that Deidra was the mother hen of the group. She was three years older than I was, but she acted as if she was much older. She was married, but they didn't have any kids as of yet. Her husband, Rafiq, was a cool guy. He worked in the family business that I later learned was real estate, both residential and commercial. Sayers Real Estate Inc. is a large company solely based in Philadelphia, but they were working towards expanding in the metroplex, New Jersey, and Delaware.

Rafiq was one of the residential sales guys working for the company. Greg, as you may have guessed, was acting CEO with a Board of Directors he reported to that consisted of their mom, our grandfather, who ran the business until he retired, Deidra, Dara and me. Yup, that's right; I inherited being a stakeholder in the company. I was vested, whether I liked it or not. I could have sold my stock but once I sat in a few meetings, I wanted to stay.

Greg and I were as cool with each other as we could be, considering how we met. We figured out a way to co-exist and get along. I stayed out of his way mostly, and he stayed out of mine. I'd been staying at the family's house out in King of Russia, but, after a month of staying there, I needed my own space. At times, I would just stay in the city and get a hotel room for a while. I still needed my space, and I was still learning my new family.

Dara was two years younger than me, and I had established a closer bond with her than with any of my other siblings. She was so feisty and full of fire. "She's my idol," I liked to say behind closed doors. She was everything I wasn't; like her fantastic looks and smoking hot body. Guys turned their heads and broke their necks just to look at her.

Dara had been on a mission to get me over Gavin. I'd confided in her and told her all about both of my exes. I had to talk her down from making a trip to "whoop some ass." She was amazing to me, and she was the main reason why I hadn't left yet.

So Dara had been dragging me to every club in Philly multiple times a weekend. I'd danced and even went out on a few dates, but no one stood out to me. I won't admit that in the back of my mind, every time I went out, I hoped I would see someone. I don't want to sound pathetic but... Oh hell! I looked for Drake everywhere I went. I hadn't told Dara about him because, well, there's nothing to tell. I mean, I know his name. I could've tried to find him, but for what? He made it clear that he didn't want anything to do with me, so there it was. What we had in Cabo was a fling; nothing more, nothing less.

"Girl, can you slow down? These four-inch heels you have me in are starting to hurt," I told her and she slowed down for me.

We were going to this club on Delaware Ave. that she said was "guaranteed filled with hotties." She said that every time we went out. Mind you, our definitions of "hottie" weren't similar.

We had to park a few blocks from the club because Dara refused to pay for valet. She figured it should be free.

Walking two blocks from the club can really sober you up...

When we got to the club, there was a freaking line. But the music coming from the place was great. I started bopping my head, waiting patiently for us to get inside. The line I will say went quick, and the moment we got inside, she and I went straight to the bar. Dara could drink as much as I could, if not more.

That night, we got wasted and drank a few guys under a few tables. We danced on the dance floor and had a blast. I forgot about who I was. I forgot about my feet hurting. I didn't even care when I was groped on the dance floor. I was so free, and I felt amazing. And that's when I saw him...

He was in all black, head shaved, and a five o'clock shadow etched his perfect chiseled features. He was wrapped around a perfect ten, and when I tell you they looked like the perfect couple, I'm not exaggerating. She was beautiful. Long black hair with a dress short as hell and tight, showing a great pair of legs and perfect toned body. He was moving his hands all over her body, and she smiled and moved her hips along his crotch. The smile on his face showed that he was enjoying every movement. He never danced like that with me in Cabo. I mean, we danced together. Don't get me wrong. But not like that.

Suddenly, I felt sick. I kind of stood there staring at them until, to my horror, his eyes left the beauty queen and fell on me. He stopped moving and just stood there, looking at me with shock on his face. He then started to smile and head towards me.

Well, I didn't wait for the embarrassment; I left the dance floor and went straight to the front door.

I couldn't tell you where Dara was. I just knew I had to leave. I hit the front door and started walking.

"Georgia!"

I heard my name, but I kept moving. My vision was getting blurred, and I didn't know where the hell I was going, but I knew I had to get away from him.

"Georgia..." I think it was his voice, but I wasn't sure.

I nearly collided with a car at an intersection and was pulled back quickly. Drake pushed me up against the nearest wall, but I wasn't having that.

"Get off me, you son of a bitch. Don't touch me..." I swung, and he backed off.

He looked so confused and hurt, but I didn't let that sway me. I was hurt too.

"Okay, baby, I won't touch you," he said calmly.

I pointed at him. "Don't call me baby! Is that who she is? Huh? Your baby?" I pushed him in his chest. Well, I tried to anyway. He was still fucking solid.

I continued defiantly. "Is that what you call her? "You men are all alike, you know that?"

I think my words started to slur, but I couldn't stop my fury.

"Hey, you get the fuck away from my sister!" I turned to see Dara coming up to me.

I smiled and folded my arms.

Drake being Drake ignored Dara and said, "Can you just talk to me for a second?" He smiled, but I shook my head.

"I don't have shit to say to you! Why don't you go back to your 'baby'? Or whatever she is to you."

As if the cards to my life fell into place, the very beauty queen appeared. "Lincoln, what's going on?"

She looked at me with disdain evident all over her face.

I looked at Drake. "Leave me alone, Lincoln."

I turned and felt a strong grip on my arm. Then I heard a voice say, "Hold the fuck up a second."

When Drake spun me around, I was so ready to light into him. Dara came between us, holding a black oblong object in her hand.

"Get the fuck back before I mace the shit out of you," she fussed.

Drake stared at me hard before regrettably letting go of me and stepping back.

"This isn't over, Georgia," he said simply.

I shook my head and replied, "It is now."

He didn't say another word, so I turned and started to walk away. I heard Dara's footsteps behind me, but I didn't turn around to see if she was catching up. I was about to lose it right there on the sidewalk, and I refused to let that happen over him.

I thought Dara would drill me about Drake, but she didn't. She stayed uncharacteristically quiet, but I was thankful for that. We went to the hotel that I booked for us, and I closed myself in the bathroom for a while just trying to get myself together. All this time I had been hoping to see him, but never did I think he would be with someone else when I did.

# CHAPTER 11

## DRAKE

"So what did she do?" Angel asked.

We had just come back from a meeting with his father and a few other bosses from a couple of families around Philly. I went to his father's refrigerator and pulled out some covered dish sitting there and some water.

On the way back from the meeting, I told Angel about last night, only because of course he heard about it from Eleanor, the chick I was with.

"She didn't do anything. She left with some woman that claimed to be her sister. But I know for a fact she doesn't have any siblings... or at least that's what she told me anyway."

I grabbed some plates and started piling it with some anti-pasta seafood dish. Angel did the same, laughing. "Yeah, well, Elle said you were pissed."

I frowned. "What hasn't she said? Damn, that bitch runs her mouth."

Angel shrugged. "Not really. She told Lucy and Lucy told me."

I grunted and warmed up my food.

*Georgia.* I never thought I would see her again, much less last night. I had just come back from taking care of business for my uncle overseas which took weeks. I traveled all over Italy and didn't get a chance to enjoy the sights or the women. So when I got back, I needed to get into something. Lucy, Angel's "sometimes," hooked me up with Eleanor weeks ago, but I just never called. She seemed too hungry, you know? Like she wanted to be with a bad boy so bad she'd do anything; one of those users.

When I called her last night, she practically jumped through the phone; she was so fucking eager. So I took her to dinner... Pleasant enough. Then we went to the club I'd just opened up and hung out there. I introduced her to some people, and she loved it. It was like she was made for this life. So having all the drinks I could get in me, I took her out to the dance floor for a little foreplay. What I didn't expect, as I was feeling her body, was to see the very woman that had been haunting my dreams ever since I left Cabo.

She looked sexy as shit in that dress, but when I traveled to her eyes, that's what made me move toward her.

I don't chase women. I just fucking don't, but I found myself following Georgia as she practically sprinted out of the club, and then almost got hit.

"So are you going to look her up? Give her a call?" Angel asked me and I shook my head.

"If she wanted to talk to me, she would've. I don't have time to be chasing her."

Angel grunted. "Uh huh. Whatever... Did you at least seal the deal with Eleanor?"

I finished my plate, cleaned it and placed it in the dishwasher. "What did Lucy tell you?"

"She said you stayed the night with her all night long."

"Then you know I didn't 'seal' anything," I told him and walked out of the room.

I headed for the office of my uncle, checking in before I left for the night, and I heard my cousin talking to his father.

"Pops, we need to act now. If we don't, we're going to seem weak."

I told you I hated Eddie, right? Well, I'm not exaggerating. If I could, I would gut shoot him and watch him painfully die; that's how much I fucking hate him. He's a hothead who's always so quick to react to someone or something, and the reaction is always violent. And guess who has to always clean up his mess when he fucks up? And believe me, he fucks up often.

"Son, you need to calm down first and think about what would happen if we do something now. Things are too hot for them. If we get involved, it's going to put attention on us; unwanted attention."

"I know, Pop, but this is a steal. They are heavy hitters down south. If we can supply to them what they need, that solidifies us in the south market."

My uncle nodded just as I walked into the room. Eddie looked over at me and frowned.

Yeah, the feeling is mutual. He hates me too.

"I'm having a family discussion with my father. You ain't family," he scuffed.

I ignored him and looked at my uncle. Eddie wasn't worth a pot to piss in. He was one of those goons that used his power for everything, to get respect, and most of all to get women. He was shorter than both Angel and me. No matter how much he tried to work out to bulk up, the muscle mass gods looked past him all the time.

So instead he took Jujitsu lessons all his life. I will say he was a bad motherfucker, but I'd beat the shit out of him any day of any week.

"Uncle, I'm heading out for the night. Do you need anything else before I go?"

My uncle was as tall as Angel and me and built solid just like us. I guess Eddie took after his mother's side of the family. Uncle Bruno was feared among Philly for the power his father and father's father had throughout this city for decades. The name Leonetti was synonymous with loyalty, fuck that up and you're gone... and not just you... It could be your entire family right along with you. Back then, this family didn't play.

My uncle was into gambling, guns, and the lending business, if you get my meaning. My uncle, with my help, had invested in a few legitimate businesses as well. We'd invested in a lot of lucrative markets overseas that was bringing us millions, as well as the illegal stuff.

We still got our hands dirty from time to time, but it had been a long time since someone tried to take what we had. You have no idea how at home I felt with this family. Ever since the incident with the CIA, my Uncle and this family welcomed me. I'm not saying the shit was easy, but I'm fucking glad I'm among like minds, minus Eddie, of course.

"Sit down, Lincoln." Uncle Bruno grabbed a Cuban from his personal stash and handed me one. He and I were the only ones in the family that smoked cigars. Angel; it just wasn't his thing, but, Eddie, he fucking hated that I had that bond with his father. He tried to smoke one and threw up for days... Fucking pussy.

I took the cigar, clipped it and lit it. Angel came into the office right at that moment and sat down too. Angel and Eddie were about three years apart; Eddie being the oldest. Angel was nothing like his brother. He was more like his father. Angel went to college and actually got his Master's degree in business and international finance. He was also just as ruthless and callous as I am. If my uncle lost his life that day, it wouldn't be Eddie that would take over; it would be Angel. Guess who would be his right-hand man?

"What's going on, Pops?" Angel asked.

Uncle Bruno took a few puffs and let the smoke slowly escape his nose before he spoke. I leaned back and enjoyed a fantastic fucking cigar.

"Your brother has connected with a cartel in Miami that wants a shipment of my guns delivered within the next few months. It's a rather large shipment that we would probably have to bring in."

Angel nodded. "Okay, we've dealt with the Russians the same way in New York. You don't think we can swing it?"

"I know we can. The problem is this family has some unwanted attention after them."

"The Feds?" I asked.

"That hasn't been communicated; just some internal turmoil that's plaguing them."

Eddie rolled his eyes and leaned closer to his father's desk from his chair. "Pops, it's not like that really. I mean, yes, they have some internal shit, but what family doesn't." He looked over at me. I smirked as Eddie continued, "All I'm saying is, let's set up a meeting. They are willing to pay a lot of money, and I think we can capitalize on this deal and be set for life. They will pay big dollar, and they have connections in South America too. I know you've wanted to get connects down there. This is our shot."

I watched Eddie adamantly talk to his father and something seemed off about everything. He knew his father wouldn't be pushed to do anything he didn't feel comfortable doing. But Eddie was trying to do just that.

I took another pull and blew the smoke toward Eddie to get him to shut the fuck up. He started waving at the smoke as I said,

"Uncle, do you want me to look into it for you? See what's really going on, see how volatile the situation is?"

Uncle Bruno took a few puffs of his own cigar, then studied me for a minute before he nodded. "Yes. Find out what's going on and report back to me. Sooner rather than later, eh nephew?"

I nodded. "Understood. Who am I looking at?"

I looked over at Eddie, who, by the way, was fuming with rage.

He said to his father, "We don't need him to do anything for this family. He's not even a Leonetti, for fuck sake."

My uncle, ever the calm, cool and collected one, just looked at his son. Nothing ruffled the man. He was like steel. He had the patience of a hawk. Me; I barely had enough patience to deal with life.

Uncle Bruno stood, walked around the desk and said simply, "Give Lincoln the information that he needs." Then he walked out of the room.

When he closed the door, Eddie's eyes fell on me. "Don't fuck this up for me, Lincoln. So help me God, you will regret it."

"Stop being a bitch. If the shit is legit, there will be nothing to fuck up." I leaned forward in my chair and blew more smoke in his direction, being an asshole, of course. I said to him, "Before I start digging, is there something you want to tell me?"

Eddie coughed and stood. "Go fuck yourself!" Then he walked out of the room.

I smiled to myself and leaned back in my chair.

"You know you're playing with fire, right?" Angel asked me.

"How so?"

"My brother thinks you're taking his spot in the family. He already knows he will never be number one; over my dead fucking body. But he won't let you be number two."

"I *wish* he would make a move."

Angel stood and moved over to me. He sat on the desk in front of me. "What do you have against Eddie?"

"I don't have anything against him. He is the one with the problem. From the first day I came here, he's been in my shit. Throwing who my mother is, his fucking aunt, in my face. Throwing who my father is in my face. But one thing is, and best believe this on your left nut, when the fucker comes at me at any point, his life is forfeited."

Angel studied me closely. I didn't trust Eddie. Both my Uncle and Angel knew this. He was a loose cannon, someone who screamed for power and money, but wouldn't make the right decisions to survive. He was a fucking idiot, and I knew one day he was going to bring this family down.

Loyalty is what this family was founded on, and it was what I believed in. Fuck that up, and it's game fucking over.

Angel stood, "Yeah, for his sake, I hope he doesn't test you. See you tomorrow."

I kept myself busy for a few days, but I couldn't stop thinking about Georgia. What the fuck was she doing in my city? Why did she run away from me?

I could answer that last question on my own; Eleanor.

Back in Cabo, I figured Georgia was starting to catch feelings, but I figured we both subconsciously agreed her seeing me outside of the island was a bad idea. But seeing her hurt like that, I felt compelled to find her and tell her what she saw was nothing. But finding her wasn't going to be easy.

I called in a few favors and checked every hotel in the area and surrounding cities. I got nothing.

*Maybe she's staying with someone. That girl she was with the other day maybe.*

I searched for Sayers in the area just for kicks, and a few came back that I could check out. But before I did that, I thought about something she told me the last night we were together. I asked my contact to search for Chloe McDaniels. He came back with a hit for the Hyatt downtown, not too far from my apartment.

I drove there hoping for the best but preparing for the worst. I parked at the curb and climbed out of my black on black Charger that I called "monster" and walked toward the hotel. I saw a truck pull up to the front door. A tall, well-dressed Black man got out and walked around to the passenger door. He looked familiar to me, but my mind suddenly went to shit when I saw Georgia walk out of the doors of the hotel and right to this man.

What the fuck?

It was my turn to stand in that spot fucking stunned. I wasn't prepared for the fucking worst.

She was stunning in an all-black dress that hugged the curves that I can't seem to take my mind off of. The man looked over at me, and he stood there staring. Just before Georgia got in the truck, she turned as well.

Our eyes met, and I willed her to do the same thing I had done. It didn't matter to me that I was dancing with Eleanor, the moment I saw her, I went to her instantly. But she didn't move from her spot. She frowned at me and got completely inside the car.

It took me a minute to gather myself. I didn't realize how pissed I was until I unclenched my fists and saw my hands were red. The thought of someone else touching her was driving me mad. I had half a mind to follow the truck, pull her out of the vehicle and to make her talk to me.

I moved to the car with the intention of doing just that when my cell rang. I saw it was Angel, and I answered.

"What?!" I barked loudly into the phone as I watched Georgia be driven away.

My cousin chuckled, which fucking pissed me off.

"I take it you didn't find her?"

Again I don't know why I talk to this son of a bitch.

I walked back towards my ride, regretting everything I'd told him. "What the fuck do you want?"

"I see you didn't which may be a good thing for me... We have a problem. Do you think you can get to the warehouse off of I-495 in Delaware?"

"What's going on?"

I heard Angel start up his Mustang through the phone, "A little territory dispute."

I grinned. "I'll be there in twenty."

# CHAPTER 12

## GEORGIA

I wanted to cry.

This had to be the fourth time I'd emptied my stomach through my esophagus and throat, and it wasn't even twelve o'clock yet. Hell, I wasn't even eating anything. I was drinking water and still that wouldn't stay down. I felt run down and tired all the time. I'd been waiting for the flu, cold or allergies to hit me for a few days now and nothing. Just tiredness and I couldn't keep anything down.

I crawled back into the bed and pulled the covers over my face. I didn't want to leave that spot, but I needed to grade papers and get my lesson posted online before the end of the day.

I didn't know what was going on with my body. I assumed it was torturing me for ignoring Drake the other day, but I couldn't help it. I was still hurt from seeing him plastered all over that woman. I knew I shouldn't have been. I could have easily given him my number in Cabo, but I didn't. So I shouldn't have been mad at him for doing what any full-blooded fine ass male, such as himself, would do.

But a part of me wished to God that Drake had held out for me. I wish he thought of nothing but me. I kept dreaming that the moment I saw him again it would be amazing. I felt like a fool. And it's my own damn fault.

Seeing the look on his face when I left him there, I can't forget it and wonder if that's the reason why I'm sick all the time now. I swear, the moment I started throwing up was the same night I saw him outside of my hotel.

I turned over, and I swear the room started spinning like crazy. "Oh no. Not again."

"Hey, Georgia. Are you feeling any better?"

I lifted the covers from my eyes and saw Dara and Deidra walk in. Deidra held some tray with something I could only imagine was food.

*Oh... no... Is that...?*

I raced from the bed and got to the toilet just in time to throw up absolutely nothing. This blows... literally.

As I came back out Deidra looked at me and said the words that almost made me pass out. "Do you think you may be pregnant?"

I blurted, "Um, excuse me? What?"

"It's not uncommon, you know? Have you had sex with anyone in the last few weeks?" she asked me.

I started to shake my head, but instantly got dizzy, so I opted for words, "No, I've not been with anyone but you guys. No, this is just some stupid bug."

Dara and Deidra looked at each other again, then Dara spoke up, "Why don't we just rule it out and take this test?"

I didn't want to argue. I wanted them out of my room and for them to take that God awful chicken noodle soup with them.

"Fine go and get one, and I..."

Deidra stood. "I have one right here."

Fifteen minutes later, I was sitting on my bed trying to figure out what the hell happened.

*I can't be pregnant... I just can't be. There's no way... Immaculate conception? I think not. My name isn't Mary.*

Deidra called her OBGYN and scheduled me an appointment for the next day. I couldn't speak. I just nodded trying to get myself together. I was pregnant with Gavin's baby... This can't be happening.

Deidra left, but Dara stayed with me. "Are you going to be okay?" she asked.

I nodded. "I'm going to lay down for a little while longer," I told her as I crawled back in the bed. I'd been avoiding Gavin for so long that the thought of seeing him again, of talking to him again, was making me feel worse than I already did. I had no clue what to do.

The next morning, Deidra had to get me up, or I would have missed the appointment. Both she and Dara came with me, and Deidra held my hand as the doctor splattered some goo on my stomach. She said, "Since your periods are irregular, Georgia, and you can't pinpoint when your last period was, let's see if we can tell

,
using the machine. I don't want to have to make you uncomfortable for any reason."

"Yes, I'm uncomfortable as it is right now, and you haven't touched me. Will you be doing some type of um... vaginal exam?"

Dr. Platt just smiled. "No, dear, not yet. Let's see how far along you are using this machine. If not, then, yes, we will have to use a different method."

We all watched as she maneuvered the device on my stomach and stopped when she saw a tiny picture, then smiled. "That's your baby."

I couldn't breathe. "That little blip on the screen is my baby?"

"Yes it is. And let's see... Do you want to hear the heartbeat?"

All I could do was nod, and the next sound that came through was a heartbeat so fast I looked at the doctor alarmed. "Is it supposed to sound like that?"

Deidra laughed and smiled. "Yes, girl."

"Now let's get some measurements and we can determine roughly how far along you are."

As Dr. Platt did her thing, I looked at my sisters. Everything in my life was happening so fast. I found out I had a whole family that I knew nothing about. I gained so much in a few months that finding out I was pregnant made everything so much better.

"Okay, my dear," the doctor said as she started wiping off my stomach. "I'm going to give you a tentative date of March, roughly the second or third week. When we get a more thorough examination of the baby, we can confirm the due date."

I looked at her confused. "I'm sorry, but is that right? I expected to be a little further than that."

The doctor shook her head. "Uh no... I may be a few weeks off, but you're roughly about three and a half months pregnant."

"I'm what? No, that can't be. I should be about five months pregnant. That's the last time I slept with Gavin." I looked at Dara and Deidra, "He put us on a sex hiatus about two months from our wedding day so... and I haven't been with anyone else since him."

Dara and Deidra looked puzzled at each other, then at the doctor. I started to say something else when it suddenly hit me... "Oh... My... God..."

My hand instantly went to my mouth, and I hopped down from the table, stumbled, trying to catch my balance, and went right for the garbage can. I threw up the breakfast Deidra made me eat as well as the Ginger Ale I drank.

"God, this can't be happening," I said softly to myself, but I wasn't alone in a small space, so they heard me.

"Georgia, are you okay?" Deidra asked, and I just put up my hand for her to give me a few minutes.

*I can't be... I can't be pregnant with Drake Lincoln's baby... I just can't.*

During the ride home, I remained quiet, sitting in the back seat of the car while Deidra drove. Every time I began to try to say something, I got sick to my stomach. I couldn't believe this was happening. Yes, we had unprotected sex, but I didn't think I could even get pregnant so easily. I was always told it would be hard for me to conceive so the thought of Drake even being a possibility just didn't click. Maybe my mind discounted him because of all the bad things Dara said about him.

The day I saw Drake at the club, Dara had told me he belonged to some very bad people. She told me that he owned the club we were at as well as a few others, and his uncle was this big shot mafia guy. She said he was as dangerous as they come.

I wasn't an idiot. I knew when I approached him in Cabo he was bad. Living in one of the worst neighborhoods in Baltimore told me he wasn't a stand-up citizen. But because of the way he treated me, how he touched me and kissed me, and the things he did to my body and my soul, I became blind to what he really was.

Now I'm having a baby by the man.

When we got to the house, their family's house, my father's estate, I instantly went upstairs, and I heard footsteps following me. When I got to my room, I left it open for Dara, and she closed it when she walked through the doorway.

"Do you know who the daddy is?" she asked.

"Yes, I know who he is."

She frowned. "Is it your ex? It would suck if…"

I shook my hand frantically. "No, it's not him either... It's ... Argh..." I fell back against the pillows on the bed and wanted it to swallow me whole if it could. I couldn't say his name.

Dara accepted my moment of silence. Tears started gathering in my eyes, and I closed them. I asked softly, "Do you remember that guy I saw at the club?"

"Um no. Not really. We've been to a lot of clubs, Georgia... Wait... Do you mean Lincoln, the guy I said was bad news?... The one that Greg said was in the mafia?"

I nodded my head first, and then said, "Yes."

She shrugged. "What about him?"

I didn't reply.

My silence told her what I couldn't, and she said, "That can't be possible, could it?"

I didn't reply, still not wanting to admit anything.

"How, Georgia? I mean, you were with us the whole time you were here."

I sat up and looked at her, wiping my eyes. "Drake and I met in Cabo two weeks before I got here. We..." I took a deep breath trying to swallow down the preverbal knot forming in my throat. "We spent so many nights together, tangled together... but this one night...." I put my head down and didn't say anything else.

Dara was quiet... Then I heard her say, "Jesus H. Christ, Georgia... How could you be so irresponsible?  Not only did you fuck one of the baddest, no good dudes on the planet, but you went raw? And never mind the fact that he's white. Shit, girl... Weren't you engaged at the time?" Dara got up and stepped back from me, shaking her head. "I can't believe this. You fucked up big time, just in case you didn't know." She turned from me and left the room.

I stared at the place she once was dumbstruck. I couldn't believe what she was saying to me. I get what I'd done was reckless, but I would have expected this from Greg, maybe even Deidra, but not Dara. We've shared so much together. For her to judge me like this, to treat me like this was hurtful, to say the least.

I stood up on shaky legs. Tears were streaming down faster now as I went to grab my bags and started stuffing clothes in them. Here I thought I was surrounded by family. Granted I didn't know them all that well, nor them me, but I thought I would be able to trust them, to lean on them.

I guess not.

I carried my bags down the steps and found Dara's voice ringing through the house. I sat my bags at the door and thought about just leaving. Considering the names I could hear her calling me right now, I knew no one would care if I just left. But I didn't want to end it like that, not on my end anyway.

When I walked in the family room of the house, Greg had his arms crossed in front of him, and he looked more pissed than he ever did before. He was standing by the mantle, staring out through the sliding glass door into the backyard. Deidra was sitting on the couch, and Dara was pacing the floor.

"That bitch ruined everything. You're the one that told me to hang out with her, and I did. But I draw the line with a crime family. No fucking way."

I cleared my throat now wishing I did just leave instead of hearing that shit. "I thought about saying goodbye and telling you where I'd be, but never mind about that." Dara folded her arms in front of her and looked at me as if I was a piece of shit. Deidra looked sympathetic with a sorrowful look on her face… No, pity is more like it. And Greg; hell, Greg just looked like Greg.

"I don't know why life brought me here and brought us together. At first, I thought it was so I could really and truly feel what a family is like. But fuck it. If it's like this, I don't want it. I can do bad all by myself."

I turned and started to leave when Dara said, "He's going to ruin your life. He's going to destroy you and get you, and that baby killed. That's all he's good for. Don't be stupid enough to go to him. That's suicide."

I didn't turn around fully. I just turned my head and said, "Then I guess I'll be stupid because so far, he has been the only loyal person I've had in my life."

Greg then had his parting words, "If you go to him, you're not welcomed here again. I will not bring that kind of life in our home."

That made me turn around. "What life? The life of fierce loyalty and love? The kind of people that put family before anything? Yeah, I know Drake isn't good for me… And hell I may never tell him

'

about the baby, but damn it I know if I did, he would do his best to protect the both of us. That's something I do know."

"All they know is how to destroy. You're naïve to think otherwise," he said to me.

"He protected me when he knew nothing about me," I told them.

"He wanted some ass... If you spread your legs for scum, that's what you become," Greg bit out. "And that's not wanted in my father's house."

"Wow," I exclaimed and backed out of the room still looking at them, "Your father cheated on your mother, probably not just once... He left his daughter out there and didn't bother to ever look for me to make sure I was okay. That makes him admirable in your eyes?"

"Hey you..." Greg started, but my voice got louder and I spoke to him. The hell if he wasn't going to hear what I had to say.

"I was raped ... in the home I was left in when my parents died of an overdose; the ones I discovered when I was nine and had to wait with their rotting bodies for four hours before the cops came and took them away. I was fourteen when I was raped, and some seventeen-year-old kid thought it would be fun to fuck the fat, quiet girl. I had no one to turn to, no family in my life... but if I had a father that gave a shit about me... that bothered to stay connected with me... maybe, *just maybe*, I wouldn't have gotten raped. So before you pass judgment on someone you know nothing about, think about your own fucking house."

I practically ran out of the house dragging my bags with me. I don't know where I was going to go or what I was going to do, but I needed to think about not only me but the child I was now carrying... Drake Lincoln's child no less.

# CHAPTER 13

## DRAKE

"Come on, Lincoln, just let me make you feel good. You know that I can."

Eleanor raked her red nails along my black, silk shirted chest. She and I were in my office at my club drinking and listening to the club music downstairs when she decided she was going to seduce me. She came and sat on my lap and had been there for a few minutes, her pussy grinding slowly on my dick. I told you it's been a minute since I had some pussy... It's really fucked up, something I didn't plan, and something that I don't do often. I'm in something mostly every night, or partly anyway, but ever since I fucking met that crazy girl, fate had been cutting me off at the balls.

I was in Italy for business. I didn't get a chance to do anything because I was so busy traveling the countryside doing business for my uncle's interests. I had to sleep with one eye open for a few nights so I couldn't be distracted, not even for a little ass.

When I came back home, it seemed every time I was about to get some, my uncle would summon me. It's like he fucking knew that I was about to fuck someone and that maybe I shouldn't and he was stopping me. But right now, there was nothing stopping me. Eleanor wanted to be fucked in half.

I was willing to oblige.

"Unbuckle my pants, baby. Let's see what kind of skills you have," I told her. I inhaled my elixir, my soothing medicine and blew smoke above her head.

She smiled back at me and started with my belt buckle. I didn't plan on fucking her that night. I actually had someone else downstairs for the night. But I wouldn't mind getting my dick sucked.

*Maybe if she does it right, I'll fuck her too.*

Eleanor, I will say, is smoking hot. Her tits were fake no doubt but were large and practically hanging out of her tight ass dress. I prefer the real feeling of tits, but this would do for the night.

*Maybe I'll fuck those first before her pussy... Yeah, that will be nice.*

"Holy shit!" Her shocked voice brought me out of my daydream, and I looked down at my dick.

"What?"

She started squirming in my lap and sort of moved back a little.

I smiled. "Don't be scared of him, Elle. He won't bite."

I saw her swallow hard. She was psyching herself up, which I found fucking hilarious.

"Hey…" I snapped my fingers, and she brought her eyes to mine. "I don't have all day. Are you going to suck my dick or what?" Yeah, that was crass but, shit, I didn't care.

I was about to grip her hair and make the decision for her when my office phone buzzed. I growled and pushed the button on the intercom. "What the fuck?"

My head bouncer came back on the line hesitantly, as he should. "I know you said you didn't want to be disturbed, but you also told me to let you know when she came back, and she's here."

One thing I had never felt in my life is my already hard dick get harder at the thought of the one woman that I knew could send me spiraling into the depths of fucking hell.

"I'll be down," I told him and looked at Eleanor. See how fate has a way of working?

"Get up," I told her. Now she started to touch my dick like she was going to do something with it.

"Lincoln, I thought you and I had something going here…"

I grabbed her by her arm, helped her off my lap and stood. I tucked my dick back in my pants, zipped and buckled my belt. "I have business, so if you don't mind my bluntness, get the fuck out."

I walked to the door of my office and opened it. I looked back at Eleanor and waited for her to move her ass. She finally did, giving me the finger and said, "You'll never get a chance at this pussy again."

I scoffed, "You've been ran up into so many times, sweetheart, my dick would probably fall out."

She looked back at me, giving me her dirtiest look, and I just laughed.

I locked my office door and made my way downstairs. I bought this club a few years prior, and it had been very lucrative for me. I'd actually bought a few clubs along a street called Delaware Ave, the home for most clubs in Philly, but this one was my baby. I'd designed this place, "Champagne Life," from top to bottom and hired and fired everyone in this place. I mentioned loyalty is everything to me. So if I find out you're stealing from me or trying to take from me, I'm not someone you'd want to deal with. Most people knew who I was, though, so I didn't have much of a problem. But there was always one that tries to test you.

I love being tested.

Right at that moment though fate was testing me, and I had to say I didn't fucking like it. I don't like feeling powerless, and dealing with Georgia made me feel like I had no control.

I moved slowly through the club, weaving through a lot of bodies. I swear in two hours this place had doubled in size. I looked at the bouncer, hoping he was keeping count. I didn't want to give the cops any reason to come here trying to shut me down on a fucking fire code.

My club was huge, with the main dance floor pitted and VIP circled above it. There were tables all on the main floor with enough places for some people to sit or just stand around and watch. There were three bar areas; one very large, one on the main floor (that's just as big as the dance floor), and two smaller ones on the VIP level.

I wasn't sure how I was going to find her, but actually I didn't have to. The steps to my office brought me just beyond the main bar area. As I walked toward the bar, she was coming to me. She looked awful and scared. My instincts suddenly kicked in, and I looked around the club looking for trouble.

I waited until she got close to me. Then I took her hand in mine and led her back upstairs and into my office. When we got there, I closed and locked the door. Georgia walked around my office slowly taking in the space. The room was nothing really; laminate floor under her feet and oak desk towards the back of the space with a large leather desk chair. There were two chairs facing the desk and a leather couch to the right of the desk. I had some pictures up along the walls. Pictures of the Eagles stadium, old and new, the Philadelphia skyline and as she stared at one other picture, I could no longer hear the club music, but my own heart pumping in my ear. She was staring at the picture of her on some shelving cabinet I had against the wall.

Of course, I needed to be an asshole to her. I didn't forget the way she just left me on the curb of her hotel a week ago. That shit still bothered me. She could have at least told me to fuck off or gave me the finger. I would have taken that better than her just looking at me, or through me and then leaving.

I put my unlit cigar in my mouth and walked around her. "What is it that you want?"

Unfazed by my tone she asked me, "When did you take this picture?"

I looked back at the picture, and I knew the very moment I took it. She was leaning over a boat railing of the sunset cruise we had taken. She was just staring out into the ocean, but her face seemed so angelic-like, soft, so beautiful and innocent. I stood there watching her for a while before I took that picture with my phone. People that come in my office keep telling me to put a picture in the frame, thinking it was the paper picture that you usually get in a frame when you buy it. They had no idea that the picture is real.

I ignored her question though and reiterated mine, just in a different way, but the bored tone was the same. "Are you going to tell me why you're here?"

She turned to me. Fear still etched her beautiful face. I won't lie to you; it was bothering me as each second went by.

She moved slowly and sat down in one of the chairs in front of my desk. I started to light up, but she put her hand up. "Can you not light that? I've ...um... been feeling sick lately, and it seems every smell triggers my stomach to unload."

I put my lighter down and my cigar in the tray. I looked at her and leaned back in my chair. I waited and watched as she battled with whatever she needed to tell me.

Before I was going to prompt her, she said, "How did you find me? I mean, at the hotel... How did you know I was there?"

I touched my fingers together and placed my elbows on the armrests of my chair. "Why?"

She squirmed in her seat. "Did you tell anyone about .... um..."

I shook my head. "Georgia, I don't know what you're asking me. I knew you were there because you told me the name you use when you want to hide. I couldn't find you anywhere else in the city using your name, so I tried Chloe."

"And you didn't tell anyone? I mean, how did you search for me?"

"Fuck, Georgia. What the hell is going on? Why are you asking me these questions?" I sat up, losing my fucking patience.

She closed her eyes and said, "Someone broke into my hotel room the other night."

I looked at her and began to frown. "And you think I did that shit?"

She shook her head, "No... I don't but..."

"But what?" I pushed.

She frowned back at me. "Damn it, Lincoln. I'm trying to tell you. No one else knows me by that name but you."

I scoffed. "Not your boyfriend?"

"What? I don't..." She stopped and shook her head. "No one knows but you. And when my room got broken into I thought that maybe someone found out about that name."

"Georgia, I didn't tell anyone about the alias you use. Yes, I have some old connections that I trust with my life, and they were the ones that tracked you down for me."

"Then I need your help."

"Why do you need my help?"

"Because the people that broke in..." She trailed off, and I picked up the ball.

"...were maybe from my life. You think I can ask around, see if I can shake some trees for you? Why don't you go to the cops, Georgia? This is their kind of thing,"

She sat up in her chair and put her arms on my desk. "That's just it. I did call the cops. They did a thorough investigation and everything. They looked at the security feed from the hotel and asked me if anyone looked familiar and one person did. He wasn't seen entering my room. He was just sitting in the lobby, but it was too much of a coincidence."

"Okay, did you tell the cops this?" I asked her, knowing what the answer was.

"No, I couldn't. Anyway, the hotel accused me of letting someone in the room, and they trashed the place because there was no forced entry. They thought I might have dropped and lost my key, or I was with some man and he went crazy. They charged me for the damage. Do you believe that?  My things were destroyed, and they have the audacity to make this my fault."

"What do you expect me to do, Georgia?" I asked again.

She went into her purse and pulled out a folded paper. She pushed it over to me and stood. "I don't know what you can do.  I just..." Tears started gathering in her eyes, and she looked down at her wringing hands. "I'm sorry to have bothered you."

I looked at the picture just as she turned to leave.  When I saw the face, I sat up. "What the fuck? Is this real?"

I looked up, and she kept moving to the door.  I stood quickly and reached her just as she moved through the door. "Georgia, are you telling me this man was sitting in the lobby of the hotel you were staying?"

She nodded.

"Fuck!"

I looked at the picture again and saw Manual Agosto, the bartender from Cabo.

"I'm scared, Drake," she said softly to me. No longer thinking about being mad at her, I pulled her into my arms and held her.

My mind was moving a mile a minute, thinking about what I needed to do first.  If this son of a bitch was in Philadelphia, then so was the other one, I assumed.

I moved her back and looked at her. "Do you have a place to stay?"

She shrugged. "I've been sleeping in my car during the day and driving around the city at night."

"What?! Georgia what the ... Where's that son of a bitch I saw you with outside your hotel?"

She rolled her eyes and moved back from me. "That didn't work out. That's why I was at a hotel. I didn't want to get another hotel in either of my names. I'm afraid they will find me again."

I stared at her, pissed as shit at the son of a bitch that she was with and the fact she was living out of her car in my city. I didn't want to even know how long she was doing it, for fear it would push me over the edge.

I went back to my office and locked my door. I then walked to her and grabbed her hand again. "Come on." She came willingly, and we moved through the club to the front door. I saw my bedtime rump look at me, but I stared at her, letting her know with my eyes we were done.

When we got outside of the club, I looked at her, asking, "Where's your car?"

"Around the corner."

"Do you have anything of value that you need in there?" I asked her, nodding at the valet guy to grab my monster.

"No, the little bit of clothes I bought are right here in my bag."

I looked back at her and asked because I had to, "When did all this happen?"

She hesitated, then answered, "I think a week ago."

"No, baby, when did you start sleeping in your car?"

She hesitated again, and then said, "Three days ago."

"Shit, and you're just now coming to me?"

I turned and faced her. Looking into her teary eyes had me shook. I took a deep breath to try and calm down. I was going to end up killing someone with my bare hands, and it's going to be Manual Agosto the moment I find this son of a bitch.

I put my hands in her hair and moved her closer to me. I tilted her head up, so her eyes were directly on me. She looked so lost and scared, and that bothered the hell out of me. At that moment, I actually felt every bit of the fight I had to not let her close to me dissolve instantly. I said months ago that she was mine and damn it if I wasn't going to claim what was mine starting this moment.

My car came into view. When it got to the curb, I opened the door and told her to get inside.

"What about my car?" she asked me.

"Give me your keys." She handed her keys to me, and I nodded at the bouncer at the door. He immediately approached him. I handed him the keys, telling him which car they belonged to. "Give these to Rock and have him take the car to my place. Tell him to take precautions when coming to my house and tell him to put the car keys in Lucille. I'll get them later."

"Yes sir."

"Who is Lucille?" she asked when I got in the car.

"My pickup truck," I said simply and turned on my car, feeling the V-eight cylinders spark and come to life... I love my car.

As we drove through the city, she remained quiet next to me. I wanted to ask her so many questions, but I knew whatever I said to her wouldn't come out right. I was steaming, fuming and if I didn't calm down soon, one of these non-driving idiots were going to get ripped apart.

I cleared my mind and took soothing breaths before I asked, "How long have you been here?"

I looked over at her, and she looked down at her lap. She then brought her eyes to me and said, "Three months, I guess."

"So you came here right after you left Cabo?"

"Yes."

Yeah... seems I should have kept my mouth shut.

*So she was here all this time, and I knew nothing about it.*

I turned on the radio to my favorite rock station and as Linkin Park screamed at me about being "victimized," I tried not to let the murderous feeling I was getting curse all through me.

I drove to my condo on Arch St. close to I-95, and once I parked in my parking spot, I looked over and found Georgia sleep.

I watched her for a moment, wondering how in the hell did I leave her that morning without giving her my number. I kept telling myself that it was for her sake, but right then I just didn't know. If she wasn't supposed to be in my life, why was she there? Why after months did I see her in my club of all places? Philly is a big city; the odds of us running into each other had to be off the charts. But there we were. I was not going to second guess it anymore. I was going to see where this went. I hoped she was in for the ride because it was going to get rough.

I called her name, touched her arm, and she practically jumped out of her skin. "Whoa, baby. It's just me. We're here."

She stared at me for a second longer, and then gathered herself. She looked around the garage. Then as I got out, she asked, "Where are we?"

I closed my door, and when I opened her side to help her out, I said simply, "My place."

She stopped, halfway out of the car. "Oh no. Drake, I can't stay with you."

"Yeah, you can. Come on." I pulled her up, and I took her hand, but she snatched it back.

"No, you don't understand...," she started but I moved closer to her caging her between my car.

"No, it's you that doesn't understand. First, you're not going to some damn hotel; not while I'm breathing. Second, I'm not letting you out of my sight for a while, at least until I can assess the threat. And third, and this is the most important one, you will not spend another night in your car. Now, get *the fuck* out of the car, Georgia."

I tried to drive home my point with the fear of God in my eyes, but she just looked back at me like a deer in headlights. She blinked and again tears started forming in her eyes. I didn't remember her being this emotional.

"Shit, I'm sorry... It's just... I don't want to put you in danger," she said softly.

"Baby, if I'm helping you, I'm already putting myself in danger. I'd rather be in danger knowing where you are than not." I wiped at her eyes. "Now, come on. I know you would love to have a nice hot bath."

Her eyes lit up as if I was giving her diamond earrings or something. "Oh, yes please."

I smiled at her. "That's my girl... Now come on."

We rode the elevator to the top floor of the building. There were only two apartments on this floor, and one was owned by some old rich guy who seemed to always have a steady stream of young girls in and out of his apartment.

When I opened my door, I let her walk in before me and she sort of just looked around in awe. I closed and locked my door, turned off my alarm and moved to the kitchen. I hadn't been home in a while, and I wasn't sure if I had any food in the fridge.

My apartment had an open floor-plan. As soon as you walk in the door, you see the living room, dining areas, and kitchen. The space had bamboo flooring throughout with a nice size kitchen and island, ten-foot ceilings, and oversized floor to ceiling windows. All three bedrooms were upstairs. Going around the corner to a set of stairs is where I led her.

"You're apartment is..." She paused and when we reached the top of the stairs, I looked at her.

"Surprising?" I added.

She smiled for the first time since I've seen her in Cabo. "Um... Yeah okay. We can go with that."

"I'm not in Philly mostly, but when I am here, I like to be in something nice."

"I get that. You just don't have a leather or suede sectional downstairs. You do have a very large screen TV, but you have pictures and plants and lamps... pillows even."

I laughed as I opened my bedroom door and moved aside so she could enter. "I had a decorator come in, so don't give me too much credit. I just told her not to make me look like a dumb ass bachelor or make it seem too feminine, and this is what she came up with."

"Well, it's very masculine. It suits you." She then looked at my four-poster king size bed. "This suits you too."

I smiled "Come on. Let's get you bathed. Are you hungry?"

She paused, looked at me, and then touched her stomach.

She nodded. "Yeah, I think I am."

I chuckled. "Okay, take as long as you want. I don't know what's downstairs, but if there's nothing to make fast, I'll order out. Chinese okay with you?"

Georgia was no longer paying me any attention. She was looking at the huge ass tub in the corner of my bathroom.

"Do you need any help getting undressed?" I asked.

She looked back at me and frowned.

You can't blame me for asking.

"Just show me how to work this," she replied and moved further into the bathroom.

This bathroom was redone to my specifications. Since I owned this condo, I made sure to make it feel like me. The walls and floor contain gray slate tiles that cover the large whirlpool tub, and the walls and floor of the large two-person walk-in shower. I had large his and her porcelain sinks that sat on top of the large vanity cabinet with chrome faucets.

I showed her how to use the tub, and then brought her a towel and washcloth.

"This is my lucky Eagles t-shirt, so please take care of it."

"Yes, sir. I will." She shook her head and sat on the edge of the tub.

I watched her for a minute as she ran her hands under the faucet letting the water run through her fingers. I wasn't sure what she was thinking about, but I hoped she knew I wouldn't let anything happen to her.

I finally moved on, and as I made it into the kitchen, I called Angel.

The phone kept ringing, and then went to voicemail. I hung up and called him again. It was about 1 a.m. He was probably into someone, but, hell, I don't give a shit.

I was right when he answered on my third try. "What the hell is wrong with you? Can't you get the hint that I'm busy?" The way he was breathing told me I probably just interrupted him deep in his swing.

I smiled. "Oh, shit. Sorry, I didn't mean to disturb you."

"Yeah, why aren't you busy doing something else or someone else?"

"Well, that's the reason why I called you. Georgia came to see me."

Angel got quiet, and I heard him moving about. When he settled, he said, "So, yeah, why aren't you busy doing her?"

*Yeah, don't I wish?*

I sighed, gave up on cooking and looked at my many takeout menus. "She didn't come for that, unfortunately. She came for my help." I told him what she told me, the edited version, of course.

When I was done, Angel was all business like I needed him to be. "Okay, you know we have to play this shit cool. You don't need any bodies, understand?"

"Of course... Not yet anyway, besides I wouldn't do it here in the city. I have a place in mind though. But we have to find him first."

"Do you think he's alone?" he asked me.

"Not for long. I don't know what his end game is or the game that was being played in Cabo, but I'm done with this shit. Hold on a second." I grabbed my house phone and placed an order for shrimp fried rice, beef and broccoli, teriyaki chicken, white rice, and three egg rolls. I wasn't sure how long she would be, but I wanted to get everything ordered so when she did come down, the food would either be here, or it would be on its way.

"Do you have a plan to smoke him out?" he asked me when I got back on the line.

"I thought about a plan, but I think I can find him easily. If he was just sitting around the hotel that day, he's sitting someplace else, eating or having a beer. I'll call my connections and will probably have a location by tomorrow."

"I need to talk to Pops. You know he hates freelance jobs. Besides, aren't you still working on that Santiago family business in Miami? Eddie is chomping at the bit."

I grunted. "Yeah, something isn't right with that family, Angel. Eddie has something going on behind this family's back; I can smell it. I'll check with my contacts tomorrow to see what they've found so far."

"Alright. Do that. In the meantime, I'll talk to my father about your... uh... girlfriend?"

I grunted again. "Yeah, you do that."

He chuckled and said, "So are you done messing with my night? I have more fucking to do."

"Yeah. I'll call you tomorrow."

I hung up the phone and turned on the television. I had watched CNN for about thirty minutes before the food came. About

'
fifteen minutes later, Georgia still hadn't made it downstairs, so I went looking for her. I walked in my room, and I saw her curled up in the center of the bed with just the t-shirt on I gave her, fast asleep.

I pulled the cover over her body and made my way back downstairs. I had a lot going on, so sleep wasn't an option for me that night. Besides, I know me; if I had crawled in the bed with her, she would be violated for sure. Looking at her bare legs had my dick screaming to feel her again.

I grabbed my laptop and sat at my dining room table. While I ate, I started finding everything I could on this Manual Agosto, the Santiago family and that black guy I saw Georgia with.

By morning, I had more questions than answers. There were so many emotions flowing through me. I couldn't think straight. I needed to prioritize. Otherwise I was going to lose my mind. As I heard footsteps coming down the stairs, I figured I'd start with her.

When she came into view, she smiled. Damn, she still looked amazing when she woke up. I don't know what it is about her, but damn.

"Good morning. Sorry about yesterday."

I didn't waste time. I said, getting straight to the point, "Who is Gregory Sayers to you?"

# CHAPTER 14

## GEORGIA

I froze in my tracks and stared at him, eyes wide, hand in mid hair rake.

This was a great time to ask for a time out to get myself together, but I don't think he was going to give me one. I sighed and finally moved toward him. I thought about sitting far away from him; I could see that he was pissed and honestly looked like he had been up all night.

I should be upset that he was looking into my business, but what did I expect? I knew for a fact he felt threatened by the unknown of Greg and my implications didn't help anything yesterday. And, wow, the murderous look in his eyes at that moment; I thought it better to not beat around the bush and just say it.

"He's my brother... or rather my half-brother."

"What? I thought you had no siblings."

I laughed slightly. "Yeah, me too."

I then explained everything; from the call I received at the airport in Cabo to me coming here, the meeting I had at the attorney's office, the shares I own... I told him everything... Well, almost everything. When he asked me why I left, I just said we had differences that we couldn't work out.

"Greg doesn't like me at all, and when he found out I knew you... he became a little crazy."

Drake sat up. "Crazy how?"

Seeing the murderous look again, I started waving my hands. "Easy... not like 'crazy'... Just ... you know... 'I don't want that kind of thing around my father's family'..."

Drake grunted. "Yeah, well, baby, he needs to stop being a hypocrite. I knew I recognized him from somewhere. His father has done business with my uncle for years. As a matter of fact, his father made a deal with my family in order to pay off his gambling debt. Junior knows all about it."

*Uh what?*

"What kind of deal?" I had asked before I realized it.

Drake however ignored my question and asked, "So do you know how much your stock is worth?"

I shook my head. "No. I don't know anything about the business. I just go to the meetings because that's what my father wanted."

He nodded his head. "So you found your family?"

I gave him a weak smile. "Yeah, I thought I did. Can we just drop the topic of them?"

"Okay... Tell me about the break-in in your hotel room."

"What do you want to know?"

"Did they take anything of value? Or did it just look like someone went in there and just tore up the place?"

I leaned back against the chair and started biting my nails. I hadn't had that nasty little nervous habit since I was fourteen.

"I don't know, Drake. The room was in shambles. It was like a hurricane ran through the room. A Tasmanian devil would be more like it. Do you know that cartoon character?"

He nodded with a half-smile. "Yes, I remember... Did they take anything of value? Watch, money, jewelry? Anything like that?"

"No, nothing like that. But they made sure I couldn't use any of the clothes I had right down to my underwear and bras. It's like twenty thousand worth of damage... I can't pay for that."

He frowned. "You won't have to pay for it. Don't worry about that."

"How can you say that? I've already heard from their lawyer. They're suing me."

"Baby, I promise you, you won't have to pay them a dime. Now I need you to think hard... Do you remember having a feeling of someone following you or watching you?"

I didn't hesitate. "No, nothing like that. I know what you're getting at, but I didn't see anyone suspicious around me. And I was staying at my father's house for most of the time I was in town. I only got a hotel room when Dara and I would hang out in the city."

"Dara was the one with you at my club?"

I nodded and brought my hand back up to my mouth; thinking about that night, seeing him with that woman.

Drake took my hand from my mouth. "Listen, I'm getting close to getting this solved, okay? Don't worry about anything. You can stay here until this whole thing blows over. We'll get you some clothes, so you aren't living from that small ass bag you're carrying. Is that car a rental?" I told him it was, and he added, "Okay, well we'll take that car back. You can drive my car; I'll drive the truck."

A complete feeling of warmth came over me like the feeling of a warm blanket when it's below freezing outside. I felt myself tearing so I turned my head. Those hormones were driving me crazy. I'd never cried that much in my life. I was completely embarrassed to tell him. I actually cried myself to sleep that night because of how much he was taking care of me.

"Georgia," he said softly.

I shook my head. "I'm fine... it's just..." I met his eyes. "Thank you so much for helping me... I don't know what I would have done if you turned me away."

Something washed over his usually hard features that I couldn't begin to explain to you. It was something that I've never seen before, and it made him look less scary, less mean, less bad. The moment that it appeared, it was gone.

He said to me, "The moment you came to me, I knew I wasn't going to turn you away. This bartender and I have unfinished business, and I hate having loose ends. They always find a way of coming back."

I didn't want to take that personal, but with all of those hormones I kind of did.

Drake closed his laptop and stood. "Make yourself at home. There is food from last night in the fridge if you want to heat up anything. There's also eggs in there but the milk, I wouldn't risk it. I'm going upstairs to lie down for a little while. When I get up, we're out of here. First stop; take your car back. Then get you some decent clothes. Okay?"

Tears again! I just said softly, "Okay."

Drake stared at me for a long moment before he left. He was probably wishing he'd said no to me in Cabo.

But he had no idea how much I was glad he didn't.

I took a shower in one of the other rooms. Then I found the laundry room and washed my clothes. I was tired of the short sleeve shirts. It was downright cold out there.

Lately, I'd been able to keep some things down, so I attempted to eat the shrimp fried rice, which I have to say was really good, and I drank plenty of water. I took a prenatal pill after I ate, learning the hard way I needed something on my stomach before I took them and watched television until Drake woke up.

While he drove my rental, he had me drive his "monster," which happened to be a tricked out Dodge Charger, big and loud and oh so beautiful. We took my rental back to the airport, and he ended up paying cash for it, which I tried to get him not to, but he gave me one of those murderous looks, so I got quiet.

He then took over driving and we drove downtown to a place called The Galleria, which was right in the middle of downtown Philly.

Before we got out of the car, he looked at me. "I don't want you to use any of your credit cards. From now on, you use cash only."

*But I don't have any cash*, I thought. I started to say that, but I saw him come out of his pocket with a wad of money. He counted, and I just stared at all the one hundred dollar bills he had. He then handed a small stack over to me.

"That's two thousand dollars. That should be enough to get at least the bare necessities, some clothes, underwear, shit like that. Shoes and coats can get costly, so I'll take care of those. I know women like to shop, but we are on a time clock here. Do you think you can be done in three hours?"

I... was... speechless.

Timeout.

Did this man just give me two thousand dollars in one hundred dollar bills and then say he would charge anything else to his card? And did he just say if three hours of shopping would be enough time?

I don't know about you, but I'm waiting for Ashton Kutcher to come out and tell me that I'm being "punked."

Drake smirked. "Yeah, I know, but I'm trying to be sympathetic to your needs since you've been through a lot. Don't think this is going to happen all the time."

He got out of the car, and I sat there feeling like I was gut-punched twice.

*Did he say "don't think this is going to happen all the time," as if I'll be around 'all the time'?*

Drake opened my door and helped me out. "Are you okay?"

All I could do is nod and grab his hand, walking quickly into Macy's.

So I shopped for only two hours, actually he shopped for me for two hours and ate for thirty minutes before we left. I don't want to admit it out loud for fear he'd take this the wrong way, but I had the best time of my life. He nixed almost everything I picked out, reminding me I was in Philly, not Miami. Then he started reminding me how old I was and to get out of the old lady section.

He didn't realize that most hip clothes wouldn't fit on this body.

This rare specimen took a look at me, and then started shopping for me. He started handing me clothes to go try on, and I have to say he had some really great taste. When I looked shocked when something looked phenomenal on me, he would just shrug and say, "It's a gift."

I couldn't wait to get out of the clothes I had on and into the clothes he bought for me. I did attempt to tell him I would pay him back every cent of what he spent, and he gave me that murderous look again. I figured that look was used often, but as quick as he brings it, it's gone.

When we got back to his place, he was only there for thirty minutes before he told me he had to run out.

"Listen, I'm going to take you out to dinner tonight. Nothing too fancy since we didn't shop for that kind of stuff yet... but nice. I'll text you the address of the restaurant and the time to meet me." He dropped the keys to the "monster" on the kitchen counter. "I'll see you later, and please burn that jacket you have, baby. Wear one of the ones we bought, okay?"

With that bit of instruction, he left the apartment.

I took another long, hot bath and crawled into his bed again, feeling drained from the outing and all the emotions that I'd been feeling. Drake sent me a text about two hours later, giving me an address that I knew I would have to map on my phone. He asked me to meet him there at seven-thirty, and it was five o'clock at the time, so I had some time.

Unfortunately, this dang pregnancy had me crazy because I woke again to the buzz of my phone and saw it was six forty-five. Drake had text messaged me and just said, "Get up."

"Shit." I stood quickly, actually too quickly, got dizzy and fell flat on my ass.

Did I say this dang pregnancy had me crazy?

Anyway, I got dressed as fast as I could, putting on a sweater style dress and leggings with a pair of four-inch platform boots. I left the condo a little after seven and, seeing that the restaurant he was sending me too was about fifteen to twenty minutes from his place, I was confident that I would make it in time... However, yeah, that wasn't the case. I ended up having to use the restroom as soon as I got to the car, so I had to go back upstairs. I ended up finding the restaurant closer to eight.

There were no parking spaces in the front of the restaurant, so I went to find a parking garage somewhere close. It was that moment when my phone went off. I found a parking lot to park in, and I raided Drake's change to pay for the meter. I saw that Drake texted me asking where I was, and I told him I was parking.

I had to park around the corner, so I moved as fast as I could, knowing I was so late.

When I turned the corner, Drake was standing outside in a pair of brown slacks and a black sweater. He wore a fedora on his head, something that he'd done for most of the trip in Cabo, and his trademark cigar was parked between his lips. He looked so fine and sexy so much so that I almost fell, tripping over the sidewalk because I was paying so much attention to him. When his eyes came to mine, I smiled. However, my smile wasn't greeted very well. He took the cigar out of his mouth and moved quickly to me.

"Where are you coming from?" he asked me, looking behind me, and then back in my eyes.

A little thrown off by his tone, I pointed behind me. "I *parked the car*. There were no parking spaces in the front of the restaurant, so it took me a minute, but I found one a few blocks away."

"A few blocks? You have got to be kidding me. Give me the keys."

Now I was getting pissed, so I slammed his keys in his hand. He gave me a sharp look but turned and signaled one of the valets to come over to him. He tossed him his keys. "Go and get my car, and park it in the front of the restaurant."

"Yes sir," the valet responded.

Drake looked at me. "What's the name of the parking garage?"

"It's not a garage; it's a lot. I'm not sure of the name. It's around that corner though, about two or three streets down." As the guy ran off, Drake gave me another funny look, and I'd just about had it. "I don't know what the big deal is, Lincoln. I don't know why you're pissed at me."

Drake squared his shoulders in front of me. Brows furrowed, he said, "I'm not pissed at you. I'm pissed at your fucking past. I'm pissed that no one in your life has taught you how you're supposed to be treated. What you're supposed to expect from a man. Understand something; if I ask you to meet me somewhere, my club or a restaurant, and there's a valet, *you valet*. Don't worry about paying for it; consider it paid because I'll be out there waiting for you to arrive anyway, and I'll have already taken care of it. It's not cool that you parked blocks from the restaurant in the cold at night. I don't want you walking around at night alone. It's not safe, number one, and number two, I just don't get down like that. When you're with me, you're with me. If we are both going someplace and I have to park far from the entrance of wherever we're going, I'll let you off at the front door and go park the car. And I'll go and get the car while you wait inside for me when it's time to leave. That's how I roll, understand?"

I didn't reply.

How could I?

I'd never in my life been treated like he's describing, number one. Gavin always made me walk, no matter what time of the day or how hot or cold it was outside. If he parked far from the restaurant, we both walked. If I was meeting him somewhere, he was waiting inside for me. He never opened the car door for me either... *like ever*... So, no, I didn't know what to expect.

Drake didn't say another word, he just took my hand in his and walked toward the restaurant.

I finally found my voice and said, which later I regretted, "The things you just said didn't sound like they would come from a bad boy who is part of a notorious crime family. That sounded like it came from a good guy."

Drake stopped walking and said to me, "No, baby, that is just how you're supposed to be treated. It's what I learned from my father and what's been drilled and upheld in me by my uncle. Maybe that's the only thing good in me that I possess."

The sadness in his eyes made me want to kick myself. He was being a perfect gentlemen and I threw his way of life in his face.

Once we made it into the restaurant, I looked around the place and found it empty, but I could hear loud voices and kids talking and screaming coming from somewhere. I looked at Drake as he led me through the empty dining area and into the back of the restaurant where I got the shock of my life.

The back private area was packed with two very long tables filled with one rather large family. All eyes fell on us as we entered the room and as the chants of his name, "Hey, Cuz," or "Uncle Drake" rang through the room, I realized that he has brought me to a family dinner.

I squeezed his hand tight, and he looked at me. I know my eyes were wide as saucers, and all he did was grin at me. He kissed my hand and said, "Don't worry. Everything will be fine. I told you when you're with me, you're with me."

Drake spoke to everyone he passed and brought me up to a plump old woman with a little plump baby in her lap. She smiled at Drake, then at me, and I swear her smile grew like tenfold. She gave someone next to her the baby, and she stood.

To me, this woman looked like a traditional Italian grandmother, and when Drake leaned in my ear and said, "This is my grandmother, Bella," all I could do was smile at her.

She didn't just take my smile though. She cupped my face in her hands and while still smiling kissed both of my cheeks. She then hugged me tight and touched Drake's face as well.

I didn't understand that greeting, but I went with it. Next he took me to some of his aunts and uncles and a few of his cousins. Then he brought me to one of the most attractive Italian men I had ever seen. I mean, he looked as if he had just come out of GQ Magazine. He wore a pair of jeans and a jacket with a button down white shirt. His hair was thick and dark and laid lazily over his eye, which he had to move back from when he stood to greet me.

"Georgia, this is my cousin, Angel."

*Oh my.*

"Angel, this is…"

"Your Georgia…" Angel finished and reached for my hand. I watched as he brought it to his lips and said softly, "Ciao Bella." He showed me his perfect teeth and perfect smile.

*Oh my indeed.*

Drake moved my hand from his cousin's. "Enough with trying to seduce my date." He went on to introduce me to others. "Georgia, this is Eddie, Angel's brother, and this is my Uncle Bruno. Uncle Bruno this is Georgia Sayers, Gregory Sayer's daughter."

Okay, can I say that if Angel was classic Italian hottie than his father was the start of the mold because *wow*. He was tall like Angel and Drake, dark and built like a brick building. He exuded power in his eyes, his character and just his presence. I felt weak in my knees just standing in front of him as if I should be kneeling or something and kissing his ring.

He smiled at me as he too took my hand and kissed it. Again, if I could blush, I think I'd be as red as the tablecloth.

Drake's uncle said to me, "It's a pleasure to meet you, Bella. Please have a seat. I hope you're hungry. We have a lot of food."

I smiled and stumbled out, "Yes, sir, I am. Thank you.'

Drake moved to the seat across from Angel and next to his Uncle and sat me next to him. I didn't see the significance to the seat arrangements until I saw Eddie give Drake an ugly look as he sat down. I almost wondered if we were sitting in his seat or something.

Now to Eddie. Okay, can I be honest? Eddie looked adopted almost. I mean, I could see his father in him, and he had a great head of black wavy hair. It's just the bulk of muscle and stature wasn't there. It was there in the three men at the head of this table but not in Eddie. I also found it rather odd that Drake introduced all of his family as "cousin" or his "uncle" but when he introduced Eddie it was "Angel's brother." Maybe there was some bad blood between cousins and the seat that Drake was in Eddie felt belonged to him.

*Wow, the movies do have it right. There is drama within a crime family.*

# CHAPTER 15

## DRAKE

I have to say dinner was uneventful. I was waiting for the wisecracking cousin of mine to embarrass me but suffice it to say he was quiet. He was actually trying to limit the amount of wine his date was putting back. Eddie was cutting his eyes at me and Georgia, but he remained on his side of the table and relatively quiet. The night was actually surprisingly good. Being with my family like this was the only time I was able to relax around my uncle. Even when I was staying at his home, I was on alert. And, to be honest, nothing was stopping someone from taking out our entire family as we ate dinner, but they would have to be assured the entire family was there. Otherwise, retaliation would be swift, painful and destructive.

I watched Georgia with my family, and I couldn't help but smile. It shocked me how my grandmother greeted her, and I had to find out what that was all about. But I was pleased nonetheless. My aunts were very nice to her, but of course I couldn't say that for some of my cousins, but that's only because they were always trying to fix me up with their friends.

I leaned back in my seat just as Georgia took my little cousin, Nya, in her arms. Nya was precious and another person I would undoubtedly kill for without hesitation. There's not that many people I would do that for and the very people were sitting on either side of me and directly in front of me. Don't get me wrong, I will protect everyone in this room with my life, but there are only a few that I would leave bodies for. As I looked at Georgia kiss on my cousin, I realized there was one person in this room that had the kind of power over me to drive me completely insane.

Dessert came, and I found myself massaging the back of Georgia's neck. The slow groan she did woke me up in more ways than I wanted her to in front of my family. I leaned into her ear, feeling the effects of the many scotches I consumed. "Baby, I would advise you to stop moaning like that. It's been a long time for me, and you're going to make me take you in one of the restrooms here and see how loud I can make you scream."

I didn't miss the heat in her eyes as she looked at me and clamped her lips shut. Her lips... Damn, I missed them. I turned and moved closer to her. "Did I tell you how beautiful you looked tonight?" I caressed her cheek softly, wanting to feel her just for a little while. I didn't remember picking out this dress for her, but I had to say it definitely helped with my imagination on the curves of her body.

"No," she said, her voice but a whisper. I knew I was having an effect on her. I could still tell when she wanted me and how bad she wanted it.

*Maybe it's been a long time for her too.*

*God, I hope so.*

"You were too busy fussing at me," she told me, unfortunately, loud enough for others to hear.

"What?" That was Angel. "Lincoln, I can't believe you would do such a thing to this beautiful goddess. You really don't know how to treat women. Listen, Georgia, anytime you want to drop that loser and get with a real man, let me know."

I shook my head at his date... Uh, what was her name again?

Anyway, she didn't take too kindly to his words and smacked his arm. Angel, ever the lady's man, just smiled at his date, "Don't worry, baby. There's enough of me to go around."

"Angelo!" I heard my aunt admonish from across the room.

"Sorry, mama," Angel called back to her and smiled at Georgia. He said, "So what was my brooding cousin fussing about?"

"Nothing," I replied hoping that Georgia would get the hint.

However, she didn't and she said, "He was upset because I parked the car around the corner instead of getting it valeted."

My uncle and Angel looked at her puzzled at first, and then they both frowned at me. "Where were you?" my uncle asked me.

"I was outside waiting for her," I replied

"Yeah, you must have been late because if you weren't, you would have seen her pass and stopped her from parking... Damn, Cuz, that's fucked up," Angel added.

"I taught you better than that, son," my uncle said to me. Then told me how real men take care of their own, in Italian. I had to listen to the speech that I heard a thousand times. My aunt must have heard her husband berate me, and I got it from both ends. Angel sat back and grinned... the fucker... and poor Georgia looked lost but I know she could tell I was getting a lecture. She started to say something, but I squeezed her neck slightly giving her the hint to be quiet.

I took a deep breath, so much for some word foreplay. My erection definitely deflated into nothing.

✳✳✳✳✳

The ride home was quiet, except for me giving directions to my condo. Georgia didn't drink a bit of alcohol, which I thought was very strange. She told me she was too nervous to drink. I caught her biting her nails a few times, so I didn't press it. But I wanted to know how the night went for her. I wanted to know if she liked my family... I don't know why; believe me. But, shit, I really wanted to know. I started to ask her, but she said, "You have a really good family thing going on."

"Thanks," was all I said because I remembered she didn't have one growing up. *Shit.*

I added though, so I wouldn't feel like a complete ass, "They seemed to love you. Nya fell asleep in your arms. She doesn't do that with everyone."

She laughed. "I can see that. She doesn't like your cousin Eddie at all. I saw him trying to play with her, and she would just cry."

I grew quiet, not thinking she would catch on, but I couldn't help it. Yes, I'm going to say it for the umpteenth time; I hate that guy.

"I see you two don't get along." she said.

I looked at her. "Why do you say that?" I sat up in the seat. "Did he say something to you?"

"Down boy... No, he didn't say anything. But he didn't have to. The way you introduced me to him and the way he stared at you all night. If looks could kill... wow."

"If looks could kill, he would've been dead a long time ago," I added, and then regretted it instantly when she looked at me.

"Why do you hate him?" she asked me and I should have expected it. I left myself open for that.

But that story I won't tell, so I just said, "I think we both are strong-willed individuals that want the same thing; the approval of the boss man. I'm getting a little more from him than Eddie is, and he's probably pissed." That sounded good, didn't it? Let's see if she bought it.

,

She nodded her head. "I can see that. He was staring at you so hard that I thought we were sitting in his seat at the table."

I saw that, but I was hoping Georgia didn't. Eddie and I try not to show our hatred for one another in family settings for the sake of his mother and our grandmother. But the way he was looking at me, I could feel the rage pointed directly at me. He and I would have to have some words about that shit.

"So your family... they call you Lincoln? All except you're Aunt Angelica, Angel's mom, and your grandmother?" she asked me.

"Yup, pretty much. Sometimes my Uncle Bruno or Angel will call me Drake too. They use that name usually when they want me to do something for them, or I'm being chastised for something I'd done or said. But just like everyone else they call me Lincoln."

She looked over at me. "Do you want me to stop calling you Drake?"

"No," I said probably too quickly. It seemed to startle her, but instead of answering her questioning look, I just stared out the window. I didn't want to answer the question I knew she had because hell I had no way of explaining it. I just preferred to be Drake to her. As I mentioned before, it made me feel normal when she called me Drake. I wished I could be just Drake to her. And I probably could say that to her, and she would undoubtedly understand, but I didn't.

"Has um..." I looked over at her. She kept her eyes on the road and both hands on the wheel when she continued, "...Has anyone outside of your family ever called you Drake?"

We came at a stoplight, and she looked over at me. I kept her gaze and answered simply, "No."

"Oh... Okay," she said softly, and she fell silent.

I felt something starting to develop in the car, and I needed to change the air. I couldn't and didn't want to deal with what I knew was starting to happen so I said, "Tell me more about what you went through in that foster home you lived at."

She shrugged. "What do you want to know?"

I noticed her tense up and bring her right hand to her mouth. I took her hand and put it in mine. "Whatever you want to tell me."

She looked over at me quickly and said, "So are we sharing?"

I knew that was a loaded question, but I wanted to know what her life was like, so I said, "Yeah, I guess we're sharing."

"Then you will tell me about you and Eddie?"

I sighed deeply. I knew she would ask me again someday, but damn I didn't expect it so soon. "Fine, I'll tell you about me and Eddie. But you can't tell me some bullshit and think I'm going to spill my guts afterward. Make it count."

She moved to take her hand back, and I squeezed it, "No, I'll keep this with me if you don't mind."

She looked over at me and smiled. "Okay. Well, my mother and father were not very nice people. They were when the social worker would come by, but the moment they left, they were back to their mean rotten selves. They let everyone do pretty much what they wanted, as long as they benefited. Some of the boys that stayed there sold drugs and they had to give a cut to them as payment for staying there. Mother and Father would threaten them all the time that they would call the cops on them or tell the social worker they didn't have any more room for them to stay. The boys needed that house. They were either running from their own home life, or they had no place to go."

"What were the adult's names?"

She looked over at me. "You know I haven't a clue? The first day I got there, they told us to call them Mother and Father. I was never around anyone that used their first names and they never called each other anything but Mother and Father."

"So was the living area clean at least? Did they feed you and clothe you? They were getting money from the state to look out for you."

"We had food there, but most of the kids pretty much ate all the food. Now Mother and Father had their own stash of food locked away in their room. So whatever we had in the main area is what we got. Of course, they would stock up when the social workers came by but after that we were out of luck."

"And none of you guys reported them?"

She shook her head. "No. Most of us were scared of Mother and Father. They were crazy. We learned to stay out of Mother's way all the time. If she told us to do something, we did it, or we wouldn't eat or have clothes to wear. She figured out a way of punishing us. She didn't put a hand to us, but she did it in other ways. Mother always told us girls that we would be nothing but whores, addicts or someone's punching bag. We wouldn't amount to anything. She would bring suspicious men around us, paraded us around them like she would give us to one of them, stuff like that to keep us girls in line. And these were very scary men. She was useless. She never taught us how to be girls. I learned about my period from my teacher and nurse in school. They knew the situation but in that neighborhood you have to understand; no one really cared, and if they did, it wasn't received well."

She pulled into my building, and when she parked, she turned off the car. She started to get out, but I pulled her hand back. "What about the father?"

"Well, he was the creepiest of them all. We learned, some the hard way, to never be alone with Father and to never bathe when he's home. He would talk to you crazy or grab himself when he looked at you. He wouldn't touch you, and I don't think he went so far as to rape anyone, but he would do things like walk into the bathroom while you're there and say things like 'Oops. My fault. I didn't know you were in here or bump into you and grab you close to him and say 'Oh, I didn't see you' or 'Watch where you're going now.' Sometimes the guys would watch our backs and stand guard

,
for us, but they weren't there all the time. And some of them were creepy themselves."

I closed my eyes and cracked my neck. I couldn't get a nine-year-old Georgia being in a place like that for as long as she was and go through what she went through. I didn't want to ask this question, but I know it would bother me if I didn't so, I asked, "What about the kid that assaulted you? You said you never reported him. What happened to him?"

She looked over at me and said, "I'm not sure exactly, but I can guess. One time one of Jay Rock's lieutenants saw Adam bothering me on the playground. He was trying to touch me and pull on me. I managed to get away from him, but not before he ripped my t-shirt. Dawg, was his name, and he pulled off his t-shirt and gave it to me and told me to go see Jay Rock right now.  So I did and, well, that was the last time I saw Adam. I don't know what happened to him per se, but the rumor was he owed Jay Rock some money, and he couldn't pay up, so he had to pay with his life."

I nodded and breathed out. *One less person I have to search for,* I thought to myself.  I asked her, "Did any of the other kids mess with you?"

She shook her head. "No, not really.  I told you they all stayed away from me after Jay Rock, and his crew was killed.  And I told you I befriended two big ass dogs, so they became my bodyguards against Father and even Mother." She shook her head. "Those dogs were mean."

I chuckled. "I wish I could meet them."

I let go of her hand and started to get out, but she pulled my arm. "Your turn. I spilled my guts to the fullest. I think it's time you do the same, don't you?"

*Shit.*

I closed the door back and turned toward her a little. "Baby, what I have to tell you can't go anywhere. I'm trusting you, understand?"

She nodded, and I closed my eyes. I'm putting her at a huge disadvantage to lie for me if something came back on what I'm about to tell her. But as I looked at her, I knew she would have my back no matter what. I didn't want her to have to do that, so I said, "There are some things that I just can't tell you about, okay? I will tell you, but I can't tell you everything, understand?"

She was quiet a beat, and then she nodded. "Okay. I don't need the sordid details. Just give me what you're comfortable with."

I sighed. "Okay..."

"Wait... should we turn on the radio or turn our phones off? Maybe someone is listening to us talking or something."

I smiled and shook my head. "Well, baby, first thing first; there are no listening devices in my car. I get it swept often. As a matter of fact, before we left, it was swept, so we're fine. And don't worry about our phones. They are safe too. We're in the basement, and the cement walls down here make it difficult for them to use their listening devices."

She nodded, and then narrowed her eyes. "Wait... Are you playing with me?"

I tried to keep a straight face, but the look on her face made me throw my head back and laugh. I couldn't resist. She seemed so serious. She didn't find it too funny though. She smacked me in my chest. "Asshole."

"I'm sorry, baby." I chuckled trying to gather myself. "But damn this isn't the Godfather or the Wire." She rolled her eyes at me and got out of the car. She was pouting and maybe my joke was in bad taste. I climbed out of the car just as she got clear of the back, and I pulled her into me. "I'm sorry, baby. Seriously." I put my hand in her hair and moved her lips to mine. She tilted her head though, giving me her cheek. What she didn't realize is that she left her neck open for me. I moved my lips to her neck and started sucking on her, giving just enough pressure to have an adverse effect on her body.

"Drake..." she said softly trying to push me away, but I backed her up against my truck that was parked next to my car and moved her hands above her head. "Drake, please...," she moaned softly as I propped her leg up against my waist.

I grinded my hips against her, hoping I was driving her as crazy as she was driving me. I needed to kiss her. I moved to her lips this time, letting her hands go. As she grabbed me by my ears, I invaded her mouth with my tongue.

Her taste... Damn, I loved it.

I needed more.

I grabbed her ass under her dress and pressed her harder against me. Shit, I was two seconds from taking her clothes off right there.

"Wait," she said pushing me from her.

My breath was coming hard and strong, the same way I wanted to attack her pussy.

"What?" I looked in her eyes. I know she could feel I was on the brink of losing control.

"Drake..." she pleaded and I knew what she wanted.

"Damn, baby. Can't this wait?"

She shook her head. "No."

I rested my forehead against hers and closed my eyes. I couldn't calm down for shit. I wanted her. I could practically taste her in my mouth. I was salivating for her. The scent of her desires was making me go out of my mind.

*Damn it.*

I took a deep breath and without moving my head, I said, "Eddie had a huge client that was very lucrative for our family's interest. He'd been working this client for months. He felt they trusted him, and he trusted them. He trusted them a little too much though."

I pulled back from her but never stopped holding her. "Eddie believed these people liked and respected him. My uncle trusted them too. Both he and Angel felt like these people were on the up and up. He also trusted his oldest son to have vetted them before we started working with them. Me personally; I didn't trust them at all. As a matter of fact, every time I was around them, I felt like they were off. Something just wasn't right about them. So I did my own digging and found out they were actually trying to set us up, mainly Eddie, my Uncle, and Angel. These people wanted what my uncle's family had, what they worked hard to get."

I shook my head and put my hand on the side of her face. I caressed her cheek with my thumb and said, "My family is not very forgiving when it comes to betrayal. We don't forgive, and we don't forget. It's a code that we live by. We can't seem weak to anyone... Understand?"

Georgia looked at me, and I saw her swallow hard, but she kept her eyes on me. Finally, she nodded. She understood, so I remained quiet.

Finally, she said, "So does Eddie blame you? I don't understand how he could."

"Eddie had the trust of his father. With this issue, my uncle started questioning everything, saying those people should have never gotten that close. We had them in our home, around our family. That could have been disastrous for us. My uncle didn't blame Eddie, but he wanted everyone looked at thoroughly, and the job fell on me. Soon everyone that Eddie wanted to work with, no matter how much he proved the people he brought to his father were legit, my uncle questioned. Eddie began to resent me more and more, and it just festered."

She didn't say anything for a minute. I thought this session was over, and I could get back to what I was doing before, but that wasn't the case. When I moved to her, she said to me, "Okay, that explains why he doesn't like you, but why do you not like him?"

I frowned. "Because, baby, he's an idiot. The reason why we were wrapped in those people was because of some woman. Some woman that at the end of the day was screwing him in more ways than one. He wanted to believe she was good and made some horrible decisions not thinking with his head, but with his dick, and I called him on it. I still call him on any stupid decision he makes. He's trying to save face in front of his father, but he's been making some fucked up decisions that's been costing us, costing me. Baby, that kind of person, that kind of desperation; he's doomed to fuck up royally, and I think when he does, it's going to be colossal. I refuse to risk my life for that damn idiot."

I moved a little closer to her, hoping to God that was the last question. My urges were getting the better of me. But again I was wrong. I tried not to get frustrated when she asked, keeping some distance between us, "Drake, have you ever been wrong about a person? Like have you ever just gotten it wrong?"

It was a valid question, and one that held some merit. I put both hands on the sides of her face and moved even closer to her. When I was inches from her lips, I said to her, "No."

"How can that be?"

I rubbed my lips against hers. "Because I can't afford to be wrong. My life and the lives of the people I care about will suffer if I'm wrong." I kissed her softly and inched closer to her, pinning her against the truck again. "I can give you an example; like right this very moment, I'm not wrong about you. I know for a fact you can't wait for me to get inside you."

"You're a little cocky, don't you think?" she replied, but I could feel her smile against my lips.

"Baby, I'm all cocky, and I plan to fill you with every bit of my cockiness in two point two seconds."

I took her hand in mine and led her to the elevator. Once the doors closed, Georgia looked over at me as I moved closer to her. She backed away bringing the elevator wall against her back. "Did I tell you how much I've missed you?" I asked her, caging her with my arms and putting my body flush up against hers.

"Drake, there's something I need to tell you..." she said, but I wasn't listening. When the ding of the elevator signaled our arrival, I let her walk in front of me, watching her ass sway.

*Wait, did her ass get bigger?*

I closed the door behind me and reached for her arm to pull her back to me, positioning her against the wall next to the door. "Do have any idea how much I've missed you?" I whispered in her ear and bent over her to place a light kiss on her neck when I quickly pulled my gun the instant a figure came from the shadows of my living room. Georgia gasped lightly as I pushed her behind me.

"Why are you in my condo?" I said simply. My intruder walked into view, looked at me, and then behind me. I kept her hidden. "Answer my question before I put a bullet in the center of your forehead."

"Wow, you haven't changed, have you?"

"Nope," I cocked the gun and Georgia gasped again, louder this time.

"You're willing to shoot me with a witness?" he asked.

"She's loyal to me, something that you don't know anything about."

My intruder sighed and sat at my dining room table. I knew he wasn't a threat, but I still didn't trust him. "Start telling me why you're here and do it fast. I'm losing my patience."

"Come on, little brother, put the gun away."

"Little brother?" I heard Georgia say behind me, and then she moved next to me. Wouldn't you know it, she pushed my hand with the gun down. "It's okay, Drake."

I looked at her and because of the fear in her eyes, I eased up on the trigger. I walked up to the table and placed my gun in front of me, hand still on the handle.

I will give my girl a shit load of credit. She may have told me to back off, but she stayed right behind me the whole time, observant and tense.

My brother looked from me to Georgia, and then back to me. "Are you going to introduce me?"

"No, you're not going to be here long enough and you'll never see her again so..."

"But you'll take her around them," he said pointedly.

I nodded. "Loyalty, remember?  You're obviously here to show me something; why don't you show it to me so you can leave?  As a matter of fact, why are you here unannounced anyway?"

I looked at the folder on the table, and then at him. He knew my interest would peak. He smiled and tapped the folder. "I knew you wouldn't meet me, and we really needed to talk about some things."

"Like?"

"Like I need you to leave Manuel Agosto alone."

My eyebrow rose. "Why?"

My brother looked at me, and then behind me. "You know why."

I scoffed and looked back at the folder. "Yeah, well, he has some answers I need, so if you don't have them in that folder, I'm not letting up."

Daniel tapped the folder. "I think I have what you need."

"Send it over and let me look at it."

I know my brother is battling with cooperating with me, but he really doesn't have a choice. He knows what I'm capable of, and he knows I'm like a bloodhound until I get what I want.

He pushed the folder over to me. "Everything is all there."

I slid the folder to me but didn't open it. "I'll see and let you know."

He looked at Georgia again and said, "My name's Daniel, by the way."

I sighed but didn't say anything, but she replied simply, "Georgia."

Daniel smiled. "You guys have a good night."

When Daniel left, I went and set the alarm. I made a mental note to change the codes and upgrade my system to include a big ass dog.

I looked at Georgia. The fire both of us had earlier was clearly gone.

"I'm going to take a bath and let you look at your folder," she told me and headed for my stairs.

I put my gun on safety, grabbed a beer from my fridge and opened the folder. I told myself I was only going to look at it for a few before I went to bed, but the moment I started reading, I felt my anger starting to rise. No way was I putting this down.

It only took me a few hours to read through everything. As I showered and got dressed, my contacts got answers back to me that I needed to set my plan into motion. I looked at the time and made another call to Angel. I couldn't wait until he got the chance to speak more with my Uncle. I needed to act right then, that night, with the element of surprise on my side.

I thought about telling Georgia that I'd be back, but seeing her sleep, I decided not to. Instead, I left her a note telling her that I'd be back. The way she'd been sleeping lately, I was counting on her sleeping through the night.

I left my condo at 4:45 a.m. and made my way north up I-65. The length of time it took for me to get to my destination was spent thinking about everything I read. I was beyond pissed. The feeling of my rage taking over my body, eating at me, festering quickly like the most potent drug would do to your system. I was feeding off it, knowing how volatile I can become if I let myself go, but I didn't care. This shit was so fucked up. I could only respond the way I was about to respond and hope and pray they didn't piss me off even more.

I made it to the house in record time. I called my contact to give me a layout of the house and surrounding area. The fence in front of me wouldn't be a problem getting over, but if they were smart, they would have motion sensors along the ground by the fence. After getting my information, it was confirmed that they did; however, there were pressure points that didn't have a wide range of reading. So I could easily get over the fence. As long as I knew where the sensors were, I could walk along without being detected.

It took me a minute to get inside the house. Patrol walked along the corridor of the outside of the house, but they were lazy and didn't see or hear me coming. I put them both to sleep as well as the dog that was with them and made my way inside the house.

With the house alarm off, I made my way into the house and waited in the kitchen for my quarries to arrive.

Early birds do get the worm, I heard footsteps coming downstairs. The coffee machine started about thirty minutes ago and you know I helped myself to a cup.

Coffee wasn't half bad.

When Gregory came around the corner and turned the light on in the kitchen, he stopped dead in his tracks, eyes falling on the huge .45 in my hand. My other quarry came right after him and ran into his back.

"Damn, Greg. What the..." She stilled until the moment her eyes met mine.

I took the coffee cup I had in my hand and took a sip. "You're out of creamer."

"Get the fuck out of my house," Greg told me, with just a hint of bass in his voice.

Just a hint though. He wasn't stupid.

"Sit down, you two. My patience is gone at this point, and I'm so far gone, I won't have a problem killing the both of you and making you disappear without a trace." They didn't move, which was adding fuel to the raging inferno within me. "I said sit down!" I yelled suddenly, and they moved quickly to the table.

"See what you did, Greg? I told you we shouldn't have let that girl in our house," Dara said.

I looked at her. "That girl happens to be your sister. Do you even give a fuck about that?"

She didn't reply.

I looked at Greg and said, "This can go one of two ways; you can answer my questions truthfully and honestly, or I can put a bullet in your sister's head, see if you become talkative then. And please don't push me."

I stood up the moment I heard voices coming down the stairs. I waited until the older sister and her bitch ass husband came in the room.

"Make sure you don't make my eggs so runny. You know I hate that shit."

When they came around the corner, bitch ass Rafiq pushed his wife in front of him when his eyes met mine. I said quickly, "No, I'm not here for you this time. Sit down, Rafiq."

I saw the tension leave his face, but the questioning look of his wife wasn't a surprise. I'm sure she had no idea what her husband loved to do.

I waved my gun at them both, and they all took a seat at the table. I stood back, watching them and keeping an eye on both entrances to the kitchen from the back door and the front. I had my contact set the alarm anyway, so if anyone came inside, I would know.

I looked at a now fuming Greg and said, "I found out some disturbing information today."

"What did that bitch tell you?" Dara bit out. "That's why you're here, because of what we said to her?"

I ignored her and kept my eyes on her brother. "You have no idea how bad I want to kill you right now. The fact that you are setting up Georgia to take the fall for your stupid business decisions make me fucking sick."

Greg's eyes bulged out of his face and Deidra, the oldest daughter, looked at her brother. "What's he talking about?"

Greg didn't reply. He just looked at me. I told him, "I need a few questions answered, and then I'm gone. How much did you pay Manuel Agosto to kill Georgia?"

He didn't reply, so I cocked my gun and fired just above Dara's head. The women screamed and ducked. I'm sure Rafiq pissed his pants. Greg, eyes wide, yelled, "Okay, okay!! I didn't ask him to kill her, okay? I just wanted her to disappear."

"Tell me about the plan."

Greg took a few deep breaths and said quickly, "Okay, so I had found his number from someone I knew and talked to Manuel over the phone..."

"No, *Junior*, I want you to start from the beginning. I want to know when you found out about Georgia. When did you find out you had a sister?"

Greg, surprise on his face, squirmed in his seat and tried not to look at his sister, Deidra, when he said, "I knew about her for a long time."

'

"Greg!" Deidra exclaimed.

"What, Deidra?... Okay, yes, father told me about her about a month before he passed. He wanted me to look for her. He wanted to meet her and talk to her. He wanted to apologize, all that shit, but I wouldn't let that happen. No one was coming in here and taking what's mine." He bit out the last part with serious venom I noticed. Jealousy was a beast I should know.

I didn't have time for sibling spats, so I said, "Greg, over here. Talk to me."

"Okay... So, yes, I found Georgia, but I never told my father. It seems though he went over my head and found where she was without my knowledge. When I found out, that's when I called around and got a hold of Manuel. I just wanted her to disappear and not show up for the reading of father's will, that's all. I didn't want him to kill her."

"Even if she disappeared, you didn't think that the lawyers would've kept searching for her? It wasn't a matter of her just disappearing Greg. You wanted her to disappear for good."

He didn't reply. He just nodded and put his head down.

"So when that didn't work, what did you do? You came up with another plan to make her become the scapegoat for your bad business decision?"

"What bad business decision?" his clueless older sister asked.

I tilted my head and smiled. "Oh, he didn't tell you? Well, your brother here was trying to be like your father. He started dealing with the cartel, not my family like your father was; Greg here is dealing with the Russians. And, unfortunately, the Russians are not as civil as we are. They deal in things like trafficking of little girls throughout the United States and abroad. The Russians are using the empty buildings you own as a place to hide the girls."

I looked at Deidra as I went on. "There is a brothel that's being ran in one of your buildings as well that exploits these young girls as prostitutes." I pointed my gun at her husband. "Ask your husband. He's been a few times. He likes them young. Don't you, Rafiq?"

"Fuck you, man," he spat as he jumped to his feet.

I took my cup and threw it at his face. It hit him square in his forehead and shattered. Rafiq stumbled over, and I moved quickly to him and kicked him in his face.

"Don't forget who the fuck you're talking to," I told him calmly and kicked him in his balls. "Trifling son of a bitch."

"Greg, is this true?" Dara asked him.

"Of course, it's true," I told her over Rafiq's moaning. "And please don't act all innocent, young lady. You knew all about it too. Greg here had you befriend Georgia, take her around the city, and keep her here so you could set her up; make her sign some papers she had no clue about, have her sit in a few meetings, get her acclimated so you could make it seem like she was in the know since the beginning. Since she's older than you, she actually owns more shares than you. The way you set everything up, she'll be the one in the front of all this shit when the Feds come knocking at your door."

Dara squinted at me. "You don't know shit."

"Dara, shut up!" Greg told her, but her arrogant ass didn't listen.

"No, Greg, if he's going to get it right, let him get it all right. Yes, we were going to let her take the fall for everything, but not with the Feds. No, we need the Russians off our backs, so that's who we're giving her too. You know, make it seem like she was talking to the Feds to get the Russians off our backs and on to someone else; her fiancé."

I shook my head. "Wow. I have never met a whole family of ignorant motherfuckers in my entire life. You have no idea who you're fucking with. The Russians aren't some neighborhood gang; they don't just go after one person that they find has fucked them over. First, when the Feds come for them, they would already have found out, and the Feds will find nothing. Then guess who the Russians are going to go for after that? It won't be just Georgia. No, they'll go after the whole entire family. They'll make statements, large ones. You are so far over your head; it's un-fucking-real and completely sad."

I shook my head. "What I don't understand is why you would do that to your own flesh and blood. When you got to know her, saw how good and innocent she was, you still went about deceiving her, making her feel like she belonged when you clearly didn't give a shit about her. She's been living her life, thinking she was alone in this world, and finally she has this family she's always wanted, and you were setting her up. She lost her mother and the man she thought was her father when she was nine. And here your coward ass father knew all about her and never went looking for her. She didn't deserve that shit. And I know the moment I tell her what you fuckers have done, it's going to crush her."

I put my gun in my pants and walked over a still moaning Rafiq. I heard someone stand and say behind me, "What have you done?"

I turned to see Deidra standing in front of me. She said to me, "Yes, you're right, what we've done to her was unspeakable, but what about you? She doesn't deserve the life you live."

I nodded. "I know she doesn't. Once I clear this shit up and get her off the Russians, I'll send her home." I pointed to her brother. "He's going to make sure she gets the money that's due to her before the Feds come and shut you down. Then she's going to live happily with all of this and us behind her."

"Wow, aren't you the hypocrite?" Greg said to me.

"What?" I started moving in his direction, ready to put my gun in his mouth and pull the fucking trigger.

He puffed his chest out and said, "You knocked up my sister, and then what? You're just going to send her on her way to raise your kid on her own?"

My heart stopped. "What the hell did you just say to me?"

"You heard me; you call my father a coward; what about you? How can you..." I cut him off with my hands around his neck. I squeezed hard about to crush his windpipe. I was seeing nothing but red. I slammed him against the wall and squeezed tighter, waiting for the life to leave his eyes. I seethed, "You're fucking lying. She's not pregnant."

I saw Deidra next to me, and she said to me, "God, he's telling the truth. Georgia is pregnant. We were with her when she found out." I didn't look over at her, and I didn't want to believe a word she said.

I dropped Greg, and he fell to the floor. I backed up and looked at Deidra, hoping that what she said to me wasn't true. But I could see she was telling me the truth.

"Why don't you go and ask her yourself if you don't believe us," Deidra said to me, and I planned to do just that. I just hoped I calm down by the time I get home.

# CHAPTER 16

## GEORGIA

This morning was rough for me. I tossed and turned all night, but I couldn't bring myself to go downstairs and ask Drake to sleep with me.

I wanted him. Last night was unbelievable. Meeting his family was something I wasn't prepared for, but I was so glad I did. Despite what the men of the family were, I'd never felt safer than I did that night. I don't know what that says about me though. Having a feeling of contentment around a crime family had to be crazy, but I felt the same way sometimes when I was around Jay Rock and his crew.

When I woke that morning, my body was tense and sore. I felt sick to my stomach, hoping I wouldn't get attacked with morning sickness again. I thought I might have been over that by now. I moved down the stairs slowly and quietly, as to not disturb Drake, but found out he wasn't even there. He left me a note saying he would be back.

My stomach started to growl, so I headed over to the kitchen to see what I could cook. Did I mention that I can't cook to save my life? Yeah, all I can do is make an egg sandwich, so that's what I did.

I drank a glass of milk then decided to take a bath to soothe my muscles.

I tossed the large t-shirt of Drake's that I was wearing on the floor of the bedroom and padded my way to the bathroom. I decided to take a shower first to wash up. I wanted to soak and soothe my body using the jets of the tub. My shower was quick, but my bath I intended to stay in until I was all wrinkled up.

I don't know how long I was in there because I dozed off until I heard the door slam downstairs. I jumped up, afraid half out of my mind until I heard Drake yell my name. I slowly got out of the bathtub, feeling dizzy and trying not to fall again, and grabbed the towel from the rack. I wrapped it around me and walked out of the bathroom. I was met with a look that I had never seen before, and it scared the shit out of me.

I mean, I'd seen Drake mad, but the way he was foaming at the mouth had me petrified.

I stood there on shaky knees, waiting for him to kill me or something. His fists were balled up tight, his jaw was flexing, and his eyes were shooting daggers straight at me. "What's wrong?" I managed to get past the knot caught in my throat.

"Are you pregnant?"

*Shit.*

I didn't reply. I couldn't move, nor could I speak. The knot in my throat finally took over. I started to shake, and it wasn't from me being wet.

"I asked you a fucking question! Are you pregnant?!" he yelled in this voice that, oh God, screamed through my body. He'd never used that tone with me. As a matter of fact, I'd never heard that tone from him.

"Georgia!"

He yelled my name with so much intensity that I jumped clear out of my skin and croaked out a quiet, shaky, "Yes."

"What did you say?"

I nodded my head vehemently but I whispered my answer. "Yes."

He moved closer to me, and I distinctively backed up until I crashed into a wall behind me. He didn't falter his steps. He kept coming, eyes ripping through me. "You mean to tell me all this time we've spent together, you didn't tell me you were pregnant?"

"I tried," I managed to say but regretted the words instantly.

"You tried?! Are you kidding me?! You tried?! How did you try? When? Was it during the whole time you rode with me here after you found me in the club? Was it during the time we went shopping for hours and then sat down and ate together? Or were you going to tell me when I brought you around my family? When Georgia?! When were you going to tell me? Or were you going to tell me at all? Were you planning on getting me to help you, and then later you were going to leave without telling me you were pregnant? Was that the plan?"

I shook my head. "No, Drake! I was going to tell you, okay? I tried to tell you the other night, but you pulled out a gun, and you were talking to him and I just..."

"That's bullshit, Georgia. You had ample enough time to tell me." He backed away from me. The anger in his eyes was replaced with a look I had seen from him before... hurt.

"I can't believe you would do this to me."

"I'm sorry, Drake, okay? I didn't know what else to do. I was trying to figure out a way to tell you, but I was afraid, okay? I was afraid of what you may think of me. I had unprotected sex with you, and it wasn't intentional, I promise. I didn't do this to trap you or get you to be with me. I didn't mean for this to happen. It's hard for me to get pregnant; very hard... almost impossible, so I didn't think you would get me pregnant. But when I did, I didn't want you to feel I trapped you. God, and you helping me... I just... I didn't know how to say it... But I'm so sorry... I didn't mean to let this much time go by. Please..."

He just stared at me, his chest heaving up and down. Nose still flaring, fists still balled. God, I didn't know if he believed me or blamed me, and I couldn't take it anymore. I fell back against the wall and let the tears that were starting to collect in my eyes fall.

I couldn't see him anymore, but I felt him move closer to me. "Shit, Georgia..."

"I'm sorry, Drake," I mumbled before I started to cry.

"Don't," I heard him say before I felt both his hands go to the sides of my face, and his lips touch mine.

He kept wetting my lips with his. "Stop, Georgia."

Yeah, that made me cry even more, and I started to fall to the floor. "I'm sorry, Drake. I'm…"

I felt him pick me up and crash his lips to mine. My legs went around his waist, and he carried me until I felt the bed to my back. Drake didn't stop kissing me as he settled between my legs. My whimpers turned into a soft moan as confusion and fear still filled me. But Drake's kiss wasn't what I was used to from him. It was soft and tender, and full of emotion I had never felt from him.

"Please stop crying, baby," he said softly to me, and then rolled himself over to where I was laying on top of him. He held me close to him, rubbing my back, kissing my forehead and the top of my head.

He moved beneath me to get me to look at him. When I turned my face to do just that, he touched the sides of my face gently and caressed me. He said to me, "I don't want you to be afraid to tell me anything. Nothing you could say to me will ever make me think less of you. I don't blame you, baby. I had a feeling I could get you pregnant. I didn't care and maybe I should have, considering what kind of life I live, but I didn't." He looked deeply into my eyes and then to my lips. He then said to me, voice deep and dripping with something else entirely, "You belong to me now… you're mine."

"Drake," I replied and started to squirm from his grip. He flipped over again pinning me against the bed. His leg pushed my legs open, and he settled between me again. This time though, his hips started to move slowly.

"You're mine now, Georgia... You and our baby." He lifted slightly to remove the towel from its folded position, and opened it to reveal me.

I shouldn't say this, and damn it I shouldn't feel this either, but thank God he's finally touching me. Finally, my body was getting what it'd been wanting ever since I saw him at the club, ever since he left me in Cabo.

I closed my eyes and arched my back the moment his fingers touched my skin. I felt every touch, every caress all through me. It looked like this pregnancy had heightened all of my senses. I felt every nerve ending in my body come alive, sending signals to my brain that was overloading me.

"I've missed you so much, baby," his voice husky and deep. I knew I was wet the moment he touched me, but his voice always brought more out of me. He gently massaged my breasts and looked at me, "Do they hurt?" he asked me.

I opened my eyes. "A little."

"Can I kiss them?" he asked me, and I smiled and nodded.

"Please." I brought my hand up and placed it behind his head as he moved down to my breast and my nipple. His kisses were soft.

His tongue even softer, but when he brought my nipple into his mouth and sucked, I pushed into him moaning loudly.

Shit that felt amazing!

He stopped and looked at me concerned. I shook my head. "No, please, don't stop. God, don't stop."

He suddenly smiled that smile of his that lights his entire face. "That's my girl."

I can't begin to explain to you what's happening to me. My body's reaction to him had been enhanced. My nipples were craving him to touch them, to kiss and suck on them. One seems to tingle with anticipation when he's playing with the other. Please don't mistake me, oh they hurt like hell, but, I don't know, the pain was reaching right in between my legs and giving me this sensation that didn't want him to stop.

But he moved down from them and kissed down my belly. I opened my legs wider to him and arched into him, giving him better access to me. When he finally touched me with his tongue, I think I came... God, I know I did. The feeling came over me instantly. I grabbed the blanket under me and growled out the ecstasy flowing through me.

"Shit, I love hearing you come. You drive me crazy, baby, with the sounds you make... Come again for me, baby. Please let me hear you... Tell me how good I make you feel... Tell me you're mine."

"Drake, I can't... I... Oh yes! Please right there... Right there!" He lapped his tongue over and over around my clit. Then he took it in his mouth and sucked. It was taking me there quickly. I couldn't control it.

I sat up and gripped his head. "Yesssss!... Oh!.... Please have me!.... I'm yours! Please just..."

I grappled at his shirt, trying to pull it up and off him. He moved from between my legs as I pulled off his shirt and fell back to the bed. I watched as he removed his t-shirt and started with his pants. I heard the clunk of his boots, and then his pants dropped. I started licking my lips with anticipation.

Drake smirked at me. He knew exactly what he was doing to me, and I knew he loved it.

"Are you ready for me?" he asked me as he crawled up my body.

"No," I replied and he chuckled.

It wasn't meant to be funny. Hell, I was serious.

But I wanted him, that I was sure of. I wanted him in more ways than I was willing to admit to him.

He started kissing me as I brought my legs up to give myself to him. He said inches from me, "Put me inside you."

*Huh? My pleasure.*

I gripped him tight, and he moaned slightly as I stroked him with my hand slowly before I guided him to my center. His head moved to my opening and as he moved in and out of me, slowly invading me, I couldn't help but move back. It had been a while since I had him and, shit, it hurt.

"I'll go slow, baby, but I can't promise you it will be for long. I've been waiting for this pussy since I left Cabo... I need this baby... I need you... I... oh fuck yes... shit you feel amazing... hmmm." He buried his head in my neck as he created a slow and steady pace, rounding his hips as he moved in and out of me, gathering my juices, soothing me.

He stopped moving suddenly and said to me. "I'm not hurting the baby, am I?"

I shook my head, "Um no... I don't think it can feel you."

"What? We'll see about that."

I laughed at first but then stopped... The way he was going at me was not a laughing matter.

He gripped my ass as he went harder and faster, then crashed into me, and we both came like a freight train. He cried out, and I screamed in his neck.

"Did I tell you how much I missed you?" he asked me before he flipped us again and put me on top.

I looked in his sated eyes and smiled. "I've missed you too."

"Yeah? Show me." He pushed me up and started moving my hips.

*He can't be hard again already,* I thought to myself but I felt him grow inside me.

*Damn... Yes, oh how I missed him.*

’

$$***** $$

After our hearts had settled down, Drake asked me, "Do you know when you're due?" I was laying my head on his chest with my arm around him.

"The doctor gave me a tentative date around the middle of March. She couldn't make it definitive until I have an ultrasound."

He grew quiet, and then said, "So you're about what four months?"

I nodded. "Yes, about that."

He rolled over on his side and faced me. I moved on my back, and he started caressing my belly, then he bent down and kissed it.

He looked in my eyes. "I didn't hurt you, did I?"

I shook my head.

"How are you feeling? Are you feeling sick?"

I shook my head again and said, "I'm feeling okay right now. I haven't been sick in a few days, but I never know until I get up. Which I need to do now or I'm going to explode."

He kissed me on my lips and moved from me so I could get up.

"First thing tomorrow we need to make you a doctor's appointment. They can do the ultrasound or whatever they need to do so we can have an official date. How are you working?"

"I'm teaching an online class. Which reminds me, I need to get to that and grade papers. I'm falling behind."

My bladder was about to explode so I slowly got up and I heard him gasp. I looked back at him. "What?"

"Shit, you have a bruise on your hip. I didn't think I gripped you that tight."

I shook my head. "Oh no, that's not from you. I fell a few times getting up too fast. I get dizzy spells sometimes."

"What?!" he exclaimed and I quickly moved into the bathroom seeing he was about to explode. "Georgia?!" he called after me.

"Sorry, Drake. I have to pee."

"Fuck!" I heard him exclaim just as I closed the door.

I did what I needed to and washed my face and brushed my teeth. I then decided, just to keep him waiting, to take a shower. What I forgot to do is lock the door. Anyways, a few seconds under the stream and I heard him come inside. He walked into the shower with this pissed off look on his face.

"If you weren't pregnant, so help me, I would bend you over my knee and spank your ass!" he told me.

*Um... what was that?*

"Turn around let me wash you." I obeyed and all but passed out from how tender he was with me. This brut of a man had a sensitive side. Who knew? Probably no one alive.

I started to chuckle.

"What's funny?" he asked me.

"Nothing," I said quickly.

"Yeah right. Turn around," he demanded, and, yup, I obeyed.

Once we got out of the shower, he held my hand and guided me into the bedroom, put lotion on my body and helped me get dressed before he dressed himself. I did tell him I could get dressed myself, and he just grunted and ignored me.

Drake made me breakfast, and as I ate, he was sitting next to me on his laptop. He then made a call and actually found me a doctor. I didn't think he would get an appointment that day, but it seems I know nothing. He hung up telling me we had an appointment that afternoon.

"Drake," I called to him, got up and took his hand. I led him over to the couch and sat down. When he sat next to me, I took a deep breath. "I'm sorry I didn't tell you about the baby. I was waiting for the right moment and quite honestly telling someone that you're having his baby isn't an easy thing. But I should have told you."

He just nodded but didn't say anything. I took another deep breath and said, "The moment I found out, I panicked. I didn't know what you would think of me, but I was more afraid of losing your trust in me. I didn't want you to feel like I trapped you..." He started to protest my last sentence, but I stopped him. "Just hear me out... I felt like I let you down. I don't know much about you, and you don't know much about me. I didn't want to stick you with this, with me. I wanted you to be free to live your life. That's what I want to tell you. You don't have to..." I stopped talking because put his fingers against my lips.

His eyes narrowed. "Don't you finish that thought. I'm getting more pissed with each second that's going by. First, Georgia, yes, you don't know everything about me, but I hope you know enough. I hope that you know I will not do anything I don't want to. And I mean anything. I can't get tricked because I don't give a shit. I do what I want when I want. Secondly, I know more about you than you think. I understand you were afraid, but I don't want you to be, not with me. I wouldn't think negatively about you because I know you, I know your heart. I know what you're capable of and what you're not. I'm as much responsible for getting you pregnant, if not more, as you. But baby, I'm a grown ass man. I will take care of you and the baby. It's not about obligation. I told you before I don't do obligations. Whatever you need, you need to know that I have you."

I should be thrilled. I should be excited, but I'm not.

Drake kissed my cheek and stood. "Come on. I have some errands to run before we get to the doctor."

A few days passed and Drake had kept his promise. We found out I was just sixteen weeks, but we didn't want to know the sex of the baby. We got lots of pictures and heard the baby's heartbeat. I thought Drake would be shocked at that sound of the baby's heart beating but he wasn't. He just told me he used to take his cousin to her appointments, so he'd heard Nya's heartbeat before.

Anyway, he'd been a saint to me. He catered to me, cooked me meals whenever I was hungry, and I have to say that's a turn on in itself. This man can burn. It doesn't matter what he's doing; he'll

,
leave from wherever he is or stop what he's doing, and cook for me, if time allows. I tell him he doesn't have to do any of this but one day he saw me struggling with boiling eggs and he banned me from the stove. I can reheat in the microwave, but that's it.

He rubs my feet if they're sore, he runs my bath water for me and the sex... Oh my God.

We hang out all the time. Just talking about the baby and who he/she would look like. I mean things were great. But I had noticed something different with Drake that still had me on edge. So what's changed you ask? It was in his eyes. It was the way he looked at me that had me paranoid. He continued to tell me that I was his, but I didn't feel it. I felt like he was faking. I feel like I trapped him with something that he wasn't prepared for.

That smile that he used to always give me, I hadn't seen in a few days. He'd been in and out of the condo doing what, I haven't a clue. He worked at the club and came home smelling like smoke and alcohol and perfume. But I couldn't say anything, right? I mean, he didn't say that we were together, in a committed relationship. He just said I belonged to him. That's it.

I felt like there was a lot he wasn't telling me. It wouldn't matter if I asked him or not, he wasn't going to tell me. So I had come to the conclusion that I was going to find me a place to live. My father's lawyer called me and told me he had money for me from my shares of my father's company. He told me he would have a check waiting for me, but I asked him to wire me the funds and

gave him the banking information. I also told him to sell my shares
of the stock to my siblings. I now knew how much the stocks were
worth so he need not bother with trying to cheat me. He said he
would.

So I had money. I didn't need Drake and his fabulous condo. I
could go buy my own car if I wanted to, so I didn't have to drive his
"monster." Hell, I could buy my own monster. I didn't need him and
his glorious love stick either. I didn't... Really... I didn't.

I decided to pick the following day to tell him just him how
much I didn't need him. I figured I'd tell him that night after we got
back from dinner at his uncle's place.

I loved being around his uncle and family. I know it's weird to
say, but I did. Angel was amazing, though every time he saw me, he
hit on me. Drake always turned red with anger. Angel loved to
rattle him. Uncle Bruno always told me to sit next to him, no matter
where we were. It's not like he talked to me a lot so it was weird.
All the females of the family looked at me when he did this as if I'm
royalty. I asked Drake about this, and he just said to me, "When
you're with me, you're with me."

Hell, I don't know what the hell that means

Another thing is; he hadn't told them that I was pregnant.
Why? I hadn't a clue.

I can't cook as I stated, but I can organize the heck out of a table.
I can fold the hell out of some napkins too. And don't get me started
on centerpieces. I was organizing a flower centerpiece in the

kitchen with Drake's aunts and a few of his cousins who were actually cooking dinner for the night. Drake's family sometimes just gets together and eats. Even though Thanksgiving was around the corner, they still gathered all the time to a smorgasbord of food to chow down and fellowship. It's another reason why I loved being around them. It's something that I never had and thought I finally did with my siblings.

One of his cousins, Maria asked me how Drake and I met. I didn't want to tell her that I seduced him, so I just said, "He was actually my knight in shining armor when some creep wouldn't leave me alone."

"That's our Lincoln." I turned to see Eddie come in the room.

He kissed his mother, aunts and cousins and looked at me, not very friendly, I might add. I should have been used to it, but sadly I was not.

"Not cooking Georgia?" he asked me.

"Not really my strong suit."

"Wow, that has to be strange; an Italian man to cook for himself."

I didn't reply.

Suddenly a beautiful woman floated into the room, and I mean she floated. The whole room erupted in smiles, laughs, hugs and kisses. I sat back and looked at this woman that seemed to be a goddess. Her black hair was glossy and flowed around her face. She wore a long sleeve sweater that hugged her curves and accentuated everything about her. Her lips were pouty, and she had flawless skin as if the sun kissed her at birth.

Eddie introduced me as a friend of Lincoln's. She didn't acknowledge me. Instead, she said excited, "Where is Lincoln? I've missed him."

Eddie smiled. "He's in the den with Pops. I'm sure he'll be thrilled to see you." The woman that I learned was Dominque, smacked her lips and shook her hips.

"Oh good," she replied and left the kitchen.

Can I say I was starting to feel really sick?

I was quiet at dinner. I barely ate what was in front of me. I was too busy trying to keep my food from coming up and splattering all over the table, hopefully on Drake and this Dominque woman that kept touching him and fussing over him.

I swear I had never felt so out of place in my life. I tried to play it off, but her laugh, or shall I say hackle, was abominable. She was overkill. Maria, who looked to have felt my discomfort, asked me, "So how do you like Philly, Georgia?"

I smiled at her. "It's great. I miss the ocean and the sun, but other than that, it's great. I may even plant some roots here and get my own apartment."

I heard someone's fork clatter to a plate. Not sure if it was Uncle Bruno's or Drake's or even Angel. He was sitting directly across from me, and I could feel his eyes on me.

But I think it was Drake's because he asked, "What did you say about getting an apartment?"

Maria, oblivious to what was going on said, "She said she was going to get her own place, which I think is cool. I live in the city. I can show you a lot of great places to live."

I smiled in her direction. I felt she really was sincere about that too. I smiled. "Thank you so much, I will take you up on your offer."

"No, she won't," Drake said to his cousin.

I frowned. "Um, excuse me?"

"You heard me; you're not going anywhere."

"Oh, you think so, Drake?" I felt my face growing hot, and my ears started ringing.

"Baby, we'll talk about this later." He went to touch me, and I moved my arm.

"Don't touch me, and don't call me baby. You know I hate that..." I caught myself and said, "I'm going to be sick." I looked at Uncle Bruno. "Will you excuse me?"

He stood and pulled out my chair, "Of course."

I stood quickly and instantly felt like I was going to faint. I gripped Uncle Bruno's arm, and he steadied me. I smiled weakly.

"Georgia," Drake called my name. Concern etched his face, but I wasn't falling for his handsome face.

"I'm fine, Lincoln." Then I turned and left the room.

# CHAPTER 17

## DRAKE

As I watched her walk away, I couldn't snap out of the shock I felt. It was a complete slap in the face, something that I'd never felt from Georgia. First of all, she had never called me Lincoln in front of my family.

The shock, however, soon faded. I stood and excused myself as well.

"Drake," I heard. Knowing the voice didn't sound like my aunt or grandmother's pissed me off as hell.

"What did you just call me?" I said to Dominque.

She looked at me, then at my Uncle and Angel.

I helped her. "Is there something wrong with you?"

Defensive, she pointed to the direction Georgia went and said, "She just called you Drake. So I thought..."

I moved closer to her and said, "You're not her. Don't forget your place."

"Lincoln."

I looked at Angel. He nodded in the direction of Georgia, saying, "Go get your woman."

I ran my hand over my head and walked out the room.

I tried the bathroom on the main floor first, but it was empty. When I moved to check upstairs, I found her with her coat on heading for the front door.

"Where are you going?" I asked her. She didn't turn around. "Georgia." She got to the door, so I had to actually jog to get to her. "Baby?"

She turned around, and I saw tears in her eyes. "Stop. Don't touch me. Do you call her that too?"

"Call who what?"

"Oh, don't play dumb with me; it doesn't suit you. You know who I mean. The perfect goddess with the perfect breasts and hair. You know the one that couldn't keep her hands off you, the one with the most hideous laugh I have ever heard. I mean, goodness, I must have been stupid to stay here as long as I have. God, if you two needed some privacy then you should have said something." She moved close to me. "Is she why you are always out late at night? Coming home smelling like perfume? God, I'm such an idiot!"

"Wait. Hold on a second. You think there is something going on with Dominque and me?" I tried not to laugh. "Baby, please..."

"Stop calling me that. You call everyone that, don't you?"

"No, I don't. I've never called anyone baby but you. 'Darlin', yes. 'Sweetheart,' all the time, but 'baby'... You're the only one that's ever been that to me."

I thought that would satisfy her, but she just turned and headed for the door again.

Frustrated beyond belief now, I reached for her again. "What the fuck is going on with you?"

"Everything is going on with me. But you are the main problem."

I stepped back from her, fucking floored. "What's the problem then?"

"I want my own place."

"Why?"

"Why? Are you serious? Because I don't belong with you, that's why... There's no reason why I should be with you."

I moved on her. "I can think of one reason."

She folded her arms. "Oh yeah? And what's that reason? Because according to me, I can't think of one."

I frowned and slashed my hand across my neck. "It doesn't matter you're not going anywhere."

"You can't tell me what to do, Lincoln. We're not together."

There it is...

"Is that what this is about?" I said to her.

She didn't reply right away. She just met my stare with hers. "Give me a good reason why I should stay with you?" she finally said.

I put my hands up in frustration. "Come on, Georgia. This is ridiculous. What do you want me to say?"

"God, you are the biggest idiot I have ever met and you are so blind." She closed her eyes, and when she opened them she moved

,
closer to me until we were a foot apart. "I'm in love with you, Drake Lincoln. I love you with every part of me. It's crazy, I know, and I don't know how it happened but it has. I love you… and it pains me because I don't have a clue if you feel the same way. Do you? Can you tell me the same thing?"

*Shit.*

She watched me battle through a multitude of emotions, and not one of them was what she wanted.

"Georgia…" I started to say when I saw the tears fall. She closed her eyes and stepped back from me.

I moved forward. "Georgia, it's not that simple for me… I… I care for you deeply. You know I do. I'd do anything for you… but what you want me to say, I don't know if I can."

"I know…," she whispered. "That's why I need to go. I can't be with you and be in love with you if you don't belong to me."

"Damn it, I do belong to you, Georgia. I don't want anyone else. You're who I want. You're who I want to come home to, no one else but you. I don't understand what more you want."

She gripped her fists tight and held them up. "God, Drake, I want you to love me. It's that simple. I want you to tell me that you are in love with me too. That's what I want to hear. That's what I need from you. I need to feel it. I need to see it. I need to know."

"I don't know what that is… Do you understand that?" I replied to her, trying not to let my voice rise, but I couldn't help it. "It's easy for you but me… I don't think I can give you that, Georgia."

She started to cry and, shit, for the first time I couldn't soothe her.

"I wish I never met you... I wish you had just said no, and, God, I wish I stayed my Black ass in Miami so I would never have known what this kind of heartbreak felt like." She then turned from me and mumbled before she left, "I so need a timeout right now."

I let her leave, feeling like the biggest asshole alive. I walked to my uncle's study and grabbed his bottle of Scotch. I then walked out to the patio that sits off the study, turned on the outdoor tower heaters and sat down. I heard my "monster's" motor rev up and skid off. Only Angel drives like that in my car, so that made me feel better, only slightly.

I was on my sixth glass and smoking my cigar when I felt my Uncle's presence behind me. I leaned back in the chair and closed my eyes.

I needed a time out.

"Sorry about earlier," I told him without opening my eyes.

"Your aunt saw the cupcakes you bought. Everyone wants to congratulate you," my Uncle told me.

I nodded but didn't reply.

I concentrated on the sound of my heartbeat and the flow of the smoke filling my lungs. I pulled a few times and held it for a few minutes before I slowly let the smoke flow. I hoped doing my favorite past time would soothe me, but it didn't. I still felt like shit.

"What's on your mind, son?"

I opened my eyes and took another sip of scotch. "I'm going to be a father."

"Yeah, you are," he replied. "It's a beautiful thing."

"Yeah, well, what if I told you I didn't know if I'm built to be a good father? I don't know if I can protect them." I looked at my uncle. "I've been thinking about that ever since she told me about the baby. I've been wondering if I could protect her and protect the baby. The shit I've done could come back to me at any point in my life, and I don't want to bring that to them."

"What have you been doing these past few days?"

I shrugged. "I've been meeting with the Russians, trying to get them off Georgia and her family if I can."

"It sounds to me that you're already protecting them." I sighed, and he added, "Look, son, no one has an instruction book on fatherhood. It's a 'learn as you go' kind of thing. But one thing I know about you is how driven, dedicated, and fiercely loyal you are. I know you can do this. But it's going to take the both of you."

I sat up and looked down at my shoes. I didn't know how this shit went south. Two days ago, she and I were laughing on the couch, watching some dumb ass movie. She was laying on me, head up against my chest. I had my hand on her belly, rubbing it and thinking about how good this felt having her there, having her with me. It didn't matter that she was pregnant. It just felt right.

Yeah, well, why couldn't I say that shit to her?

I shook my head and looked over at my uncle. "I fucked up."

My uncle, leaning back against his own chair, feet up, said to me. "Yeah, no shit."

I sighed, sat back and closed my eyes. My uncle asked me, "Do you love her?"

I shrugged. "I don't even know what that is."

"I read somewhere that if you feel that your world will end without her; if you can't stop thinking about her whether she's with you or she's not; if you ache so deeply in your soul just thinking about her leaving you or being with someone else; if you would lose your mind over her, prevent anything and anyone from hurting her; if she makes you feel like you could change the world with just her smile, then, son, you know what love feels like."

I looked at my uncle. "Reading up on your sonnets, Uncle?" I smiled.

He chuckled. "You find yourself doing crazy things when you're in love."

We sat there for a little while longer just smoking and drinking until I heard my car coming back. I stood, feeling the effects of every single drink and puff I inhaled.

"Make sure Angel takes you home."

"Yes sir," I told him.

I went in the house and said my goodbyes. I got a few hugs, but for the most part I got cussed out in, English and Italian, for not telling them Georgia was pregnant sooner, for being an ass and running her off.

Angel and I started for the car when my cell rang. I thought it might be Georgia, but it wasn't. It was my old contact from Langley.

"Do you have something for me, Mark?" I said into my phone.

"I sure do. I have the information you wanted on Gregory Sayers Jr. There's nothing exciting going on that you don't know about, except he called Gavin Diego a few months ago and again about three weeks ago."

I stopped and stared at Angel. "Say that again."

"Yeah, they called each other a few times and spoke for a long period of time."

I moved my head side to side cracking my neck.

"Also, which I know you really want to know this... Gavin isn't his real name. He's actually DeGavin Santiago." Mark added.

I frowned. "Why does that name ring a bell?"

He berated me, "You are losing your touch, Lincoln."

"Yeah, yeah... Just tell me."

"DeGavin Santiago is a member of the Santiago crime family out of Miami, Florida. He is actually the son of Don Luis Santiago, the family you asked me to look into for you because Eddie wants to do business with them. "

"Fuck!"

"Yeah... he is also the cousin of the one you had me looking for in Cabo... Juan Vegas." Mark replied.

I closed my eyes and sighed, "First thing I need you to do is get me the location of Greg Sayers. Then find me the Santiagos and Vegas... I need all of those motherfuckers."

"Will do... I want to let you know that Eddie, your cousin, has also spoken to Gavin Santiago. They actually just talked on the phone about an hour ago. But as it seems, they've been talking quite frequently. Not on his phone but on some burner. We've been taping some of the conversations they've had on Gavin's end. As it seems your cousin is trying to sponsor a coo."

"Wait hold on." I signaled for Angel to get in the car with me. When we got inside, I turned on the car and put my contact on speaker. "Okay, what did you get on Eddie."

Mark said, "Eddie has already been supplying the Santiago family with weapons. He's completed two deliveries so far. The problem is the Santiago family is being looked at by the DEA. Eddie isn't trading under his own name, but he's working under yours. The DEA is building a case against you for multiple counts of gun trafficking and trafficking of women. That's what the cousin's into, by the way. He likes them exotic looking, sweet, and young."

"Do you have proof about my brother?" Angel asked. I looked at him, and I could see the skepticism in his eyes; Déjà vu rearing its ugly head.

There was a pause in my car, and I said, "Tell him."

I got a huge sigh, then we heard, "I have a lot of proof. I have phone records, taped conversations about how much he hates

Lincoln and can't wait to shame him in front of his father. I have pictures of meetings and everything. I can email them all to you tonight."

Angel gripped the steering wheel tight, but looking at his face, I saw that he was calm as the air before a storm.

"Yeah, send that info with the usual encryption," I told Mark.

"What do you want to do about your brother?" Mark asked me.

"My brother?" I asked, eyebrows risen.

"Yeah, he has his hands in trying to shut down Vegas and the Santiago family, the trafficking side anyway. You know he has a hard on about that."

"Keep an eye on him and let me know if he makes his way down to Miami or any other place he shouldn't."

"Will do. Later."

Everything fell silent. I could feel the rage coming off Angel, but I didn't say a word. We sat in my car for twenty minutes before my phone dinged. I looked at it, and my contact sent me Greg's whereabouts. He was at his office downtown.

"I have some place to be. You want to come?"

He looked at me, asking. "You okay to drive?"

"Yup... I'm sober as shit right about now."

He nodded. "Then come and get me when you're done. Go see Georgia and pack. We have a plane to catch."

I nodded, knowing exactly where we were going. But Angel added anyway, "Eddie has already left for Miami."

We switched places then I drove off to have a conversation with Greg.

When I got to his office, I didn't waste time. I barged inside to see him getting head from some chic. I pulled out my gun and told her. "Get the fuck out or die, your choice."

The girl scrambled, grabbing her clothes on her way out of the room.

Greg tried to move, and I put a bullet in his desk, next to his hand. "Shit, you crazy son of a bitch!"

I shot again. "Don't call my mother a bitch."

I moved close to him and smacked his silly ass across the face with the gun. He fell out of the chair, and I kicked him in his solar plexus.

"You are a dumb motherfucker, you know that?"

Greg crawled away from me. "She's going to call the cops."

I shook my head and kicked him in his bare ass. He fell forward and scrambled, trying to pull up his pants. I said to him, "Sorry, Junior, if she calls the cops, you would be going to jail and so would she. She's underage, you prick."

His eyes went wild as he continued to move away from me. I brought a chair around with me and sat right in front of him.

"Now you and I are going to have a lovely talk. I'm going to ask you some questions, and you're going to answer me. Fucking lie and I'll shoot you. Piss me off, and I'll fucking kill you, understand?"

He said nothing, so I fired again, close to his leg. "Okay! Okay! Shit... Why do you always like to shoot around people, scaring people half to death?"

My eyebrows rose. "Would you rather I shoot you? I mean, that's what I love the most. Actually shooting people." I moved my gun to his knee. "Now pardon me; I've been told I was getting slow. But you mentioned you were in communication with Georgia's fiancé, Gavin Santiago. Can you enlighten me on what you two had to talk about?"

Gregory looked at the gun, then his knee. The contemplation went fast, and he started spilling his guts. He told me how he found Georgia close to a year ago and when he called her cell phone, Gavin answered. Greg told Gavin about his company, about how many shares Georgia was owed, etc. At the time, Gavin wasn't trying to marry her, but after he and Greg talked, he decided it would be in his best interest to marry into the family and get a piece of the pie. That's when he roped the Sayers into a money laundering scheme.

Greg didn't know how to get out of it, so he contacted Manuel Agosto, hoping he would be able to help him. Apparently, Manuel and Greg knew each other from their college years.

I asked him, "So what did you and Gavin talk about recently?"

He sighed. "When I told him Georgia was in Philly, he asked me to stall her until he could get his crew up here. When she left, I called him and told him she was gone. I didn't tell him why she left, just that she's gone."

I aimed at his shoulder and pulled the trigger.

He screamed and writhed around on the floor, cussing at me, telling me that he was going to kill me... I waited. Finally having enough of his whimpering, I grabbed him by his shirt and put my gun to his temple.

I said calmly, "You think I'm fucking stupid?"

"No, No... Ugh... You shot me," he cried.

I let him go and said, "You lied to me... again I don't like to be fucking lied to. If you planned on setting her up with the Russians, you wouldn't have a problem telling her mafia fiancé she was pregnant by someone else."

Greg didn't reply. I screwed the silencer on my gun, and Greg's eyes grew ten times wide.

"Please don't kill me! Fuck! I'm sorry. I didn't tell him by who, just that she was living with someone and had gotten pregnant. I swear that's all I said."

I stood. "You're lucky I don't have time to beat your ass for being a pussy, but my time is up. You're right; that girl is going to call the cops; the FBI actually, since she's underage. It seems the Russians have one up'd you. So you better get moving if you don't want to get caught with your pants down."

I moved quickly to the elevator and rode down to the basement. I looked at the time. I needed to see Georgia. Hopefully she would forgive me for being an idiot, and then I needed to pack.

*****

When I opened the door to my apartment, I could feel it was empty. I closed my eyes with regret.

I was going to Miami anyway, so I'd find her when I got there, thinking that's where she may have gone. I quickly went upstairs to pack when I noticed something odd. First thing first, the bed looked slept in. I knew my Georgia; she hated leaving the bed unmade. Even if she slept on top of the covers, the moment she got out of bed, she fixed it.

I moved into the closet and saw all her clothes gone except for my t-shirt. That was another red flag. She told me the other day she was keeping my shirt forever. I know for a fact she would have taken this shirt no matter if we argued.

I went to my safe in my room and opened it. I took my laptop out and started it. I put in the codes to my security cameras inside the apartment and found that they recorded her coming in. She went upstairs, and I could see her curled up on the bed. I fast forward until she started moving, then the cameras went off. I then switched on my backup cameras that came on instantly when my main cameras get shut off. I saw my brother in my apartment talking to her, along with Eddie. I hurled my laptop across the room and made my way to see my brother.

I don't know how I got to my parent's home because I don't remember the drive. I remember getting into the car and getting out. I didn't bother with knocking or the locks. I bust the door down. My family members, being who they were, weren't prepared; especially when they saw it was me- except my brother. I moved quickly to the dining table grabbed the plate and hurled it at the hand that was going for his gun. He finally pulled it, but I took it and smashed his face in with the gun.

"You son of a bitch! I'm going to fucking kill you."

I meant every single word of that statement. My brother wasn't a slouch, so he swung at me. I pushed his hand away and went for his gut. I punched him with everything I had in me. I went in; connecting with kidneys, spleen, liver. I didn't care what I hit; I just wanted to do damage. I wanted internal bleeding. I wanted him spitting and pissing blood for months.

I was just about to take my shot when I felt two people come up beside me, guns pointed. I moved quickly, pulled my sister's gun apart and flung her into my father. They collided with each other, and I took my father's gun.

I raised his gun at him and my sister's at my brother, who must have gone for his spare because he was pointing one at me.

I then heard a click behind my back... my mother.

"Drop it, or I'll shoot," I heard her say but I didn't move. I watched my father, sister, and brother.

My brother spat blood close to my foot. "It's over you've fucked up now."

"You think I give a shit about fucking up? You think I give a shit about my fucking life?" I moved closer to him, face distorted with the rage I was feeling. My brother backed up slightly and looked over at my father as I spat, "You stupid arrogant piece of dog fucking shit. Do you have any idea what you've done? You've sent her to her fucking death and for what? For your precious career? He's going to kill her, don't you understand?"

My brother, still unable to stand up all the way, shook his head, "That's not my problem. She made her bed…"

I cut him off. "What bed? You coward, she knew nothing about Gavin being who he was. He kept that from her this whole time. She finally got away from him with her life, and you just took it from her and for what? So you could close your case? Did you send her with backup at all?"

"Yes, of course, I sent her with Eddie. Your cousin has been extremely helpful in the past, giving us information we needed for cases we were working on. They are working together on this to clear your name, you prick. When they get there, they are to call me directly."

I looked at my father. "Are you kidding me? How in the fuck did he get a badge?" I looked at my brother. "Eddie has been feeding you false information or information that only benefited him in the end. For one thing, he is working with Santiago. He sold them the guns and used my name to do it. I bet you he even gave you that information on me, right? On the bodies? The shit you couldn't stick on me because I didn't fucking do it? He set you up, he's setting me up and he set up the love of my life and my fucking unborn child for God only knows what, and you have your head so far up your own ass you can't see anything but shit."

It took a minute, but my brother finally got what I was telling him. He started looking behind me and to our father. "I... I didn't know she was pregnant, okay? She didn't say anything when I asked her for her help."

"What did you say to her?"

"I just asked her to help us. I said you were a loose cannon, and you were going to get yourself killed if she didn't help. I told her about Gavin, and she didn't react any kind of way. She just looked at me. I told her that you were going to go after him for her and that you were going to get yourself killed. Then Eddie took it from there. He coached her until she packed her clothes, making it seem like she was gone so it wouldn't tip you off, and she left with him. I drove them to the airport about two hours ago and told them I would meet them tomorrow morning." He looked at my father. "This isn't my fault."

I shook my head, put my gun away and tossed my father's on the ground next to him. "Understand something, Daniel; if something happens to her and my child, I'm going to kill you."

I looked at my father, sister, then turned to my mother. Before I left their house, I said, "And tell your boy he's on borrowed time. After I clean up your fucking mess as usual, he's next on my list."

"You can't touch or threaten a Federal Agent," my brother told me.

"You fucked up big brother... You used her to get to Vegas, when she had no clue you were setting her up. You drugged her for fuck sake... that's unacceptable and unforgivable. I have every right to threaten him. I'm telling you, just so he can have a head start." I slammed what was left of my parent's door and jumped in my car. I had a plane to catch, and I hoped to God I'd get to her in time.

# CHAPTER 18

## GEORGIA

I wanted to be wrong about Eddie, and I thought I was when he showed up at Drake's house with his brother. I didn't trust either of them but if Daniel was there, Eddie had to be on the up and up.

We touched down in Miami in the dead of night. It was cool out, but it was nothing compared to where we just left. Eddie was quiet the whole plane ride there. I was thankful of that because all I kept thinking about was my conversation with Angel.

I was surprised when I left the Uncle's house, and Angel was standing by Drake's car. I wondered that moment if everyone heard our conversation or argument.

Angel came to me. "Need a ride home, beautiful?"

I nodded, thankful I didn't have to drive myself for fear I would have crashed somewhere because I was shaking so bad.

Angel helped me to the car and once inside, he turned on the heat.

We drove in silence for a while. Then Angel said to me, "The most hideous laugh." Then he smiled and shook his head.

I groaned, "You heard us arguing, didn't you?"

He smirked. "Well, it was hard not to miss. But not everyone heard. We got rid of some of the family, sent them in the family room. They might have gotten some of it but not all."

"I'm so embarrassed." I buried my head in my hands.

"Don't worry about it. You're pregnant, so you get a pass. Besides, Dominique's laugh is hideous... it's like a hyena. Congrats, by the way. I can't wait to meet my little cousin."

"Wow, you did hear everything."

"Well, yeah, but actually Lincoln told me and Pops the day after he found out you were pregnant." I looked at him surprised. He replied, as if feeling my eyes on him, "Yeah, surprised I know. He bought a ton of cupcakes to give out to everyone tonight. There's a few back there for you."

He pointed to the seat behind us. I reached back there and pulled out the box. I opened it and found three cupcakes with pacifiers on top of them. A few were pink, and one was blue. I pulled one out, removed the pacifier and bit into it. I moaned at the taste. "This is so good."

Angel laughed. "I'm glad you approve."

I ate the cupcake and looked over at him. "Do you think I was overreacting?"

He was quiet for a minute. Then he said, "Yes and no. Look, Georgia, no one can blame you for how you feel and what you want. You want someone to love you, to express that sentiment to you. It's normal... every woman should want that."

"...you don't think he's capable of feeling it or saying it to me."

"No, I think he's perfectly capable of both things. Georgia, I know for a fact he's changed since he's met you. And he is miserable when he's not around you." I looked at him skeptically, and he shook his head. "Woman, you have no idea how much of a grouch he was when he came back from Cabo. He wasn't a pleasant man to begin with, but he was worse when he got back."

I nodded my head. "I know Drake can be a grouch..."

"Georgia, the moment you came back in his life, the grouch went away. He actually became very pleasant. Hell, he's even stopped saying the word 'fuck' as often; that's you, my dear. First things first, no one calls him Drake and lives to tell anyone about it. Even his teachers called him Lincoln. Second, he never and I mean never brings anyone to dinner or around family. No one has ever meant that much to him, Georgia, except you. And he's not a touchy guy. But he can't seem to keep his hands off you, and it doesn't matter who is around. That's not my cousin."

"Yeah, but he's not in love with me," I told him.

"Who says he's not? Georgia, think about the man you're with and think about what he's been through. You know he has feelings for you and so does he. Even my pops can see it. Why do you think he's been sitting you next to him? He's been getting to know you in his own way, letting everyone in the family know what place you have because he knows how precious you are to Lincoln; we all do. All I'm telling you is not to give up on him. Give him a chance to tell

,
you how he feels in his way and in his time. He won't let you go; you know that, right? He's a stubborn son of a bitch, and he won't be without you or that little baby. The moment he finds out he fucked up, he'll be there."

I was waiting for him to come home that night. I had planned on jumping him the moment he came through the door, so I was completely disappointed when his brother came over instead.

So here I was, back home trying to prevent Drake from getting killed.

I couldn't believe what they'd told me about Gavin. I couldn't understand how I never knew what he was, but he was definitely a great liar.

I looked over at Eddie. "How are we going to do this? Are we going to wait until morning?"

Eddie looked over at me. "Yes, we are going to wait until morning. We're going to stay at this bed and breakfast off the coast. Just sit back and enjoy being home."

I watched Eddie drive with both hands on the wheel. He seemed so tense instead of relaxed, but I could see why he would be.

*I'm going to have to tell Drake he was being too hard on him and that he was wrong about his cousin. I can only imagine what he's risking for Drake.*

Drake was wrong about this one.

I did what he suggested and laid back. I closed my eyes feeling a little dizzy, hoping this car ride wouldn't have me throwing up everywhere.

I felt the car stop, and I opened my eyes. I first smelled the ocean, then heard it. The house looked beautiful in the dead of night. There were a few cars there, but I was exhausted, and all I wanted to do was lay down and sleep, so I didn't question it.

I followed Eddie to the house, and when he opened the door, he moved out of the way so I could walk in. When I passed the threshold, a gun was instantly put in my face. I looked into the eyes of a rather large man. I turned quickly to see if Eddie was okay and wow... he was fine. As a matter of fact, he was hugging some man.

The man seemed very familiar to me, but I couldn't quite remember. The man walked up to me and smiled. "So we meet again, *Maya.*" I finally remembered who he was when I felt a sharp pain in the back of my neck.

✳✳✳✳

Thank goodness I was alive!

I could wiggle my toes and fingers, and I at least knew who I was. What I didn't know was where I was. I opened my eyes and found that I was laying across a bed and was in some room with no windows, a bathroom and a door that I knew was locked. I sat up slowly, and my head started to pound like crazy. I gripped the back of my head and felt a knot. Then as if on cue, I started to heave. I moved as quickly as I could and threw up my stomach lining because there wasn't anything in my stomach.

I stumbled to the bathroom and rinsed out my mouth with water. I stared at myself in the mirror. This was a huge mistake coming here. I should have never even entertained or opened the door for Eddie or Daniel. I just so badly wanted Drake to be wrong about both of them. I'd been without family for so long. It was a shame that he had an abundance of them but couldn't trust them.

I ran my hands through my braids, thinking, *I am so in over my head.* But when I think about everything, what if I didn't come and something happened to Drake? I would've never forgiven myself. He meant everything to me and to think of raising his baby without him tore at me. But now there was a possibility that my life and the life of my baby was in jeopardy. I just hoped Angel was right and Drake did come home to see me and noticed the subtle things I left him. I knew he had hidden cameras everywhere, and he would check to see whom I left with… I hoped anyway.

I heard someone open the door, and I moved from the bathroom just as the big guy that had the gun in my face walked in.

"Let's go!" he ordered and I obeyed.

*Here goes nothing.*

So my brain decided to create this idiotic idea to run for it. I saw the whole thing play out in my head like an outer body experience and felt, *yeah, this could work.* So my dumb ass went for it, pumping myself up by thinking, *Don't voluntarily walk the plank... I'm going to try something.* So I kicked this rather large man in his balls and cut out of the open door, only for my face to run right smack into someone's hand.

I hit the ground hard, face on fire.

*Ho-ly shit!*

"Punta!" I heard above me. I cowered and protected myself from any more blows that I just knew were coming. But they didn't come. Instead, I got yanked to my feet by my hair and grabbed forcefully and very tightly by the arm. I was walked down the hall like I was a child. What I did was childish, I know, so I guess I'm getting what I deserved.

There were more rambles going on behind me in Spanish, and honestly I wish I would have paid more attention in school or when Gavin tried to teach me. Maybe if I had, I'd have known he was in the cartel.

We came to a set of double doors, and someone suddenly opened them from the inside. I was shoved, nearly tripping over my own feet. The room was packed, and I could feel every eye on me, but there was one set of eyes mine went straight to.

I couldn't move. I couldn't breathe at first, but as I was pulled further into the room, I said softly, more so to myself than anyone else. "Drake."

# DRAKE

The closer we got to our destination, I was beginning to feel more and more uneasy. I had the feeling of deep dread on the plane ride to Miami, but I used the thoughts of Georgia to calm me. One thought, in particular, that invaded my mind was a memory of a few nights ago. I was stressed half out of my mind. Eddie and I had been arguing nonstop and going back and forth about this cartel in Miami. It felt like the Capuano family shit all over again. I made it home that night, and the condo was quiet; not empty but just quiet. It was three in the morning, so I didn't expect Georgia to be up. She'd been extra tired most nights because of the baby, so I usually just let her sleep. I needed her though- I felt it. Sometimes I just wanted to hold on to her, the normalcy she gave me sometimes was just what I craved. We didn't have to have sex. Sometimes holding her was just enough to fix me. But I didn't go to her. She always seemed so tired, and I usually felt guilty when I took advantage of her, so I decided to let her sleep.

I grabbed a beer from the fridge, moved to the couch and attempted to watch some TV. Since I couldn't have what and who I really wanted, I settled for Sports Center and smoking my cigar.

When I turned on the television, however, the station that came on was an R&B station wafting a little Luther Vandross through the speakers. I let it play.

I took a long swig of my beer and placed it on the table in front of me. I slouched down further in the cushions of my couch and closed my eyes. He was singing about some house not being a home, and I listened to the lyrics thinking, *Shit... this is what I'm talking about.*

I felt her coming into the room before I saw her. Lately, there'd been something about her that made me feel completely connected to her the moment she entered a room I was in. I didn't know what it was. Quite honestly, I was still in denial that it existed, but I was not stupid.; whatever I was feeling was real.

I opened my eyes as hers were concentrating on me. She looked beautiful. She had just gotten her hair done. She was sitting with some lady for hours, but afterward it looked good. It didn't look like the braids she had in her hair before; it just looked like she had long hair. She only wore my Eagles t-shirt, and I could see that she didn't have a bra on. My eyes then went to her hips. I watched her closely, the way she moved, how she swayed... and, shit, the look in her eyes. It seemed she wanted to devour me.

I took a few puffs of my cigar and blew the smoke back away from her. I then stretched to put it out, and she stopped me. She says the smoke makes her sick, so I usually didn't smoke around her. I was completely shocked when she pushed me back against the couch.

Without speaking, she grabbed the throw pillow I had in my lap and placed it on the floor. She then knelt in front of me and positioned herself between my legs. With her eyes never wavering from mine, she lifted my shirt up and moved her hands underneath so she could touch me.

I exhaled. *This is what I wanted.*

I wanted to feel her touch. I needed her to...

She started undoing my belt, and I sort of froze. To be honest, all the time we'd been together, she'd never given me a blowjob. She'd tried, and I never let her. Most of the time I was going out of my mind from wanting her- I didn't care about it. I just wanted to sate myself in her fast and deep. Foreplay was the pleasure I gave her. I never asked for her to give me head. I thought about it constantly, wondering how her lips would feel, but we never took it there. Now...

She got my jeans unbuttoned and unzipped. She released me from the confines of my briefs, licked her lips slowly and then gripped the sides of my jeans in her balled up fists. She yanked so I pushed up slightly so she could completely pull my pants down. She undid my boots next, took them off and freed only one leg from my pants.

My heart started to beat faster with promise of her touch. The moment she gripped me in her hand, I thought I was going to explode.

*Shit...*

My breath caught with longing as she slowly bent down and made my head disappear into her mouth. I exhaled slowly and closed my eyes.

*Damn...*

I took more of my elixir in my lungs, opened my eyes and watched her as she familiarized her tongue and mouth with my dick. I was speechless... Yeah, me; speechless.

This beautiful woman was kneeling in front of me, giving me a fantastic blowjob without a word.

She created a rhythm that drove me crazy. She devoured me and licked the side of me, then devoured me again and licked the other side of me. She did that, at the same time stroking me, and I felt like a fucking king. Damn, she was making me lose control. I started to feel my balls tightening up. I was going to come... Hard.

I moved my right hand to her neck and the scene before me made me swell even more. She didn't take all of me in her mouth, and I didn't care. She was making me feel so good all I could do was moan and say silly shit like "yeah baby...just like that" and "shit, you're going to suck me dry, baby... God, keep doing what you're doing."

I sounded like a bitch, but I didn't care. She was making me feel that good. I took one more drag of my cigar, and I refused to come without being inside my favorite place. I then sat up and pulled her from me.

"I wasn't done," she said to me and I almost lost my load in her face.

I cleared my throat and said, albeit hoarse as shit, "I want to kiss you, and if you make me come in your mouth, I won't be able to."

She smirked at me, and all I could do was smile at her. I said with grit and yearning starting to take over, "Let me feel you, baby."

She climbed into my lap and straddled me, taking me in her hand and sliding slowing down my shaft. I closed my eyes and moaned, "Hmmm."

*Now that's what I've been longing for.*

I sat up so that I was on the edge of the couch. I leaned over, stomped my cigar out in the ashtray and leaned back. My baby then took the reins and rode me just the way I loved...

As I sat on the plane, thinking about that night, I regretted how she left my uncle's house. It burned me. I should have told her how I felt about her. Maybe she wouldn't have left. Maybe I could be buried deep in her right now if I had just fucking told her.

Now, just thinking about her was filling me with the dread that started when I boarded that plane and it was growing deeper.

While I was having dreams about my woman, Angel was sitting across from me on the phone with my uncle. My Uncle, who by the way we had to practically fight to keep him off the plane, was livid. Hearing and seeing the evidence against his son was a shock in itself. He couldn't believe Eddie had that much hatred and jealousy for me.

He always says, "Family can argue and fight all day, but when the day is done, we're still family." Yeah, my uncle and I clearly had different perspectives. He raised his kids to think the same as him, but I didn't have that family background.

I knew for a fact Eddie was capable of this shit. But going behind his father's back was against what we stood for. The trust and loyalty had been rocked. I could see it in my uncle's eyes; he knew what I would do the moment I got my hands on that little shit. He put my life, my future in jeopardy for what? Because he hated that his father gave me more attention than him? He needed to grow the fuck up, and I was going to teach him what it meant to fuck with a grown ass man.

I was going to kill that son of a bitch. I hoped for the sake of my family that Angel got to his brother before I did. I hated to lose my family over this shit, but I was done.

When we landed in Miami, Angel brought me up to speed on his phone calls.

"So it seems we have the same shit happening in the Santiago's family as in our own. Your contact Mark said that Gavin has made some connections with Eddie behind his father's back. Pops got a hold of Don Santiago and sent him the information about his son plotting to take over the family business and his ideas about forcing him into a grave. He wasn't too happy about it and wanted his own contacts to confirm. So while he's confirming what we gave him, he said he'd meet us at his son's place. He gave us directions."

"Is she there?" I asked as we climbed into one of the three Tahoes waiting for us on the tarmac.

"He'll let us know."

We got confirmation she was there two minutes later and were now five minutes out from the house. I started taking deep breaths as I pulled out my guns, checked and chambered a round and verified the safety was on. We flew a chartered plane to make sure we didn't have to worry about security gates and, shit, the flight was faster.

*This shit's about to get completely messy. I just hope I can get to her in time. Otherwise, everyone in that house will pay.*

When we pulled up to the house, it was surrounded by a gate. However, no one was at the front of the gate, and the gate was open. Each driver from the trucks turned off their headlights and approached the house in the dark. We pulled up close to the front of the house, and three bodyguard goons came out.

We, of course, had our goons with us, Things 1, 2, and 3, along with a few other guys. One of the men from the house came up to Angel as we climbed out of the back seat.

"Don Santiago is waiting inside. We need to take your weapons."

*Yeah right.*

I walked past him. "You'll have to take them from my cold dead fingers. Let's go." I moved past the other two bodyguards and walked inside the house. It was one of those typical mansion type houses with a large foyer and curved staircases that lead up to the second floor, high chandelier, expensive, ugly paintings, shit like that. This place had twelve bedrooms, four living or family rooms, kitchen, formal dining area... I can go on and on. I had Mark send me the specs of this place, and I studied it on the plane, making sure I knew everything I could. There were some secret exits and rooms, and I assumed that was where they were keeping her.

We crowded into the foyer and headed straight to the back of the house with one of Santiago's men leading the way. We stopped at a closed door, he knocked and out comes Don Santiago. He was a short, pudgy man, but I could see he exuded the same kind of power and respected my uncle had.

He greeted Angel and I with a handshake and a nod. He said to Angel, "I just got off the phone with your father. He assures me this won't get messy."

He then looked at me, but I didn't reply nor did I give him an indication that it wouldn't.

If they didn't give me what I came for in the exact manner of which she arrived, it would definitely get messy. I would wipe out this entire fucking family.

My cousin, ever the diplomat said, "Sir, that will depend on your son. If he gives us Georgia, unharmed everything will be fine."

The Don scoffed, "All this over some pussy?"

I smirked at him. "It's some good shit!"

He looked at me up and down, then shook his head. "Georgia was nice to my son. He didn't fucking deserve her... neither do you." He turned and walked in front of us.

*Eh... he's right of course, but so what. She's mine.*

We made a left and walked down a long hallway. We got to a set of double doors, and Santiago's men opened it wide and we walked inside. There, Eddie sat next to a pretty, thin black woman, with long hair and a tight ass green dress, on the couch. Vegas was sitting in a chair with his two guys from Cabo standing some feet behind him, and I assumed Gavin, who was sitting on the couch opposite Eddie and the woman.

Gavin stood when we walked inside, and his father boomed. "What's this business I hear you buying guns behind my back?"

*Here we go!*

Gavin looked over his father's head at Angel and me, then he looked at Eddie.

Eddie; that motherfucker was shitting bricks. I could see the sweat beading on his forehead from a distance. Seeing him there

272

and knowing that he touched what was mine, pissed me off even more.

I shut down; void of all emotions I moved to stand next to my cousin. My guns ready and waiting for the cue from him to start this dance I knew was coming.

Angel moved and reached his hand to Gavin and Gavin reluctantly took it. "This is my cousin, Lincoln, and well you already know my brother. I'm here on behalf of my family's interests. It seems you have a few of our shipments without our approval, but we'll overlook that. Also, what you have is someone that belongs to our family and we're here to collect."

Gavin looked at Eddie and smiled at Angel. "You are more than welcome to take him."

Angel shook his head. "Not him."

The room fell silent as Gavin and Angel did the staring contest.

The Don spoke, sitting in a rather weak looking chair, too weak it seemed for his bulk, but he looked as if he sat there all the time. "Go get Georgia."

Gavin looked at his father. "I would if I could, but I haven't seen her in months. After all, father, she did leave me at the altar." He looked over at me innocently, but quickly turned his attention back to his father, seeing the look of madness in my eyes.

Vegas sat there quiet, but he seemed agitated some. He kept staring at me; I could see it out of the corner of my eyes.

*Don't worry*, I thought to myself. *You'll get your chance believe me.*

I had to give the Don credit; he didn't take too kindly at being lied to. Neither did I.

"Go and get her. I know she's here. I've been told she is. You're holding her in that room you built down the hall. Fetch her and bring her here."

I watched Gavin closely. Finally, he nodded at someone behind me, and I heard the door open and close.

As Angel sat down, he looked over at me. I nodded and made eye contact with our crew, and they moved out in the room, getting into position just in case they had to protect Angel. When I turned, I saw Gavin's eyes on me.

"So you think you're just going to come in here and take what's mine?"

I didn't reply.

"Answer me!" he exploded, and I just smiled.

"That's enough," the Don barked. "You have bigger problems it seems."

"How so father?" Gavin spat, then looked at his father.

"You bringing this petty shit to my front door over a woman that you didn't even want."

"It's the principle, father. She is my fiancée, and no one is taking her from me. She's mine."

His father scoffed and waved his hand. "Didn't you take that one for your wife already?" he asked, looking at the woman in the green dress. "You need more black pussy for what? They're not worth anything but to fuck." The last two sentences he spat in Spanish, but I got every word and made sure I had a fucking bullet for the Don to eat before this night was done. No one in this room was above reproach.

Gavin was about to say something when the double doors opened and I tensed. Shit, I could feel the tension in the air. Shit was about to go from calm to chaos. I just hoped we all could leave there with our lives.

# GEORGIA

Seeing Drake made me feel better, but the look in his eyes put me on pause. His eyes were black as night, void of any feeling or emotion. He looked like pure evil... like the pair of eyes that seemed to haunt me for seventeen years.

I noticed no one else in the room until I was placed right in front of Gavin. Gavin frowned, showing me concern and attempted to touch me, but I moved my head back from him.

He looked behind me, asking, "What happened to her?"

"What difference does it make?" I responded.

Gavin looked down at me. "I've missed you." He attempted to touch me again.

I backed away slowly. "Why am I here?"

Gavin's pleasant face turned at that point and he looked like every bad guy I had ever come in contact with; well, except for Drake, although right now Drake got the award for being and looking like the meanest evilest person I had ever seen in my life.

Gavin gripped my chin tight and pulled me close to him. "Because you're mine," he gritted his teeth, then placed a kiss on my lips.

I felt the heat from my back coming off of Drake. I knew he was pissed, and I knew Gavin was doing this on purpose, so when Gavin stepped back from me, I turned my face and spat on the floor.

I don't know why I did that. Two seconds later, I was on the floor, ear ringing, and now I felt pain on both sides of my face... *Good job, Georgia!*

Gavin laughed, and I heard him speak, I think, to Drake because he said, "Wow, I mean I just smacked the shit out of her, and you didn't even blink. Damn, do you even give a shit about her? Isn't she pregnant with your baby? "

I heard Eddie say, "Bullshit. She's pregnant?" He looked at his brother, then at Drake.

I didn't hear Drake reply.

I slowly stood on shaky legs and looked at Drake. Gavin was right; he just stood there as if I didn't exist, like I wasn't even in the room.

Gavin shook his head. "I guess it's true what they say, you don't have a heart at all."

Angel moved to Gavin's father, who I didn't even know was in the room. "We discussed this over the phone and right by your front door a minute ago. We came for what belongs to us. We'll take her now and be on our way."

Angel stood, and Drake moved in my direction when the Don raised his hand. "You don't come in my house dictating to me what you're going to do. You ask permission... And I grant you permission. So, yes I granted you permission to enter into my home, but I didn't grant you permission to leave."

More men burst through the door, moved into the room and crowded everywhere. Drake looked at me, and I finally saw what I needed from him. I watched in horror as someone came up to him and pulled his guns from his holsters. Eddie then walked up to him smiling.

"I've been waiting for this day for so long. I can't wait to fucking kill you." He then punched Drake in the face, hit him twice in the side and pulled out a gun, placing it to Drake's head.

Drake seemed completely unfazed by the punches, never moving his eyesight from Eddie's. He didn't say a word, but he didn't have to. I saw his fists balled up tight.

This was going to get bad.

The Don, who I hated every time he was around, stood. He was a dirty old man who would always look at me as if he wanted to eat me for dinner, literally. He walked to Angel, saying, "You see, you and your family seem to think you are untouchable. You walk around with your nose up in the air thinking you're better than us. Well, tables have turned. I will take everything you own. It will be mine. Your lives end here."

Don walked by his son. "Do it quick... we don't have all day." He then turned and left the room with two bodyguards with him.

Gavin moved to me and gripped me by my arm. He moved me to where Drake stood. "See, this bitch and your bastard of a baby are mine to do exactly what I want." He took a deep breath. "Oh, I hope it's a girl. You know how much money she'd be worth on the black market? What do you say, Vegas? About one hundred grand?"

I saw Vegas, the one from Cabo that I knew as Julio, walk up next to us. "At least... I may be able to get you more when they find out whose baby it is."

They both laughed, but I kept my eyes on Drake. He stared back at me, eyes unwavering, unmoving. I wanted to touch him, but I saw a slight shake of his head, so I didn't move.

"Let's go, bitch," Gavin barked and pulled me along. I turned to look and, for the first time, realized that Maya was also in the room. She was following behind Vegas and Gavin.

Gavin said over his shoulder, "They're all yours...," and they walked out of the room, pulling me along with them.

# DRAKE

"Well, well, well. The infamous Drake Lincoln has met his match." Eddie moved to his brother. "I told you and Pop that this son of a bitch would be the end of you both. But you didn't listen to me."

Angel's eyes narrowed on his brother. "So is this how it is now? You're picking them over us."

Eddie moved quickly into Angel's face. "You picked him over me!" he spat, face raged with venom. "What happened to loyalty for blood, huh?"

"He is our blood, you dumb son of a bitch... What the hell is wrong with you?"

Eddie didn't reply, but he backed away from him and moved closer to me. Looking at me and raising his gun, he said, "It doesn't matter now anyway. Don't worry, I'll tell Pops that you both died trying to save Georgia, but all three of you were killed. Then I'll kill him, and the family will be mine."

"You're a pussy!" I said to him.

He tilted his head. "What did you just call me?"

"You heard me. These motherfuckers have you exactly where they want you. Why in the hell do you think they left their men?"

Now he squinted his eyes at me. "What are you talking about?"

I moved closer to him. "You have to be the dumbest bastard I know. Look around you. When they shoot our men, then you kill Angel and me, who do you think they are going to kill next? You think they're going to let you walk out of here? You are so gullible. It's fucking Capuano all over again. Just like Bridget, they are fucking you in the ass with no lubrication, just the way you like it right."

"Shut the fuck up!"

I moved closer. "Just like before... what did they offer you? Money? Did they tell you they will give you the piece of the empire, be the boss?

"Shut up!" he yelled but I kept coming.

"They said that you were going to run this family alongside them, right? Take over more of the families in the area and become a Don?"

"I said shut the fuck up!" Eddie charged me, as I knew he would, and I grabbed the gun from him just as an explosion rocked the side of the house. I heard gunfire in the distance and inside the room, body blows and yelling but I wasn't worried. I didn't have to know who was doing the shooting and whose bodies were dropping. I knew exactly what was happening; I trained them well.

I threw two jabs at Eddie's face, then as he threw one back, I sidestepped and elbowed him in his forehead. He doubled back, and I landed a vicious kick to his chest. I moved toward him swiftly, ready to stomp his fucking face to the ground, when Angel pushed me back and moved in front of me.

"Go get your woman... I got Eddie."

I stared at him for a minute. He knew what I wanted...No, I take that back... He knew what I *needed* to do to Eddie, and I felt like they were giving this bastard a pass.

He was right though; I needed to get to Georgia. I had to trust that Angel would do what's right.

# CHAPTER 19

## GEORGIA

I kept looking back at the closed doors just waiting to hear the gunfire and my heart break.

Gavin snatched me forward. "Are you really waiting for him to come and save you?"

I didn't reply.

He stopped and came in my face. "I saved you. My father wanted to kill you too, but I talked him out of it. *Me;* I'm the one that saved you, and you're pining after that murdering cold-hearted bastard? That's how you thank me?"

I didn't reply.

"I'm the one that loved you; I told you all the time that I would love you forever, and you'd betray me like this? By going off to Cabo like that?"

I frowned. "You loved me?" I said slowly. "Is that what you think you were doing, loving me? You cheated on me the night before our wedding. You were banging that trifling skank right there, and you have the nerve to say you loved me?"

Maya came closer to me. "What did you call me?"

I turned to her. "You heard what I said. You were supposed to be my friend, my sister, and you went behind my back and screwed my fiancé the night before my wedding. What kind of person does that? What kind of woman does that? A trifling ass, skank, whore would, that's who. I hope your coochie loses its muscle traction and can't come again, *ever*."

Maya shook her head. "You don't deserve him. Why do you think he came to me? You don't know shit about men and how to please them. As a matter of fact, why don't I go and show the big one back there how a real woman feels? After you, he'd probably beg me for it like Gavin."

My hand came up quick, and I punched her square in the face before I knew it. I didn't think about being pregnant or possibly getting shot in the back by Gavin or any of his bodyguards. I swung again, and she crashed against the wall behind her. I growled loudly, going for her again when we heard a loud explosion and the front door exploded. Gunfire erupted, and as I ducked, I saw Maya go down, and all I could do was look into her lifeless eyes.

"Let's go!" Gavin grabbed my arm and started dragging me. I fought, as much as I could, but Vegas came up behind me and poked me with what I assumed was a gun.

He confirmed it when he said to me, "Move, or I'll shoot you and your unborn bastard."

I stopped fighting and let Gavin drag me. Gavin's father and his men came out of some room as we passed by.

"What the fuck is going on?!" he asked his son.

"I don't know, but we need to get out of here and fast," Gavin said, then looked over at one of his father's men. "Get my dad out of here now."

Gavin started moving away when someone started spraying bullets in our directions. I wanted to stop and get in the fetal position and cry.

*I don't want to die.*

"Let's go!" He yanked me hard, and I tripped and fell down.

"Leave her man," Vegas said to Gavin, then spoke in rapid Spanish.

Bullets started flying close by us, and I scrambled up just as Gavin and Vegas started returning fire.

I didn't know where I was going, but I kept moving down this hall trying to find an open door where I could hide or get out of someone's window.

I found a door unlocked and slipped inside. It was an office with a huge desk and a chair. I didn't bother turning on the light. I just went straight to the window. I tried to open it, but it was locked. I reached to unlock it, but the window was too high.

I looked around at the furniture in the room to find something to throw at the window, hoping it would break. I grabbed one of the chairs that was sitting in front of the desk and threw it at the window, but all it did was bang up against it.

*Shit!*

I grabbed the other chair and threw it, but nothing.

I decided to pick up something heavier and grabbed a lamp that was sitting on the desk when Gavin barged into the room.

*Double shit!*

God, he looked like he wanted to kill me. His face was red, nose flaring, chest heaving. He raised his gun and pointed it at me. This time I didn't freeze; I threw the lamp at him and knocked the gun out of his hand.

The gun clattered to the ground, and I went for it, but he was faster. However, instead of picking up the gun, he went straight for me. I tried to fight him off by kicking him in his balls, but he seemed to recover too quickly for me to get away. He was too strong, and his hands easily went around my neck.

He pushed me up against the wall, with his hands around my neck, and I felt the ground disappear from under me.

*I'm gonna die.*

I can't breathe.

I felt his hands grow tighter around my neck, and I tried desperately to move his fingers. He had a vice grip on me and by the look in his eyes, he wasn't letting up until he saw the life leave mine.

I'm going to die and the last person I will see is this maniac. The last smell would be his breath on my face as he watches me struggle to breathe. The last thought I'm going to have is fear and regret.

I can't believe this is happening. I don't understand what I did that was so awful that my life would end like this.

*Damn it, I'm stronger than this.*

I tried to fight him, gouge out his eyes, but his arms were too long, and I couldn't reach his face, let alone his eyes. I tried to kick him in the balls like I'd done earlier, but it was futile. It's like he has brass for balls or something.

God, what was I thinking getting wrapped up in him? I knew the moment I laid eyes on him that it wouldn't end well for me. I knew he would end me. I knew the moment his lips touched mine that he would destroy me, but I didn't listen and now... Oh God!

It's happening.

I blinked back the tears but as I felt them fall I knew I no longer had control of my body. I could feel the fight leaving my body. I could feel death circling my dangled feet. My brain was finally getting the message and starting to shut my body down.

I started to pray first asking for God to forgive me. Since I messed up in this life, maybe He'll have mercy on me in the next. I then thanked Him. I thanked Him for the good and bad that happened in my life; for the mistakes and triumphs, successes and losses.

It's crazy really; that this would be my end.

I'm dying because I fell in love with a man who said he would love me forever, but has taken my life instead.

# DRAKE

I found the piece of shit who had my guns, and I checked them both before I started moving through the house. I didn't see exactly who came inside, but I had a clue of who it might be... they had perfect fucking timing.

I saw a couple of Santiago's men come around the corner, and I shot them both in the head without breaking stride.

From memory, I moved through the lower level, knowing there was no way he would take her upstairs. I came to a long corridor, and I braced my back up against it. I moved quietly, ducked down slightly expecting the worse. I heard voices arguing, then speaking in rapid Spanish. I moved faster and as soon as I saw who was in the room, I started shooting.

Gavin and Vegas ducked as I watch Georgia scramble away from the room. Suddenly, there was gunfire coming from behind me.

*Shit!*

I returned fire behind me, moving to the opposite wall and doubling back. I saw one body fall, and the firing stopped. I didn't ask questions or wait around to see who shot the stiff, so I reversed and started shooting back in the room. Gavin and Vegas returned my fire, then suddenly they stopped. I released my clips and reloaded.

"Is that you Lincoln?"

It was Vegas.

"Why don't you come out and we can discuss this man to animal?" he added.

"I take it you're the animal?" I replied.

He chuckled. "I could be. Why don't you come and find out?"

I crouched down, and I peeked into the room quickly. He was alone, arms up and palms out to me.

I risked a second peek, and he was still standing there. I moved slowly into the room, guns up, and looked everywhere before I believed he was alone.

I looked at him. "Are you supposed to slow me down?"

He shrugged but didn't reply.

"You think I won't shoot you?"

He shrugged again. "I'm positive you won't. You want to teach me a lesson, don't you? Teach me all about who Drake Lincoln is because clearly I don't have a clue. I was going to sell your woman, right after I fucked her, of course, and sell your unborn child. I should be punished, don't you think? Taught a lesson?"

He was right, and I know he was baiting me into a fight, just like I did Eddie, and you have no idea how bad I wanted to.

I shot him in the chest, and he dropped. I walked closer to him and watched as he writhed around in pain looking shocked as shit.

I said, "I don't have time to teach you shit.  Find out who I am in hell."

I tapped him once in the head and thought about shooting him again, but the sounds coming from down the hall brought me back and I ran.

# GEORGIA

*My eyes are going to close. I don't think I can hold on any longer... This is hopeless.*

*I love you, Drake*, I said to myself wishing I were able to tell him again.

"See if you would have just come to me...," I heard Gavin say. I opened my eyes confused. He leaned into me. "If you would have just come back home from Cabo when Vegas went to get you, all of this wouldn't have happened. You see this is your fault."

My brain wasn't working properly, but I could have sworn he just told me he sent his cousin down to Cabo for me. If that were the case, then he knew I was there all this time. And he probably knew I was in Philly too.

He confirmed it by saying. "What more of a hint did you need to come home? Was the destruction of your room not enough? Should they have waited for you to be there too?"

*You have to be kidding me.*

Without thinking, I clamped down hard with my teeth on his nose! I bit hard on the cartilage and wouldn't let go, not when he screamed and definitely not when I tasted blood.

He finally let my throat go, and I fell on my knees and wrists. I took in as much air as I could when Gavin grabbed me by my hair.

When he pulled me up, I spun around and kicked him in the balls again. He let me go, and I reached for his gun, picked it up and turned it on him.

Gavin straightened up slowly and a devilish smile crept on his bloody face. "What do you know about shooting a gun?"

I pulled back the slide, pushed the hammer down, and then pointed the gun back at him.

His smile fell away, and he put his hands up. "Are you going to shoot me now? Do you know what it even feels like to take a life?"

He moved closer to me, and I backed away slightly. "Stay where you are Gavin or I will shoot you."

I tried to sound stern, but I could hear the quiver in my own voice, so I know he heard it too.

He smiled at me. "You can't do it, can you? Pull the trigger." I didn't move as he moved even closer to me.

The gun was starting to feel heavy. I started to tremble, and the gun started to move. It felt like I was fourteen all over again, except I had the means to shoot first, and I couldn't pull the damn trigger. I was gripping the barrel with both hands and stepped back further. "Please don't come any closer..."

Tears started to gather in my eyes, and I could barely see him.

"You wait. The moment I get to you, I'm going to fucking kill you!" I saw him move, and I jumped back and heard a gun go off.

I screamed as I heard a body fall.

My heart was banging out of my chest. I couldn't breathe.

I felt someone touch me, and I turned on them, gun still in my shaking hands.

"It's me, baby. It's okay."

"Drake," I said softly. I felt him move my arm down, and then he removed the gun from my hand.

"Yeah, baby, it's me," he said softly.

"I- I," I stammered.

He wiped my face as the tears started to fall. He became clearer, and I saw the face that I fell in love with watching me.

I shook my head and closed my eyes. "I couldn't shoot him, Drake. I couldn't... but I think..."

He nodded. "I know you couldn't. You're not supposed to."

"But he was going to kill me... he was choking me... I thought..."

"Shhh, baby, it's alright." He soothed. He placed both hands on my cheeks.

I was still erratic. "No, you don't understand, I couldn't protect myself. I couldn't shoot."

"And you're not supposed to shoot, baby. That's my job, okay. It's what I'm supposed to do."

I just stared at him until I heard some gurgling noises. I turned to look down when Drake moved my head back at him. "No... you look at me... are you okay?" He touched my cheeks and rubbed them, looking at the bruises I knew were ugly and dark.

"I'm okay, but Drake..." I tried to look back down, but he still wouldn't let me.

'

"Lincoln," I heard someone call, and Drake yelled back, "In here!"

He moved closer to me and kissed me lightly on my lips, once, twice, then pulled back. "Baby, listen to me. I need you to go with them."

I didn't know who "them" was until I saw two large men come in the room. My eyes went large, and I shook my head. "No, Drake, please don't leave me."

"Shhh, baby, it's okay. They're okay. Remember them from my uncle's and the restaurant? This is Darrell and Hugo. They're my guys, and they won't let anything happen to you. I promise."

I gripped his arm, then hugged him tight. I was afraid to let go.

He said to me, "It's only for a minute, okay? I'm right behind you."

"I'm sorry. I'm being a wimp. Just...," I said to him burying my face in his chest.

He chuckled. "It's okay...That's what I love about you the most."

I leaned back slowly and brought my eyes to his fiery ones.

I held my breath and said softly, "What did you say?"

He took his finger and caressed my cheek from my temple to my lips to under my chin. He tilted my head and leaned in close to me. "I said that I love you." He then kissed me.

I exhaled and paused.... *Finally*!!!

He grinned at me and said, "Now I will tell you all the ways I love you in a little bit, but right now, baby, I have to work. Go with them, okay?"

Unable to speak, I just nodded and moved over to Darrell.

Darrell looked at Drake. "We got her, Lincoln."

# DRAKE

I watched Georgia leave with Darrell and the anxiety finally subsided. I turned and looked at Gavin.

I guess you can call me heartless and crass, and I wouldn't disagree. I could've shot Gavin in the head or the heart; I had a fantastic shot from almost any angle. But I didn't want his death to be quick. He needed to suffer, so I shot him in the chest. I knew his chest would fill up, and his lungs would collapse. He would suffocate... An eye for an eye right?

I looked at him struggling to breathe. I walked over to him, knelt down, and he looked up at me. I shook my head.

*Maybe Mark is right; maybe I am going soft.* I stood and shot him in the head ending his pain. *Damn, Georgia.*

I walked out of the room in search of Angel and my uncle.

I knew my uncle was the one that came in blowing up the place. He liked to create an entrance. I also knew that the cops would be coming soon. The house was pretty much in a deserted spot off the beach, but someone had to have heard the explosion, if not the gunfire.

I moved through the house and found Angel and my uncle talking to a couple of their guys. Angel saw me and signaled his father. I moved quickly to them, "We need to get out of here. Did you find that fat fuck?" I looked at Angel, then my uncle.

My uncle, with a cigar in his mouth and a large semi-automatic in his hand, nods. "I found the son of a bitch trying to get away in the parking garage."

I nodded. "And Eddie?"

Both my uncle and Angel looked at each other first, and then only my uncle looked at me. Angel couldn't look me in the eyes. They both didn't reply, and that's all I needed to know.

I nodded my head and backed up, asking, "Where's Georgia?"

Angel answered, "I told Darrell to take her to the emergency room to get her checked out."

I simply nodded again as I walked away.

I heard my uncle call me. "Son…"

I put my hands up. "I don't understand this shit but it is what it is. That's your decision." I looked at them both, then walked away saying just loud enough. "We'll find our own way back home."

# EPILOGUE

## DRAKE

*Thank God I'm home.*

Tonight was hectic. I opened up my second nightclub in Philadelphia called "Silk" and that place was packed. "Champagne Life" of course was still my baby, but "Silk" was Georgia's. She designed the place, named it, and I even let her hire some of the staff. This place was chic, upscale and definitely not my flavor. It's not as large in size as "Champagne Life," so we were able to do more with it. The designs are more to cater to the "grown and sexy," those were Georgia's words, not mine. I also opened the same club in Miami, and that's been a huge success.

After the kidnapping, she and I stayed in Miami for a while until I felt it was okay for her to travel. She had some bumps and bruises, but the baby was okay. She needed some rest because she started spotting. What better place to stay than on the beach? I rented a house right on the beach and made sure I catered to her every need.

I didn't mind it... I loved her..

Yeah, I've been saying it more and more, and now it's second nature, like me saying please and thank you. Actually, I say I love you to her more than I say please and thank you, so I guess I'm evolving.

We received no backlash on the bodies we dropped. We had a meeting with all the bosses in the area and told them what happened. Apparently, Don Santiago and his son made quite a few enemies that my uncle found out about, so as a gift and a show of faith my uncle dropped off a very alive and breathing Don Santiago to his rival Latin cartels. My uncle was assured they would take care of Don Santiago and the beach house.

I drove by it three days later just to make sure they held up their end, and I only saw a shell of a house left. Apparently there was a huge fire.

There were some alliances made, and I think my uncle is trading with some of the cartels down there, but I wouldn't know.

My relationship with my Uncle and family doesn't exist as of right now. They made their choice by keeping Eddie alive. I couldn't be around Eddie and not want to kill him, so I parted ways. My uncle calls me, invites me to family dinners, but I don't go. Georgia though, she goes. My family loves her. My grandmother told me she knew Georgia was pregnant the first day she met her. She said it was something glowing and ominous about her. Georgia is always like that to me, so I just took her word for it.

Georgia loves my family too; especially my aunt Angelica and my grandmother and they can't seem to get enough of her. I will say they have been there for her every step of this pregnancy. I knew when she was there with them, no matter where she was, they were taking great care of her.

I wish I could be as forgiving as her but... Yeah, well, you get what I'm saying.

I walked into our condo and paused at the door. I heard music coming from upstairs, and I instinctively grinned.

I reset my alarm and moved to the steps. When I got to my bedroom, I saw my wife dancing with my four-month-old son in her arms. She was singing to him some slow song that I didn't know. Maybe Celine Dion or something- my baby has weird taste in music. I'm not speaking of my son, mind you.

I leaned against the doorway and just watched her. She was in a tank top and red bikini underwear, which stirred my deep desires for this woman. I get hard actually every time I see her. She just turns me on that much.

She turned around and smiled at me. "You had a long night I see."

I walked into the room and went for my son, "Yeah, baby, you know it was hell. Packed, but hell."

She put her arms around my neck. "Well, if you let me get back to work I can..."

I shook my head, "Uh-uh, baby. All I want you to do is take care of Junior, okay? I'm just tired; I'm not overwhelmed."

"Are you ever going to let me work?"

"No," I said to her. I moved to the bed and sat down with my back against the headboard. I held up the baby and looked at him. I have a handsome son, bald just like his father. His complexion is golden, but I swear he looks like his mother. When he's pissed, though, he frowns like me.

Georgia and I got married before the baby came. I didn't want her to have him without officially becoming mine. We were in this together, and I wanted that to be forever. We went back to Cabo, where it all started, and had a wedding on a private beach. We stayed for a week, just the two of us. I asked her if she wanted to invite any of her siblings. They had a case pending against them, but they were cooperating completely, so they may get off with a fine. I didn't tell her the entire plot they had against her, and they did reach out to her, but she only sees them sparingly. She sold her shares to them, so she has no dealings with them, except her father's grandparents who she adores.

She flipped the script on me and asked if I wanted to invite Angel and my family, but at that time, shit was too fresh in my mind.

Now, shit is still fresh in my mind. I don't know if I can get over it either. My trust and my loyalty have been rocked. I never felt it would go down like it did.

"Angel came over to see the baby right after you left this afternoon," I heard her say.

I grunted my reply and laid my son on my chest.

Georgia came on the other side of the bed and crawled up to me. I sighed, knowing what she was going to say.

"Don't say it," I told her.

"Then don't make me. Look, Drake, I get it; you're hurt, you feel betrayed. But think of this... Now that your son is here, and you are able to physically hold him, see him, can you even fathom letting him go?"

See? I knew she was going to say that.

Angel has been calling and texting me from time to time wanting to talk, but I ignore him.

I'm being a bitch, I know.

"Baby..." She called to me, and I looked at her.

Yeah, by the way, *she* calls *me* baby now. That shit is crazy, right?

"You have to try to forgive. I could see it in Angel's eyes, he misses you. You two were so close. Can you imagine how hard it was for him?"

I did think about that, and I knew it was... but still...

My cell rang, and I couldn't reach it. I leaned over so Georgia could get it off the clip of my pants. "Put it on speaker," I told her. I figured it was someone from the club calling because I couldn't recognize the number.

"Lincoln..." I answered.

There was a pause, then finally I heard, "Lincoln, don't hang up."

It was Eddie.

I could feel the hatred starting to rise in me. Georgia saw that I wasn't going to say shit, so she said, "Hey, Eddie. It's Georgia."

"Shit, Georgia, thank fuck you're there. Look, Lincoln, I know I'm the last person you want to hear from, and I get it..."

I wanted to put my son down, so I could hurl the fucking phone against the wall, but my wife seems to know me too well. She stood and moved away from me.

"Uh huh, Eddie, he's listening," she responded. "But you better get to your point quick."

Then I heard him say, "Angel's missing."

My heart stopped. "What?!"

"Look, Lincoln, we need to put our differences aside." He took a deep breath. "Pop needs you. He's going out of his fucking mind and... shit man... we need you... your *family* needs you."

I looked at Georgia. Her eyes began to water. I saw the fear in her eyes, but she nodded her head. So, I replied, "I'm on my way."

*To be continued...*

To receive text message alerts of future BWWM releases from Jessica Watkins Presents, text the keyword "femistry" to 25827.

Add Author S.K. Lessly on Facebook: S.K. Lessly

## BECOME A PUBLISHED AUTHOR:

Jessica Watkins Presents is currently accepting submissions for the following genres: African American Romance, Urban Fiction, Women's Fiction, and Multicultural/Interracial Romance. If you are interested in becoming an author, send a synopsis and the first three chapters to jwp.submissions@gmail.com.

40308681R00176

Made in the USA
Charleston, SC
31 March 2015